Richard was born on the Gaer estate, Newport, Gwent, South Wales. He is married to Barbara. They have two married children, Nathan (Sarah) and Bethan (Matt); and four grandchildren, Lucy, Isaac, Sophie and Jessica. Storytelling has always been a strong part of Richard's life, which came into its own after his children were born. It was during this era, especially when his daughter was growing up, that the stories of 'The Land of Pleasant' began. Many years later, 'The See Thru Man' became a key figure in them and the stories were given a new lease of life.

I dedicate these stories about 'The See Thru Man' and 'The Land of Pleasant' to my children, grandchildren and our friend's youngest daughter, Kate, for their patience and encouragement as they listened to them.

Richard Davies MBE

THE SEE THRU MAN AND THE LAND OF PLEASANT

AUSTIN MACAULEY PUBLISHERS™

LONDON • CAMBRIDGE • NEW YORK • SHARJAH

A CIP catalogue record for this title is available from the British Library.

ISBN 9781528900553 (Paperback)
ISBN 9781528956833 (ePub e-book)

www.austinmacauley.com

First Published (2019)
Austin Macauley Publishers Ltd
25 Canada Square
Canary Wharf
London
E14 5LQ

When I first started to write these stories, I had no idea of the journey I was embarking on. And for this first book of short stories to become a reality has taken a lot of encouragement from my wife and family to persevere with them; a huge thank you goes to them and to my publisher for all their hard work, patience and dedication to these stories, for their willingness to put them into print and for seeing their potential. Thank you.

Table of Contents

Volume 1
The Ogre of Gulberia

Introduction

The Land of Pleasant

The Land of Pleasant isn't perfect but it is pleasant. It has some main characters called Stabmows, a King, a Queen, another group of citizens called Stesomrams and a variety of outsiders who must be dealt with so that the land remains pleasant. And not forgetting T.S.T.M.

Chapter 1
The First Tunnel

You wouldn't know it was there. You could quite easily miss it, on foot, in a car, on your bike or on a double-decker bus like the number 22. The main road ran past it close enough to see it, but if you didn't know what you were looking for or where to look then you wouldn't know if you'd passed it or not, and on foot you could walk over the top of it and not even realise. Well, I had done all those things many times, but one day while I was out walking on my own, just minding my own business, I paused, I don't do that very often when I'm walking, I tend to get there and back again without a rest, but on this particular day I didn't, I paused. It was then I realised there was something odd about this path because I was walking over a bridge, now bridges always take you over something, like a river, a road, a valley, or a railway track. There were none of these where I was looking, so I was curious. Before I went down to investigate, I went to the opposite side of the path because surely there should be something worth looking at; whatever this bridge went over, there should be something to observe. A bit like coming and going; if my bridge crossed a river, well, there should be water going under the bridge and the same river coming out the other side, and if that was the case, then children would race stick boats down the river, wouldn't they, and watch them come out the other side. Well, there was nothing, and this was a bit of a mystery, and I was very inquisitive. So, there was nothing else for it; I found my way off the bridge and went to explore under it, or more like into it because it was a tunnel. As I crept in, I was very surprised to find there was no daylight at the other end.

The reason soon became clear; the tunnel didn't go in a straight line. I thought I would walk into the tunnel and quickly come out the other side but this didn't happen; but it did lead me to The Land of Pleasant; but I didn't know that straightaway. What happened was this; very suddenly and unexpectedly, the tunnel went around sharply to the left and then after a short distance, it turned sharply to the right, which was all very confusing. Then without warning, I was out in the fresh air but not in a place I knew, which was more alarming but not in a bad way because everything seemed very pleasant. The air was warm but not muggy; the grass was green, a very rich green, what I would call Lincoln Green and very soft; the trees were all full of different shapes of leaves, shapes I hadn't seen before and didn't recognise; flowers that were amazing in colour, giving off such a gorgeous scent it was truly amazing and very pleasant. Suddenly, it hit me; whop!!! When I set out for a walk, it was a bright but very cold, early November, Saturday morning. *What's going on?* I asked myself, *Where am I?* I turned around quickly spinning, in fact, on my toes, I started walking back the way I thought I came, but I couldn't find the tunnel. It was nowhere to be found. *How am I going to get back home?* I thought. *What if I can't get home? How will my family find me? Oh dear, what am I going to do? And if I do find my way home, who will believe me when I tell them where I've been? And if I find my way out, will I be able to find my way back in again? Because after all, this is a very pleasant place.* Then I began wondering. Who lives here? How many? What do they do? What do they look like? What language do they speak? I had so many questions I wasn't certain which one to try and answer first.

And then I asked probably the most important question I could think of; Why me? Why have I found this place? Why has no one else found it and put it on the map? While these questions continued buzzing around in my head, I kept on walking and looking at my newfound surroundings. One thing was very clear, everything was very pleasant. The grass was pleasant, the trees were pleasant, and the small hill in the distance was pleasant. The fruit on the trees looked pleasant. The path I was following led me into a wood, not densely populated with trees and bushes, but pleasantly populated about the right number. One of the trees I was walking under had fruit hanging from its lower branches. I was feeling just a little peckish, and so I reached out to pick one of its fruit. As I did, the branch on which the fruit was hanging rose upwards, moving it out of reach. That startled me. "Trees don't do that," I said in astonishment.

"They do here," replied the tree.

"Trees don't speak," I spluttered.

"They do here," replied the tree again.

"No, they don't."

"Yes, they do."

"O no, they don't."

"O yes, they do."

"No, they don't."

"Yes, they do."

"No, they don't."

"Yes, they do." While this yessing and noing was going on, I thought I would try out the old well-worn trick. "No, they don't."

"Yes, they do."

"No, they don't."

"Yes, they do."

"Yes. They do," I replied more quickly.

"You are right," replied the tree. "We agree."

"Well that didn't work," I muttered to myself. "Alright then, Mr Clever Tree, where am I?"

"Firstly," replied the tree, "I am not now nor have I ever been Mr Clever Tree. I am, in fact, just so as you know for future use, I am a Nugumba tree, which is a descendant of the great Mungawumba Tree of Gulberia."

Chapter 2
Stabmows

As he was answering, I noticed a large and impressive oak tree just a little way off to the side with an open door; that's right, a big door in the bulky trunk opened outwards and a small stairway consisting of six stairs unfolded, and standing at the top of the stairs in the doorway was a curious figure. His fur coat had ginger and white stripes, he stood on his hind legs, his head was very round, with two not so large round ears with big, bright, sparkling brown eyes. He was about the size of a large badger, with the curiosity of a meerkat, and while standing on his hind legs, he was about a metre and a half tall. But, in fact, he was neither badger nor meerkat. "Who are you?" I asked.

"Since you are trespassing," he answered, "I should be the one asking the questions, so tell me are you one of them from the other side?"

"Ahh, I, ummm—"

"Speak up man, don't be shy, let's hear what you have to say for yourself. Just as I thought. Your kind can put men on the moon, explore the depths of the ocean, but you can't answer a simple straightforward question, can you? Right then. Let's take this slowly. Now watch my lips. Are you one of them from the other side?"

"I understood the question the first time," I retorted.

"Tut-tut, there is no need to be like that. Look around you and you will discover that everything here is pleasant, not perfect, just pleasant."

Suddenly, another voice called out, "Will you be quiet please, I'm trying to watch the telly."

"Who said that?" I cried.

"That's my friend; come out here, Boggle, we have an intruder." And with that, another of these creatures appeared in the doorway. Identical, except his stripes were grey and white. "Where did you come from, are you from the other side?" he demanded.

"When you say the other side," I asked, "do you mean over the hill and far away, or do you mean the afterlife, the other side? Will you speak more plainly because I am feeling rather confused right now."

"Allow me to explain a little of what we mean when we say the other side. We simply mean the place where you and your kind come from?"

"Well," I replied, "I live in the outer-west of Newcastle. Does that help to make things a little clearer?" I asked.

"Perfectly," he replied. "Why didn't you say that first instead of making it all unnecessarily complicated? Does your kind always make a song and dance over everything?"

"But I am still confused," I said. "How did I get here? Why am I here? How will I leave?"

"First things first," replied the ginger and white striped creature. "Let me introduce you to my friends," and with that he gave a shrill whistle and out from the big oak tree came three more furry creatures; one was brown and white, another black and white, and the third creature was red and white.

"Now let me see," said the ginger and white creature. "We are a group of five as you can see. We are Oggle, Foggle, Boggle and Wise." Then, standing as tall as possible and swelling his chest, he waved his hand in a very grand and proud manner to the red and white furry creature, "And this is Brave."

"We are all Stabmows. I am called Wise, the grey and white fellow is called Oggle, Foggle is brown and white, and Boggle is black and white. We have all been here as long as we can remember and we can't remember being anywhere else, except for Brave that is because he is often somewhere else on a mission. But here in The Land of Pleasant, everything, no matter where you go, is pleasant. The one thing we never worry about is time; we don't have clocks or watches or calendars because everything here is pleasant all the time, but as for seconds and minutes and things like that, we don't have them because this is a place of no time. If you remember that, which you won't, it will help you enormously. It will help you not to worry about how or when you will get home because when you leave, it will be exactly the same time as when you arrived, which means right now no one knows you are missing because as far as they are concerned, you are not, you are just out for a walk. But there are some things you should know about the land, The Land of Pleasant. Firstly, it is very pleasant but not perfect; we face challenges and adventures, which means we must depend upon each other from time to time. Secondly, we have our own language, it's called Rorrim, more about that later, and we also speak English, which is good for you. Thirdly, we have a few very simple principles which we live by. Two of these in our language are: '*semitemos inaligiv syawla tnarelot*'; in your English language it is: sometimes vigilant, always tolerant. And here, in The Land of Pleasant, every day is a good day but some are better.

"But now it's down to business, because you've been allowed into The Land of Pleasant for a reason," said Wise. "Brave has been asked by our King, Suoegaruoc III, to go to the neighbouring Kingdom of Gulberia because an old Ogre who was imprisoned in their most secure dungeon in The Dark Castle has escaped and is spreading terror and panic everywhere. Brave must go and capture him and imprison him so that he can never escape again."

"But where do I come in?" I asked.

Continuing, Wise answered, "The only way this Ogre can be imprisoned forever is for him to be enticed to the edge of the river near where you live, and then he will become a huge piece of stone for anyone to look at when they are enjoying themselves on the river bank."

"But how am I supposed to make that happen?" I stammered.

"Firstly, we need to go inside, sit down, have something to eat and drink, and then we can start making our plans," said Wise. And with that he turned and led the way into the large oak tree. The inside seemed to be much larger than the outside; because my new fury friends are smaller than me, I was expecting to duck through doorways and to find ceilings very low, but they weren't, everything was just right. At the end of the long hallway, hanging on the wall was a full-length mirror. "That," said Wise, "is the mirror of Ecitsuj." They showed me into a very large, comfortable lounge, offering me an easy chair on which I sat down. It was a very comfortable easy chair. Wise asked, "So what's your favourite meal then."

"Mixed grill," I replied immediately.

"Foggle will sort that out for you and for a drink we have two favourites here in Pleasant. Woodland Surprise, it's amber with a hint of bright red and made up from a selection of wild berries and fresh strawberries. And Sunrise Special, this is a mixture of oranges and lemons mixed with honey."

"I will leave the choice of drink to Foggle," I said. "He will know which one is best with a mixed grill." Five minutes later, the full mixed grill and my drink were brought in by Foggle. "Goodness me, how did you manage to cook a meal like that so quickly?" I asked amazed.

"You will be surprised at what we can do in The Land of Pleasant. But before we get side-tracked, we must get down to business."

Chapter 3
The Mission

"Brave, as we have said, must go to Gulberia. The Kingdom of Gulberia is made up of rolling hills, steep valleys, rivers and lakes, but all of this is surrounded by a formidable wilderness, which is not totally barren but very harsh and dry, with some interesting wild life, making it dangerous; it's called The Dartknoy Wilderness.

"In the middle of the kingdom is a very splendid castle called The Castle Narcaervon, or The Dark Castle, because it is made out of black, highly polished marble. In the middle of this huge castle is a grey stone tower known to the locals as Stabille. Deep underground is the most secure cell; in this inner cell was the old Ogre. He was a prisoner there for over 100 years; how he escaped no one knows, but now he is wreaking havoc everywhere.

"Now what Brave has to do is entice him away from Gulberia and into your world, because in your world he cannot survive. We have already discussed where you must entice him to, which is not too far from where you entered The Land of Pleasant, just a little further down the road on the edge of the riverbank.

"To give you an idea of where Brave is going," continued Wise, "you must climb to the top of our tree." I've always liked climbing trees, but I was in for a very pleasant surprise. I went outside and looked up at the tree; firstly it was much bigger in circumference than I realised and was much, much taller.

"Reach up for that branch there," encouraged Boggle.

"That one," I said. "It's far too high for me to get a hold of, I will find another way of getting to the top."

"Trust me," said Boggle, "Reach up to that branch there." Reluctantly, I did. And as I stretched up to the branch, it lowered right down to where I was standing.

"Very pleasant, very pleasant indeed," smiled Boggle. "Now climb onto the branch, stand up and hold on." Doing as I was told, I climbed onto the branch, which was now hanging very low.

"Move towards the end of the branch and hold on tight," encouraged Oggle. I did so and suddenly the branch moved upwards and stopped in its right place.

From the ground, Wise shouted up, "Talk to the tree, tell it you want to go to the top to see the view."

"Talk to the tree?" I answered.

"Don't sound so surprised. You did so when you first arrived here."

Looking at the main trunk of the tree and feeling rather silly, I spoke, "Take me to the top of the tree, I want to see the view."

"Don't forget the magic word," shouted Brave. "And it's not abracadabra, it's—"

"Please, Mr Tree, will you take me to the top, I want to see the view. Thank you." Suddenly, the end of the branch I was standing on lifted upwards, taking me to another branch higher up.

Wise shouted up again, "Climb onto the next branch and say the same thing again. Keep doing that until you get to the top."

"Right-ho," I yelled. Onwards and upwards, I went from one branch to another until at last I was clear of the foliage. The view was breathtaking. I stood there taking it all in, the river, the hills of The Land of Pleasant, their Great Lake, and the King's Castle and in the far distance the edge of the wilderness. "What are you thinking," said a voice in my ear. Shocked, I spun around on my branch, almost losing balance and plummeting to the ground below.

Wise with his friends sat there grinning at me. "How did you all get here so quickly?" I demanded.

"We prefer climbing, it's quicker," replied Foggle chuckling.

"I can see you've spotted the wilderness," cut in Wise.

"The challenge we have is this. Brave has to leave here in ten minutes, get to the wilderness and cross it, arrive near Narcaervon Castle, but he must not be seen by anyone. Then he must start playing music on his flute. The Ogre will hear the music and follow him all the way to the very edge of Gulberia. If you look closely, you will see," said Wise pointing with his right paw the Burnew Bridge. "Brave must arrive at the far side, and you must be waiting at what appears to be this side. You will hear Brave playing the flute. The moment the Ogre steps onto the bridge, Brave will stop playing and you must start playing this." And with that he gave me a mouth organ. "Don't worry about tunes and rhythm, all you must do is blow out and suck in with it in your mouth, and you will lead the Ogre to the chosen spot. But he mustn't see you. All this must be

24

done by midnight or just after and certainly before it starts getting light."

"That doesn't give us much time," I said. "Brave will have to travel fast to even get close to the edge of wilderness." Wise smiled.

"It's closer than you think, and we have a shortcut to the centre of the wilderness, but now we must get back down the tree. Are you ready? When I get to three, you must jump."

"Jump, now you are joking."

"No joke, you're in for a pleasant surprise, ready 1...2...3... JUMP," they all shouted. I did and instead of falling like a stone, I gently floated to the ground. Once again, we gathered inside their tree trunk home. Brave was busy drinking huge amounts of cool Woodland Surprise.

"How can he consume so much fluid?" I asked.

"It's very simple really, us Stabmows are able to store fluid in our fur because every individual hair is hollow and used for this purpose. Then when we are thirsty, we bring what we need into our mouths. Brave will need as much fluid as he can hold; the heat from the sun in the wilderness is terrible. The fluid stored in his fur will help to keep his body cool and fresh as well as giving him a supply to drink."

"Right, I'm ready," said Brave.

Chapter 4
The Short-Cut Adventure

With Boggle and Foggle, he went behind the oak tree and into the bushes. In the middle of them was a large gorse bush, pulling the centre branch towards them and twisting it slightly, the bush fell backwards revealing a large hole and a sudden rush of cold air. Peering down into the shaft was like looking inside an ancient well; the bottom of the shaft disappeared into total darkness. Without warning, Brave shouted goodbye and disappeared head first, the claws in his four paws gripping the sides of the shaft as he scampered headlong downwards into the long, black shaft. "What's he doing?" I shouted. "He hasn't got a torch with him."

Wise smiled at my concerned ignorance and said, "All us Stabmows can see in the dark."

"See in the dark?" I stammered.

"Why of course, we've all been to night school," replied Foggle grinning.

At the bottom of the shaft was a large tunnel cut out of the rock making the walls incredibly solid but for some reason unknown to Brave, very damp. This made the going more difficult as Brave often slipped and missed his footing. Undeterred, he pressed on, keeping up a steady pace. As he rounded a sharp bend, the tunnel floor dipped downwards. At the bottom of this descent was a large puddle. Crossing it wasn't a major concern; where the water was coming from, was more alarming. Brave looked quickly up to the roof of the tunnel, water was starting to pour through. Quickening his pace, Brave made it through the puddle. Behind him, he heard a loud strange rumbling noise and an increase in the volume of water pouring through the roof into the tunnel. Brave kept running upwards, gaining as much ground as possible. As he reached the top of the rise, he glanced over his shoulder. The pressure from the water was causing the roof to cave in. The rumbling sound was the movement of rocks being pushed by the water. Suddenly, the roof caved in completely, rocks were flying from the roof, and water was gushing in like an angry waterfall. Brave braced himself for the race of his life, frantically hurrying towards the far end of the tunnel, around one bend after another, down one slope, up the next, ever onwards towards his destination with the flood waters coming after him.

Above the ground, we were trying to listen for him, but as Brave had started his journey along the tunnel, his sounds disappeared from our hearing. We were just about to go inside when Foggle caught Wise by the arm. "*Ssshhh*," said Foggle. "Listen to that noise."

"What's going on down there?" asked Boggle.

"I think," said Wise slowly, "there's been a cave-in in the tunnel. We can only hope now that Brave is safe, we can only wait and hope. And give Brave time."

"Whatever happens, we must assume that our plan will go ahead as we've decided."

"I will be in my position at the end of the bridge at the right time. It's business as usual," I added with grim determination.

"Good man, we knew we could depend upon you," said Wise.

Meanwhile in the tunnel, Brave was racing along faster than he had ever run in his life. His exit shaft shouldn't be much further. The noise of the rushing water was getting closer and closer by the second. Around a few more bends raced Brave, the sound of the raging water signalled him it was much closer. He raced on through the tunnel. Then he saw it up ahead; the exit shaft was just 150 metres away… 125… 100… 75.

"Keep going, Brave, not far to go now," he encouraged himself, 50, 40, 30, 20, 15… The sound of the water was deafening… 10, 5, 4, 3, 2, 1. Brave leapt at the wall of the shaft, but it was too late; the surging, rushing water caught him. There was no tunnel left for the water to go down, it had to go up the shaft. Brave found himself being carried upwards at an incredible speed and with tremendous force. Instinctively, for his own survival, he curled himself into a ball. Onwards and upwards, he was carried at a dizzy speed. Still he kept himself tightly curled up. Without any warning, the force of the surging water blew out the escape hatch at the surface. The water came bursting out with such force that it shot into the air like a huge fountain. It went up and up and up, almost 350 metres.

Thrilled to have survived the ordeal, Brave let out a shrill of delight as he shouted, "What a gusher, what a gusher, this is totally amazing." For a brief moment, sitting on the top of this fountain of water, Brave was able to glimpse The Dark Castle. The spouting water eventually and slowly subsided spreading out across the ground, which was so dry that most of it disappeared instantly.

Chapter 5
Dartknoy Wilderness

Brave's first task though was to plug the hole only as a personal safety precaution. He didn't want to risk falling down it while completing his task later. After a few minutes searching, he found the original wilderness bush, which was similar to the gorse bush at the back of his oak tree home. Firmly locking it in place, Brave looked around carefully taking everything in, particularly good hiding places and useful points of cover. Working out his plan, he pressed on towards the Kingdom of Gulberia and Narcaervon Castle. The heat and the dry air in the wilderness were unbearable. "The temperature must be close to 50°C; I'm really pleased I've packed as much Woodland Surprise as possible but I must make it last, I've still got a huge task in front of me," muttered Brave to himself. After several hours of careful progress and planning, his wilderness journey was almost over. A little way ahead, the landscape was changing. The bushes were greener, flowers were greater in number and more colourful. As Brave entered this more fertile area, the air changed from hot and dry to hot and humid, but with the rolling hills came a breeze, which helped to lower the temperature slightly. Climbing over the top of the next hill, the view he got was not what he expected; at the top of the next hill was the famous Mungawumba tree. It was far bigger than he imagined. To say it was huge was an understatement. This tree was awesome. Brave pressed on; he wanted to climb the tree to get a better view of Gulberia. Reaching the Mungawumba tree, Brave paused to catch his breath and to quench his thirst. Leaning his back against the massive trunk, he looked back over the ground he had just crossed. Making the return journey wouldn't be too difficult; he would simply follow his scent, but what he really needed was a specific landmark that would help him find his side of the Burnew Bridge. "It must be further away than I thought," mused Brave. "Now to tackle this tree; I wonder if anything lives in it." With this thought in his head, the challenge before him and the urgency of his mission, Brave started his climb.

Chapter 6
The Royal Visit

Meanwhile, back in The Land of Pleasant, Wise had gathered the rest of the group. "We must make plans for your part in this adventure," he said looking at me.

"Is it that challenging or demanding?" I asked.

"Not really," he replied, "but there are certain things to be aware of for this to be totally successful. Firstly, you will leave here by a different route to the way you came in. That is for our protection. Secondly, we will lead you so far but at a certain point we must leave you to complete your departure on your own. Thirdly, you must only start blowing your harmonica when Brave finishes playing his flute and not before. This will only happen when the Ogre steps onto the Burnew Bridge, and fourthly—" at that moment there was a sharp constant knocking on the front door. Boggle went to the door.

"Your Majesty," we heard him say. "Please come in, what an honour for us for you to come to our humble home." We all stood in absolute silence as we waited for King Suoegaruoc III to make his appearance. Majestically, he swept into the room we were in. Instantly, everyone bowed low. As we straightened up, it was easy to see why he was the king. He was half a metre taller than them. His natural fur coat was gold and purple. On top of this, he wore a long velvet cloak, which was gloss black like highly polished black marble, edged with thick golden thread. The buttons on the front of his cloak and on the sleeves were rubies. His bright eyes twinkled with delight as he took in our surroundings and the small group standing in front. Wise was the first to speak. "Your Majesty, to what do we owe this great pleasure?"

"As you know," he spoke in a very crisp, distinct voice, "Brave was commissioned to rescue the Kingdom of Gulberia from the rampage of the escaped Ogre. I was hoping you could give me some news regarding his progress." Then turning slightly towards me, he said quietly, "If you succeed, we will forever be in your debt. Have you been briefed with your task and equipped correctly?" His eyes shone with hope as he spoke.

Again, Wise spoke, explaining exactly where we were up to in our plans and preparations. "But do you have the all-important harmonica?" he asked.

"Not yet, sir," I replied, dipping my neck slightly as I spoke.

"That's excellent and exactly what I was hoping to hear."

"Has there been a change of plan, Your Majesty?" asked Wise.

"Not at all. Not at all," he replied. "It is still business as usual. It is just that I have a harmonica that I would like you to have for the task and for you to keep to remind you of your first of many visits to The Land of Pleasant. The important thing with this harmonica is you don't have to be musical, just think of a song and start blowing and the right tune will be played." Then with a regal flourish of his well-groomed paw, the King took from the inside of his cloak the best harmonica I had ever seen and proudly presented it to me. "You have been chosen for this task and many more not for any special or specific reasons but just because you have been chosen. If you try and understand it or explain it, you will make it far more complicated than necessary. Therefore, the best thing to do is accept it as the truth, and you will be fine. Wrestle with it, try explaining it and you will be more confused, you will have more questions than answers and above all else, lose the pleasure of enjoying The Land of Pleasant. Not perfect but pleasant." And with that he bowed slightly, turned and headed for the door. As he reached the bottom of the steps, he half turned and said over his shoulder, "Now we've met, I want you to know that from time to time your services will be in demand, and in responding favourably, you will meet some very interesting individuals." We bowed, we cheered, we waved, we shouted and we clapped, and in a few moments he was gone.

"Well," said Wise after a few moments of silence, "I'm going in for a drink."

"I'll do halfunhalf," said Boggle, "that's my speciality."

"What's half and half?" I asked.

"It's 50% Woodland Surprise and 50% Sunrise Special," chipped in Oggle. "We simply call it halfunhalf."

"I'm for halfunhalf," shouted Foggle.

"Me too," said Wise.

"I'll have halfunhalfunall," I asked expectantly.

"You can't have halfunhalfunall because we only do halfunhalf," said Wise.

"I understand that," I replied. "But if Oggle, Foggle and you Wise want halfunhalf, then I'll have halfunhalfunall."

"But we don't do halfunhalfunall," interrupted Foggle.

"I know that," I said. "But if you are all having halfunhalf, and I am having the same as you, then I will have halfunhalfunall."

"But we don't do halfunhalfunhalfun…" The penny suddenly dropped and Foggle understood what was going on. "Maybe by the time you come again, I will have concocted a new drink and just for you I will call it 'Halfunhalfunall'." Boggle eventually brought drinks in, which proved to be a very interesting and refreshing combination.

Wise called the meeting back to order and quickly did a recap on the first three points, then he gave point four without any interruptions. "Fourthly, the Ogre must not see you and he must not be seen by anyone from the other side."

"What if something goes wrong?" I asked. "What will happen to the Ogre, and what will happen to me?"

"If this goes wrong," replied Wise slowly, "it will be disastrous for everyone."

Chapter 7
Snake Attack

Back at the great Mungawumba tree, Brave was busy climbing. It was more difficult than he anticipated. The trunk was incredibly smooth and very, very hard. He had the impression from its smoothness that something or someone used this tree a lot. It jerked in his memory but as it surfaced, it disappeared again; this cause for concern made him climb slower than normal while exercising more caution. Inching his way up while keeping a watchful eye all around him caused him to forget how far he had climbed and what the view around him was like. Suddenly, Brave realised why the tree was so smooth. A long time ago while undertaking another commission for his king, Brave encountered the Donacada Snake. A huge tree-dwelling snake, 12 metres long, which could swallow most animals it encountered. The memory caused Brave to shudder. He also remembered how he overcame it. With that thought in mind, Brave began selecting a suitable branch. He needed a piece of branch about 10 cm in diameter and at least 40 cm in length but not more than 90 cm. Finding the right piece, Brave set about using his teeth in the same way a beaver would. Ten minutes later, the job was complete. Brave now had a short shaft of wood, which would be very useful in an emergency. Gripping it firmly between his teeth, he continued his climb. Pausing for a moment to look around, Brave realised how high he had climbed and how far down the ground now was. He must have climbed well over 150 metres. Far out on the horizon, he was able to see the tops of the towers from The Dark Castle, but he wasn't high enough to get the full view. Brave continued climbing. Above him, the branches moved slightly, the leaves rustled as if the wind had disturbed them, but there was no wind. Again, Brave paused, focusing his attention further up the tree. *There it is,* he thought, *that's where the movement is coming from.* As he looked intently, he saw the body, the great long snake slithering silently through the branches. *So that's the way it's going,* thought Brave, *but where is its head?* Freezing amongst the big leaves and with great difficulty, Brave began tracing the snake's long body with his eyes through the thick foliage of the great tree. The problem was made harder because the snake was dark green with a light green diamond pattern running over its body, and in this environment, it made it almost impossible to see. Brave sat patiently watching, following the body of the snake until he saw its head; it was huge, its tongue kept flicking in and out quickly as it followed Brave's trail. A few large fruit bats were hanging upside down near to where the snake was. In one lightning fast movement, the snake reared its head, opened its mouth, shot forward and snap, snap, snaps; opening and closing its huge mouth in rapid succession, all the bats were swallowed up. "At least, I now know what I am up against," said Brave with grim determination. And again, he sat and waited. He couldn't afford to keep climbing because he wouldn't see the snake slithering up behind him. "No, I must sit this out until either the danger is passed or I have my face-to-face encounter with this monster. He might not know I am here but to move will now give the game away." Gripping the wooden shaft he'd made, Brave continued to sit motionless as he watched the snake slithering slowly closer and closer to him. *What's that ancient pearl of wisdom we have back home?* thought Brave. Then quietly reciting it to himself in Rorrim, he murmured, "*Tsiser eht ekans dna eh lliw eelf morf ouy.*" With renewed determination, Brave sat and watched and waited. It seemed to him that hours and hours were passing by but a side-glance at the sun told him that he had only been watching for just under an hour. His lips were getting drier but Brave resisted the urge to wet his lips from his supply of Woodland Surprise in case he revealed his hiding place too soon. His main concern was the sweat coming from his paws; he was hoping that wouldn't give him away.

Slowly, the big monster came closer and closer, its great head swaying from side to side, its long black tongue flicking in and out constantly, and its beady eyes penetrating its surroundings. Brave sat motionless, gripping the shaft of wood. The snake was about 10 metres away. Brave sat like marble, totally immoveable. The snake slithered closer and closer, now it was just five metres away. Brave didn't flinch, not a muscle, not a strand of fur, motionless like a stone, he continued to sit. Closer and closer the snake slithered, two metres away. Now its head was raised up, its beady eyes were peering through the leaves where Brave sat, as if he were made of granite rock. Brave eyed the snake not taking his eyes off it for a moment, waiting for the moment, the right moment when this

35

monster would lift its head and open its huge mouth. Closer still the snake slithered. Brave sat, steadfast, immovable. The wooden shaft gripped in his right paw as if it were clamped in a vice. Half a metre was all the distance between them. *Any moment now,* thought Brave, *it's make or break. Just hold your nerve.* Like a whip being cracked, the snake reared its head, opened its huge mouth, which was cavernous and shot forward. In a split second, with nothing to spare, Brave thrust the wooden shaft upright into the snake's huge mouth, wedging it open and paralysing the snake. Instantly, its huge head dropped forward, hanging over the branch of the great Mungawumba Tree. "It won't trouble me any more on this trip," said Brave as he breathed a huge sigh of relief. Then with a big satisfied grin on his round fury face, he said speaking to himself, "They don't call you Brave for nothing." Brave continued climbing up this huge tree a little more quickly and confidently, then making his way to the end of this very high branch, he took a fresh look at his surroundings and the view he was now afforded. "WOW! THIS IS AWESOME! But I'm not here to see the sights, I have a task to fulfil."

Chapter 8
Narcaervon Castle

Focusing his attention, Brave was able to use another unique feature that Stabmows have. When focusing with specific purpose, their eyes act like binoculars; this advantage was now being put to good use. The Dark Castle and the surrounding area was now very close in Brave's vision. He was able to see Gulberians dashing about frantically, some were hiding in odd corners of the Castle Square, some were trying to find their way into the towers, and others were trying to climb over the walls to find a safe hiding place. While Brave was observing this, he wondered why the people were behaving in such a frantic manner, but he didn't have to wonder for long. A loud bellowing roar filled the air, metal rings were being flung far and wide, these were the remains of the shackles which had kept the Ogre imprisoned for such a long time. Brave sat silently watching this giant as he terrorised the people of Gulberia. Male, female, young, and old were terrified of him. All at once, the Ogre slumped to the floor half curled up and fell asleep. All the locals who were in hiding came out, gathered around him and stared at him in awe and amazement, then they all promptly ran away, scurrying like frightened children.

This is as good a time as any, thought Brave and began his quick descent down the great tree, passing the paralysed snake on his way. Once on the ground, he hurried on towards the Dark Castle. Over one hill, across a river, down a steep valley, across a ravine, up another hill and finally in a valley of its own, he saw the Dark Castle. Close up, it was much bigger than he imagined. He could make out part of the King's palace, the curtains were drawn, and in some cases the shutters were against the windows. Brave hid himself in the long grass and crept towards the castle gates; they were still open. Just outside the gates, were two Gulberians; they were dressed in what Brave thought were palace costumes. The one said to the other, "Did you know that our king sent for help the other day."

"What do you mean sent for help?"

"What I mean exactly is that our King went himself in person to King Suoegaruoc III in The Land of Pleasant and one of their citizens, a Stabmow called Brave, that's Brave with a capital B, has been instructed by both kings to remove this Ogre and imprison him, so he can not cause chaos, carnage, and catastrophe again."

"The Land of Pleasant, that's kids' stuff and nonsense," replied his companion in disgust.

"Well, we have to wait and see," answered the first character. Just then, they both heard a noise different to each other. The first heard what he thought was the Ogre stirring, the second thought he heard music.

They looked at each other in bewilderment. "What's going on?" They asked each other. They quickly stepped into the castle courtyard. The Ogre was slowly standing to his feet, looking like he was in a trance. Outside the castle gates came the sound of soft music, mystical, magical and enticingly melancholic.

"Where's that coming from?" whispered the second companion.

"*Ssssshhhhh,*" his friend whispered in reply as he led the way out through the gates to a secure hiding place behind some very large water barrels. As they watched, the music seemed to be drifting away. The Ogre followed, almost as if he was compelled. Slowly he followed the music and slowly the music seemed to lead him further and further away. As the music led the Ogre away and the distance between the Ogre and the castle grew so, more and more Gulberians filled the Castle Square and the gateway. The King, by now, was present, keeping order and everybody quiet. In total silence, they watched as the Ogre became smaller and smaller with every great lumbering step he took.

Chapter 9
Setting the Trap

The haunting music from Brave's flute enticed the Ogre while maintaining the trance he was in. Eventually, Brave passed underneath the great Mungawumba Tree. The snake was still there, very still, but not for much longer because the saliva in its mouth was slowly softening the wood and the pressure on the wood from its great jaws would cause the shaft to break and the snake will return to normal. Unfortunately, it will remember Brave and it will seek revenge. But that's another adventure.

Back in The Land of Pleasant, no one was speaking. Everyone was thinking about Brave. Had he escaped the cave-in? Had he reached the Dark Castle? What adventures had he encountered on the way? Was the Ogre now following him? All these and many more questions were buzzing through their heads. Wise broke the silence. "You have two harmonicas now then," he said.

"Yes, I do, but unfortunately, I'm not musical," I replied.

"If I were you, I would use the one our King gave you," interrupted Foggle, "because with his harmonica you only have to think of the tune as you begin to blow, and the right tune will come out. It's really that simple," he concluded.

As I reached into my pocket for it, Oggle joined in the conversation. "I wouldn't play it," he said, "because its music will travel much further than we actually know and if the Ogre hears it, it will make him confused and he might realise it's a trap, then he would get into a right rage, which Brave doesn't need at all." I hesitated, not certain what to do. Could I get it out and look at that which was given to me to help me in my part of the quest and in my part of the trap. I moved my hand towards my pocket.

"We have another phrase here in Pleasant," said Oggle, halting me in my actions. "It's this: do you want to be right or do you want to be happy," continuing Oggle went on, "we decided here in The Land of Pleasant that our happiness and contentment was better than defending our individual corner proving we were right. But right now, that's your choice." I sat and thought long and hard, pondering deeply over Oggle's comments and finally, I agreed with them. Their happiness was more important than me having my own way for my benefit when there was a bigger picture to consider.

"I'm sorry. You are right, and I am wrong," I replied.

"Thank you, that is wonderful to hear," they all responded in unison.

"Tell me," I asked, "What did your King mean when he mentioned meeting more interesting people?" Three Stabmows looked at Wise and waited for his answer.

"Well," said Wise slowly. "Chances are you will…meet at some point…ummm…someone known in short as… TSTM."

"Who or what is TSTM?"

Wise was about to answer when Oggle suddenly went, "*Ssssshhhhh* everyone, what's that noise, I can hear music floating on the evening air." We all rushed outside our big oak tree and listened. I couldn't hear a thing, Oggle could, and then Wise raised his eyebrows and nodded knowingly, followed by Boggle and Foggle together. Boggle took a few steps forward and focused his attention on a far distant point on the landscape.

"Look," he said pointing in the direction he was staring. Again, I couldn't see what he was pointing at, but the others could.

Boggle continued, "The music is coming down through that gorge. That's the way Brave is heading, which means he has survived everything and the Ogre is following him."

"How much time do you guys think we have?" I asked. The sun was setting low in the distant sky, dusk was now upon us, the shadows were getting longer.

Wise took all this in then answered my question. "We have just under an hour to show you the way. When we are near the bridge, we must leave you. You must stay in hiding and always out of sight."

Chapter 10
Through the Rorret Gorge

The huge Ogre was passing the Mungawumba Tree; seeing the snake paralysed with its huge mouth wedged open, he hit the snake across the side of its head, causing the shaft of wood to come free. The snake shook its huge head like something coming out of a deep sleep then it slowly slithered down the tree. Brave kept up a steady pace, constantly playing the flute and zig-zagging his way from cover to cover. It was while he was doing this that he noticed in the side of the hill he was passing a steep narrow gorge. While still playing the flute, he wandered into it for a closer look. *This is the Rorret Gorge,* he thought to himself. Far off in the distance, he could make out the river; it looked like a dark, squiggly, pencil line on nature's canvas.

This is what I've been looking for, thought Brave while continuing to play the flute. "That's the mighty River Enyt. Now to make my way down this gorge, and I've no idea what lives in it." So, pressing on downwards he made his way. It was painfully slow, fraught with boulders across the path, which were helpful for hiding behind and for giving him the right cover. It was on this part of his journey that Brave had a proper look at the Ogre. He had secured cover behind a massive rock fall. Once behind it, Brave stopped to examine it. The way the rocks piled up gave a small peep-like hole right through them. This meant that Brave could see without being seen. Looking at the Ogre from this vantage point, Brave realised how enormous he looked and just how terrifyingly ugly he was. He was about four metres tall, his head was large and shaped like it should belong on a shire horse. His face was covered in lumps and bumps and sores. His shoulders were huge with great big long arms and hands bigger than shovels. His legs looked like twisted tree trunks and on his massive gnarled feet he had seven big toes. As the Ogre continued in its trance, following the music Brave was producing on his flute, a howling noise was heard. Brave continued watching and playing from his hiding place. The howling grew louder and fiercer. Suddenly, over the rocks further up the gorge, rushing at great speed came a pack of wolves. Brave stayed rooted to the spot in his temporary hiding place watching the events unfold while still playing the flute. The 13 wolves launched themselves at the Ogre, trying desperately to bring this monster to the ground. But the Ogre grabbed one, then another, throwing them against the rocks with such force that they were killed instantly. Others he threw high into the air and a few he threw down the gorge. All of them ended up the same. None of them survived. With the excitement over, Brave continued down the gorge playing the flute and secretly leading the Ogre on its downward journey.

Chapter 11
Celebration

Meanwhile in Gulberia, the King had ordered a tidy-up of the castle. What was repairable was moved into the workshops; everything beyond repair, which could be burned was taken outside the castle and stacked up like a great big bonfire. A stuffed dummy was made looking like the Ogre and placed at the top of the bonfire. Stalls were set up, feasting, music, dancing, and all manner of events were prepared, and the King declared an annual holiday called The Ugly Ogre's Day.

There were jugglers and jesting and jokers galore.
Acrobatic dancers, dancing all over the floor.
There were locals dressed up in fancy costumes
Looking like Ogres being chased out of town.

There were musicians and music and a big brass band,
All playing the freedom song of their land.
There were performers and actors
Upon a grand stage,
Telling the freedom story to every age.

The king was happy and the queen a delight,
They led all the dancing both morning and night.
The celebrations lasted a whole week long,
All taking part the weak and the strong.

All playing their part telling their history,
How Brave came from Pleasant and brought them victory.

The jokers were on top form telling all the latest Ogre jokes like:
"What do you give an Ogre with big feet?"
"We don't know. What do you give an Ogre with big feet?" shouted the happy crowd.

"Plenty of room," replied the Jokers.

"Here's another one for you. How does an Ogre count to 14?"

"We don't know. How does an Ogre count to 14?" shouted the crowd again.

"On his toes," laughed the Jokers.

"Here's another one," shouted another joker. "Did you hear about the two-headed Ogre, who got so angry that he was beside himself with rage?" Once again, the crowd shrieked with laughter.

And of course the celebrations lasted longer than a week and they took place every year.

Chapter 12
Back in the Gorge

Back in the gorge, Brave was on the move, still playing his flute as he moved cautiously from boulder to boulder and rock pile to rock pile, totally unaware of the celebrations taking place in Gulberia. Another quick glance over his shoulder and he could see the Ogre following him, still in the mystical trance as he followed the music. Without warning, the air was filled with a deafening screeching sound. Brave glanced to the sky and saw five big birds of prey called Ked Rites swooping down on the Ogre, their great beaks pecking savagely at him; then climbing high in the sky and diving at the great monster using their big claws to tear at its flesh. Eventually, the Ogre caught them in his massive hands and flung them against the rock wall of the gorge. By this time, his face and arms were bleeding where the lumps of flesh were ripped out. As soon as the interruption was passed, the Ogre resumed his steady plodding. Brave was about 200 metres in front of the Ogre, the Burnew Bridge was half a mile in front, Brave could see the ideal hiding place. He kept up his steady pace, continually playing the flute at the same time.

At the other side of the bridge, I had carefully selected a good hiding place. As you come over the Burnew Bridge, there is an old stone building called the Boat House. On the outside wall is a mark which was made a long time ago by the owner after the river had flooded. A bit further along is a small bridge going over a brook, which feeds into the main river. Beyond this is a wide concrete ramp called a slipway, which is used for launching small boats safely onto the river, and just beyond that is a play area; near the play area was my hiding place because I had to trap the Ogre at this chosen spot. My challenge was to make him stand still long enough for the full moon to shine on him. Hopefully when this happened, the Ogre will turn and look straight at the face of the moon, at the right time, I must stop playing and let everything else take its course. And so I sat patiently, watching and waiting.

As Brave reached the bottom of the gorge, there was a huge rumbling sound behind him, the ground was shaking violently. As Brave looked back up the gorge, he realised the massive stone, which was standing upright like a huge monument, was the reason for the rumbling sound. The Ogre had caused a rockslide, tonnes of rocks, boulders, rubble, and stones of all shapes and sizes were gathering in size, speed, and volume. The Ogre with his great arms rotating in an anti-clockwise fashion like a windmill and his legs peddling as if they were in reverse, was making the rockslide worse. Brave continued playing, racing for his final hiding place. The Ogre was too preoccupied to spot Brave, which was just as well. Brave slid over the side of the riverbank. The hiding place was better than he'd anticipated, set in the riverbank surrounded by bushes, brambles, and shrubs, the hiding place was a hollow. From his vantage point, Brave could watch everything while still playing on the flute. The Ogre was an amazing sight as he continued with his frantic arms and legs actions. How he stayed upright was remarkable. Closer and closer he came to the end of the gorge. The moon was completely blotted out by the night's cloud cover. *Will the residents hear the noise and wake up?* Brave thought to himself.

Brave was in high spirits as he watched the Ogre hurtling down through the gorge. Closer and closer he came. Already boulders, rocks and stones were landing in the river, stirring the water up so it looked as if it was a witch's boiling pot. More and more rocks and boulders were hurled into the river. Greater and greater the water appeared to be boiling and closer and closer came the old Ogre. Arms spinning like demented windmill sails and his legs continually rotating backwards as he tried maintaining his balance.

From the other side of the river, all I could see from my secluded spot was a huge gathering of a thick dust cloud, and I could just distinguish the sound of the flute. Listening intently, I waited. I just hoped and prayed Brave was safe. From my hiding place, all I could do was watch, wonder and wait for the right moment. The anticipation was mounting. "Be patient," I kept telling myself. "All things come to those who have patience." The dust cloud was now mingled with water from the constant crashing of rocks and boulders pouring into the river.

Brave kept playing the flute. The Ogre was still hurtling through the gorge; how he still stayed upright was a miracle. The boulders kept crashing into the river, the dust cloud kept on rising, and Brave kept playing. *Not much longer now,* he thought, *and my part in this adventure will be over,* and without any warning, it was. The rockslide ended. The river slowly returned to its normal flowing self and the Ogre steadied himself and continued walking towards the bridge as the flute music was seamlessly replaced by the haunting music from the harmonica. All Brave could do was hold his breath and watch as the ugly Ogre continued stumbling along in his trance-like state.

Chapter 13
Grand Finale

From my hiding place, I continued playing 'Blue Is the Way That I Feel'. It was the only melancholy tune I could think of. But it was working. One slow lumbering step after another, he came across the Burnew Bridge. At the end of the bridge, without hesitating, he turned left onto the footpath, passing the old stone public house. His great, big shadow was cast over the building like a black cloak. I kept playing the same tune. He kept walking, reaching the bridge over the brook, which he easily cleared with one of his huge slow strides. I kept playing, he kept plodding in his trance-like state ever closer to the spot I had previously marked out. It was on the grass, just off the path where it bends to the right, almost on the edge of the riverbank. I kept slowly playing the harmonica. I was feeling quite impressed with my musical ability. For someone who can't sing, doesn't play anything and can only whistle a bit, I was doing quite well.

The Ogre was passing the concrete slipway. He was something out of a nightmare. Now he was back on the path about forty-five metres from the spot. I kept playing. He kept walking… 30 metres… "What was the advice from Wise…" 25 metres… I kept playing. He kept walking… 15 metres… I kept playing. He kept walking. "Oh yes, that's it, throw a stone into the river, this will cause a distraction, and he will step off the path and onto the grass." I held the stone in my right hand while still playing the harmonica. He kept walking. I prepared to throw… 5 metres… I kept playing. He kept walking… almost there… I kept playing. He kept walking. *Now*, I said in my head. The stone whizzed through the air, landing in the river, making a loud splash. The Ogre growled and turned to his left, stepping on to the grass. Instantly, I stopped playing. At that precise moment, the clouds parted and the full moon shone in all its nightly brilliance. The huge Ogre turned his face to the moon. The moon was shining down on this ugly creature, illuminating him in the blackness of the night. As this was happening, the ground beneath the Ogre's feet started gurgling and bubbling and turning into sinking sand. Slowly, he sunk into the ground up to his ankles. The gurgling ground had a deep, dark reddish brown colour to it. The Ogre was transfixed staring at the moon and slowly sinking until the ground was around his calf muscles. Totally paralysed, he kept staring at the moon, its yellowish face smiling down on him. The bubbling, gurgling ground was just below his knees. Still he kept staring at the moon, and the Ogre continued slowly sinking into this strange mess. The Ogre kept slowly sinking, the gurgling ground was just above his knees. The Ogre didn't flinch, he was transfixed, and his gaze at the moon was expressionless as if he were hypnotised. He continued sinking until the ground he was sinking into reached a little further up his thighs. Without warning, the ground stopped sinking and became like a large rectangular slab of brownish, reddish marble. Like a big foundation base. The Ogre didn't struggle; he was paralysed as he stared at the moon, and as he stared a further transformation took place. His whole body became like off-white marble, his arms and hands seemed to melt into his body as his head, shoulders and neck became as one as they slowly melted into this marble-like structure. Within 30 minutes, this transforming process was complete. To this day, you can still see his horse-like face as the Ogre looks like an off-white statue set in concrete on a large base on a grassy bank alongside the famous River Enyt. And if ever you are visiting the Burnew Riverside Park, you will see the statue with the horse like head engraved in it.

I yawned, stretching myself in a slow satisfying manner. As I did, I heard my wife saying, "You've woken up then. You've been sending them home like a goodun, so I decided to let you have a lie in this morning. Breakfast is ready when you are."

I sat up in bed and asked, "What time is it?"

"It's 10:30 and it's pouring down, it's the ideal day for sorting your boxes in the attic," replied my wife. As she turned and went downstairs, my hand accidently slid under my pillow; it touched something made of metal and plastic. I pulled it and to my amazement, it was the mouth organ, inscribed on it was the following: 'From your new friends in The Land of Pleasant'. T.S.T.M.

But who is T.S.T.M? In the next story, you find out.

Volume 2
The Screaming Woman

Chapter 1
The Train Journey

I yawned, stretching myself as I slowly woke up. I was in B carriage travelling from Newcastle in the Northeast of England to Penzance in Cornwall. I've always enjoyed train rides but this was for business not pleasure. As I slowly came to my senses, I realised the carriage was totally empty, well, almost, because I was in it. *Well, I thought to myself, I did book the quiet carriage.* Then I wondered how far had the train travelled, *we must be quite a way down the country now because I have slept for hours.* As these thoughts were going through my mind, the train driver made an announcement, "The next station stop is Durham. Would all passengers leaving the train take all their belongings with them and please mind the gap as you step off the train. Durham, the next station stop."

Durham. I sat bolt upright, looked at my watch and declared, "That's impossible, I've been on this train for five hours and Durham is a ten-minute journey from Newcastle." I slumped back in the seat. *Maybe, I thought, I've slept deeply for ten minutes or my watch isn't working.* As I stared out of the train window, I drifted off to sleep again.

"The train will shortly be arriving at Mahrud," the announcement woke me with a start. *Mahrud, never heard of it, I thought.* As I surfaced to a state of consciousness, I was aware of a man sitting opposite me. He looked out of place dressed in Victorian clothes with his long, black frock coat, tall black hat, and scruffy black trousers and polished but very worn-out black boots. I was about to smile at him politely when I noticed the carriage I was travelling in wasn't the modern comfortable type of the twenty-first century but the old-fashioned sort with the compartment off the corridor and two long bench seats, the one facing the other, and now I was facing backwards, which was definitely the opposite way I was facing when I set off from Newcastle. Panic gripped me. "When and how did that happen?" I stammered to myself. "What's going on?" I pinched myself, thinking I was dreaming. I started to sweat;

looking up at the old out-of-place man opposite me, I got a bigger shock. Blinking quickly and looking away for a few seconds to try and compose myself, then slowly, very slowly, I looked back in his direction. I had not been mistaken. I could see through him. He was hollow. From the top of his tall black hat to the tips of his black pointy boots, he was hollow. I could…I could see straight through him. Oddly enough, he looked strangely familiar. I must confess, I was in a right state. What had happened to the train I got on at Newcastle? Where was I now? How was my journey going to end? And would I reach my destination on time? Probably not and who was this stranger?

I tried to get my brain in gear, I tried thinking logically, and I tried thinking laterally. I tried thinking inside the box and I tried thinking outside the box.

I turned the problem upside down and inside out. Finally, I plucked up courage to ask The See Thru Man if he could give me any answers. As I opened my mouth to speak, another announcement was made by the train driver. "Would all passengers please sit down and secure their seatbelts. Thank you."

"Why do we need to fasten our seat belts?" I asked, not to The See Thru Man, I just spoke the question out loud. Under normal circumstances, this might have broken the ice, but things weren't normal today. The See Thru Man just sat there, staring into space. As I fastened my seat belt, the train accelerated like a rocket. It was excitingly terrifying.

Somewhere down the train, a woman's voice screamed out, "The bridge is gone."

Finally I spoke up. "What bridge?" I stammered, "And who's that woman and is she like you?"

"Transparent," he smiled. Not an unpleasant smile. Not ghostly, just odd. Odd because he was see thru.

"Of course, the bridge has gone, that's why we are accelerating," he smiled again, then added, "You are in for a big surprise when we land on the other side."

"On the other side of what?" I replied.

"Well, you should look out of the window," he snapped. I turned towards the window and for the first time I realised the window blind was down but the carriage wasn't dark, in fact it was quite bright. *How strange,* I thought, *but then lots of things were strange today.* I opened the blind and was shocked at the speed we were travelling; we were flying along. The hedgerow was whizzing past. Without any warning the train swerved to the left making a big bend. It wasn't on the tracks any longer, it was in the air flying over a wide river and heading for a small hill in the distance. The See Thru Man smiled again and reached inside his long black coat. "Let me give you this," he said. "You will need it when you get off at the next station," and he pulled out of his coat a mirror.

My eyes popped out of my head. It was two metres by a metre. "How did you do that?" I stammered.

"Take it," said The See Thru Man. "Put it in your inside pocket, you will need it when you get out at the next station."

"I can't put this in my inside pocket," I exclaimed.

"You will discover it fits quite snuggly. You need to keep it safe, it will help you on your travels," he said calmly. I unbuttoned my coat and made my first attempt. I banged the mirror against the ceiling. I hit it against the wall. I got it wedged in the corner of the carriage and all the time The See Thru Man just smiled. I repeated my attempts with dismal success. "It's simple to do," he encouraged. "You put it in your inside pocket, you don't wrestle with it." *Put it,* I thought. *That's easy for you to say, you're not the one in a state of confusion.* "Put it," he repeated, "in your inside pocket." I listened carefully to what he said, and I finally paid attention to the way he said it. *Put it, hmmm don't struggle with it, just put it.*

I opened my coat, picked up the mirror and said to myself, "Put it in your inside pocket." I did and to my amazement, it fitted, snuggly. The train came to an abrupt stop. I looked out of the window and realised we were at the station. "This is your stop," said The See Thru Man. "Now listen carefully, wait until the train has disappeared, then stand with your back to the station name plate and take the mirror out of your pocket and look in it. I think you are in for a pleasant surprise." I picked my bags up and opened the sliding doors from the compartment to the corridor. "See you again soon," he said. "Oh, by the way, the mirror is called 'The Mirror of Hturt', and watch out for the screaming woman." And with that farewell, I left the train and started walking along the platform following the way out sign. The fresh air and sunshine brought on a sneeze. I dug my hankie out of my pocket and *Aaaaagh Chooooo*; when you sneeze, you close your eyes. It's one of those strange things we all do. I blew my nose and put my hankie back in my pocket. All of this took just a few seconds, but when I looked around, the train had vanished. The track in both directions was straight for hundreds of metres. I couldn't believe it. Where had it gone? This was one strange day. My business trip to Cornwall was out of my mind. All the training I was going to do with the group in Penzance was a million miles away. I looked up and down the length of the platform. It was one of those country type stations, old-fashioned, overlooked, forgotten, tired and forlorn. But it seemed to take an age walking towards the way out. As I got close to it, I began looking for my ticket. When I remembered what The See Thru Man had said about the station nameplate, I walked further down the platform looking for it. It took me 90 minutes to reach the end of the platform and, no sign. "Well that's really helpful," I declared. I now began to look around me; the view across the track looked familiar. I turned around; this view had the same affect. Familiar. It was at that moment I realised the train station was deserted. There was no one about. Not a single soul, no station staff, no passengers, not the barking of a dog, no singing of birds, not the sound of a car or a bus, nothing. I then had this awful thought. What year is it? When I left Newcastle, it was May 2014. But this was anything but that. And yet everything looked familiar but old-fashioned. Then I remembered again the station sign. I must find it before I do anything else. So, with that resolve, I started walking back down the platform. I went just a few metres when I saw it. How could I miss it? It was a very long sign in upper case and underlined.

ꓕИAꙄAƎ⅃ꟼꟼOⱯИAⱯƎHTOTƎMOⵛ⅃ƎW

What kind of place is this? I thought. I tried pronouncing it and failed miserably. "It's a bit of a tongue twister," I said. I tried again but without success.

Then I remembered what The See Thru Man said. "Wait until the train has disappeared, then stand with your back to the station name plate and take the mirror out of your pocket and look in it. I think you are in for a pleasant surprise." Well, let's see what happens. I reached inside my pocket for the mirror, then I remembered I would need both hands, so I put my bags down, stood with my back to the sign and took, or should I say, pulled the mirror slowly out of my pocket. There it was, two metres by a metre. Amazing. I held it up so I could see the sign in the mirror. It took me a moment or two before I was able to read it.

WELCOMETOTHELANDOFPLEASANT
WELCOME TO THE LAND OF PLEASANT!!!
The Land of Pleasant. I told my children and their friends' children and my grandchildren stories about The Land of Pleasant.

Now I realised why things seemed out of place but familiar; I'd been here before.

My arms were suddenly aching; I was still holding the mirror. Remembering the instructions from The See Thru Man, I 'put' the mirror back into my inside pocket. Picking up my bags I turned and walked out of the station.

The sun was shining, there were a few white fluffy clouds in the sky, and the birds were singing in the treetops; in fact, everything was very pleasant and the native language of this pleasant land is Rorrim, which crops up from time to time. But for the benefit of my readers, I will mainly use English.

Chapter 2
The Land of Pleasant

"*Pssssst. Pssssst. Pssssst.* He's here, I knew he would come." I turned around looking in the direction of the voice but I saw no one. I kept walking slowly because I was taking in my surroundings. This was a pleasant place. The path through the woods was soft beneath my feet. The air was sweet to breathe, and not too hot, the smell of woodland flowers seemed to fill my nose with delight. My eyes took in such rich colours; deep pinks, vibrant orange, distinctive yellows, sunset reds, gorgeous greens and brilliant blues, and so many other colours which were equally amazing.

"*Pssst, Pssst.* Go on, stop him, go on before it's too late." Again, I looked in the direction of the voice and again I saw nothing. Standing perfectly still, I started looking more intently. While doing this, I heard the voice again. "It must be him. The See Thru Man said he would bring him." Now they really had my attention.

"Where are you?" I asked.

"Up here."

"Down here."

"Over here," came their replies.

"Well, that's three of you and I know there should be four. So, which one of you is missing? Let me guess," I said. I spent a few minutes working it out, using my fingers to name them. "It must be Foggle," I eventually said.

"Well that took you long enough," they all replied together.

"Come on, we'd better show him where he's staying, then once you've settled in and wearing the right clothes, we will tell you all about our adventure and how it turned out."

"I would love to stay and hear all about it, but I'm supposed to be in Cornwall for two days and I'm due back home on Friday."

"Now don't you go fretting about Cornwall and your business trip. All that will happen and you'll be back by Friday as if you'd never been away."

"Do you know," they continued, "you sound just like Robinson Crusoe."

"Robinson Crusoe?" I said.

"Yes. All his work was done by Friday," they chuckled. "But firstly, we must ask you if you have the Mirror of Hturt."

"Yes," I replied. "I 'put' it in my inside pocket."

"Fantastic, you must have listened well to The See Thru Man."

"I did, eventually, but it took me several attempts to get it right," I replied.

"That's good news because we'll need your help soon."

Before I go on, I think it's about time I introduced you to my friends in The Land of Pleasant. They are Oggle, Foggle, Boggle, and Wise, plus one more who isn't around just now, he's rather busy.

Firstly, they are all similar, like humans, similar but different. They are all about the same size as adult badgers and they are called Stabmows. They usually walk on their back legs. They have big round faces with sparkling eyes, which are always brown in colour. Their paws are very soft with long claws for climbing, which they are very good at. Their fur coats are always striped; black and white or brown and white or grey and white or ginger and white, and always very, very, very soft; all very pleasant.

Well now, that's enough of their description. Let me introduce them to you one at a time. So this is Oggle. He was given his name because he is so inquisitive and always curious. Yes, that's right, he's always ogling at something. The next in line is Foggle. He was given his name because in general terms, he always gave the impression that he doesn't have a clue what was going on; you got it, he doesn't have the foggiest. But that's not really true. Then we come to Boggle. He was always watching the telly, always boggling at the box. But he was also called Boggle because of his love for word games. And finally, we come to Wise, who has so much wisdom he should have been called Namron, and he has more common sense than most for his age, so he was called Wise and it really suits him. Well now, the introductions are over and I must settle in, unpack and put on more suitable clothing. "Right then, boys, can you show me where I am staying please." With that a door opened in the trunk of the massive oak tree, which was a short distance away, followed by an unfolding of steps. Not a rope ladder, a proper set of steps, six in total. Standing in the door was the fifth member of this group. "Hello, Brave," I called out. "It's good to see you. Are you fit and well?"

"I am doing, champion, thank you," he replied. "I'm like a lion; it is so good to be back in The Land of Pleasant."

"When did you get back?" I asked, "Have you been anywhere exciting?"

"Exciting, you bet I have," he replied. "But before I tell of my adventures, you'd better come in, sit down because we need your help. Now make yourself comfortable." I quickly climbed the steps and stepping over the threshold of their home, I found myself looking into a full length mirror and to my utter amazement, I was wearing a long fur coat just like theirs except mine was removable and it was black and white stripped.

I smiled to myself and murmured, "Hmmm, pleasant, very pleasant indeed."

"Come in, come in," said Brave. "Take your coat off and settle down in that easy chair over there. Wise has got your supper ready and it's mixed grill, your favourite." I settled in and Wise brought my supper with a special drink of Woodland Surprise. It's an interesting colour, amber with a hint of bright red. As I sat enjoying my supper with my friends sitting around, Brave started telling me of their recent adventures.

Chapter 3
The Mountains Beyond

"As you know," started Brave, "if you go out through the back door, down the garden path, through the hedge, down the bank towards the river and climb the big Weeping Willow tree, and when you get close to the top, if you look way out west, you will see a mountain range called The Naddibrof Mountains. We never knew they were there, not until Great Uncle Woggle, or Woggle the Wanderer as everyone called him, climbed this tree some time ago. Everything here is pleasant as you know, from the weather to those who live here. What we do and how we do it. How we work and how we play. Everything is pleasant. Not perfect, but pleasant. What we eat and drink. It's all very pleasant. Then one day, while he was resting on the riverbank, which was unusual for him and feeling adventurous and inquisitive, Woggle the Wanderer decided to climb the Weeping Willow tree and when he had, he discovered that in the distance far across the River of Ecaep is a very dark mountain range. Dark grey, jagged, rocky mountain peaks, no sunshine, no trees, bushes or grass, no birds, just forbidding towering mountains rising high into the dark grey sky. As he sat on a branch looking at this terrible sight, he was aware that he was not alone. Looking over his shoulder, he had the shock of his life. Sitting behind him, dressed in the most peculiar fashion, was The See Thru Man.

Now, Woggle the Wanderer was known for his courage, but this intrusion took his breath away. "Who are you?" he demanded.

"The See Thru Man, of course," replied The See Thru Man, with his non-ghostly smile. "I have a very special commission for you. It will test your strength, your courage, your cunningness, and your bravery to the limit."

Now, at this point, The See Thru Man paused for effect, knowing that he had Woggle's full attention. "Speak up, man. There's no need to be shy about these things," demanded Woggle.

"You see those mountains beyond the river; well, they are called the Naddibrof Mountains. The wind is never silent, it howls like baying wolf, night and day. Trapped in a cave, beyond the tallest jagged mountain peak in a strongbox are the ancient secrets to The Land of Pleasant, and they were stolen by and are now guarded by the Screaming Woman. Your job is to rescue the secrets and entice the Screaming Woman away from those mountains, setting a trap for her so she will disappear forever and life will return to the mountain range once more, and The Land of Pleasant will be kept safe. It's up to you; you are the only one who is right for the task."

Again, The See Thru Man paused and this time he watched Woggle the Wanderer closely. Woggle never flinched. He didn't move a muscle. He just sat on the branch of the tree, motionless, staring firstly at the river, then at the mountains and back again.

Finally, he broke the silence. "What will I need to take with me? When do I set off? How much time do I have? Do I travel alone? And who is the Screaming Woman?"

"Time is not important, success is. You travel alone, but I will have someone here ready for you to complete the task when you get back.

"As for the Screaming Woman, she is old, very old, 510 years old to be exact. She wears an old, full-length, dark grey cloak with a hood which covers her dark grey straggled hair. And all you need to take with you is this," and with that The See Thru Man put his hand into his inside pocket and took out a very, very, very long thin box. "This," he said, "is called the Eveilebylno Box." Woggle the Wanderer stared at it saying nothing. Suddenly, The See Thru Man held in his hand a short spiral, black and silver cane.

"Where did that come from?" demanded Woggle.

"What, this black shiny thing," chuckled The See Thru Man, "Up my sleeve, of course. Now watch carefully." And with that he gently tapped one corner of the box. The lid slowly opened, rising silently on its gold hinges. As Woggle looked inside the box, his face showed serious disappointment. The box was empty; in fact, it was worse than empty, it was see thru. Woggle stared in disbelief at The See Thru Man.

"Am I missing something?" he asked.

"Not at all," came the reply. "This box contains everything you need to be successful. All you have to do is 'put' your hand into the box and take out what you need." Woggle looked again and again; he saw nothing in the box. "Are you having a laugh?" he snapped.

"Listen, this box is called the Eveilebylno Box."

Woggle hesitated, thinking carefully about it, taking it all in, then he 'put' his hand into the box and carefully took out a big coil of rope. "Well done," cried The See Thru Man. "But remember, you only need the box, that way you can travel light, and when you've used something, don't try and put it back, it won't happen that way around. You simply leave what you've used when you've finished with them."

"What? Leave it on the ground?"

"That's right, you leave them and they disappear, which means all you need is the Eveilebylno Box."

"Well, that sounds clever but where do I keep it?" replied Woggle.

"You don't keep it, when it's not in use you 'put' it in your inside pocket or for you, in your pouch," replied The See Thru Man. And with that instruction, Woggle picked up the Eveilebylno Box and balancing carefully on the branch made a half-hearted attempt at putting it in his pouch and failed. The See Thru Man smiled and said, "Don't be half-hearted with it, just 'put' it in your pouch. Woggle contemplated this for a moment, thinking to himself it must be possible. Then, with renewed confidence, he 'put' the box into his pouch and it fitted very snuggly indeed.

"That's amazing," declared Woggle. "So, am I right in thinking that I can set off as soon as I like?"

"Whenever you're ready. Just use the rope first to get the idea." So, tying the rope around the branch and then throwing it to the ground, Woggle lowered himself off the branch, and quickly, he slid down the rope to the ground. As soon as he landed, The See Thru Man called out, "Now walk away just three steps and turn around." Woggle the Wanderer did so and to his amazement, the rope had vanished and so had The See Thru Man.

For a few moments, Woggle stood there scratching his head. Then with a firm resolve, he headed for the riverbank. Sitting there for a few moments, reflecting on all that had happened and the commission he was given, he decided to make some plans. The first thing he did was to leave a note for Brave explaining all that had taken place and where he was going. "Which is why," said Brave, "we are able to give you the story."

The next thing Woggle did was to reach inside his pouch and carefully and slowly take out the box. Using the short shiny black and silver spiral cane, he softly tapped the one corner. Once again, the lid slowly opened. Woggle looked inside and looked at the river, then putting his paw inside, he lifted out with a paddle a one-man canoe.

"Wow," was all Woggle could say. Closing the lid, he 'put' the Eveilebylno Box back into his pouch. Next, he gently placed the canoe onto the river, then he placed one end of the paddle on the back of the cockpit and the other on the riverbank. He sat on the paddle and swung himself into the canoe. Then using the paddle, he pushed himself out into the River of Ecaep. He found his heart racing with excitement, his breathing was quick and fast. This was the kind of adventure he needed.

It didn't take Woggle very long to paddle across the river. As he climbed out of the canoe onto the opposite river bank, he felt inside his pouch. "Hmmmmm, it's still there," he murmured. As he scurried up the bank over the dark grey rocks, he remembered the canoe, turning back and looking at the spot where he left it. He was startled; it had vanished. Remembering what The See Thru Man said, he allowed himself a small smile. Turning around, he started for the rock face. The wind was suddenly ice cold; the rock face was very forbidding and unfriendly. The howling wind was suddenly shrieking wildly. It was howling like the wind had a wolf's head. It was a horrible noise; it made Woggle's blood run cold. Plucking up his courage, Woggle headed for a narrow crack he spotted in the rock face.

"I wonder where this will lead me," said Woggle to himself. If you want to find out, read on if you dare.

Chapter 4
The Screaming Woman

As Woggle started climbing through the narrow crack in the rock face, he heard a chilling, screaming voice howling, "Beware, beware, beware." Woggle the Wanderer paused for a moment and seeing no one, continued climbing. Now Woggle and everyone else from The Land of Pleasant are very capable on their hind legs, but they are also very able on all fours when it suits them and because of their soft bodies, they are able to get through and into very small spaces and gaps. The rock face was slimy, and the smell was awful. Woggle remembered, success was more important than time. Right then, let's calm down and think this through properly. Sitting on a grey, slimy rock, he began reflecting on the challenge. 'Trapped in a cave beyond the tallest jagged mountain peak in a strongbox are the ancient secrets to The Land of Pleasant.'

Hmmmmm, thought Woggle to himself. *Right now, I'm not certain which direction that mountain peak is in.* At that moment, the rock he was sitting on heaved, almost like an earthquake, and roared. Woggle almost lost his balance. Gripping the wet, slimy rock face, Woggle pressed himself into a narrow crevice. Again, the rock heaved and roared, as if it were trying to break free. Suddenly, a deafening scream filled the air, and the wind started howling again like a baying wolf. From his hiding place, Woggle watched with intense interest. The scream wasn't saying anything this time; it was just a continuous wailing sound, which rose above the noise of the wind. Again, the slimy dark grey rock heaved and roared like a monster trying to escape, then with a sudden sigh it settled down. As it did, Woggle was distracted by another movement off to his left. As his keen eyes penetrated the dark surroundings, he saw her; squeezing himself further into the crevice but leaving just enough space to use one eye, he kept a careful watch.

As far as he could make out, she was hideous. Occasionally, she would slowly straighten her huge bent back and peering out from beneath her dark grey hooded cloak, she revealed her ugly face, with her beak-like nose and twisted thin-lipped mouth. Her long dark grey hair was unwashed and unkempt, and her skin was wrinkled and dry. Bone dry. Woggle shuddered as he watched her. Pondering for a moment, he realised that she didn't know he was here. Well, not yet. That could be useful. But he didn't know if anyone else lived in this dreadful place. As Woggle continued to watch her, she straightened herself completely. She was almost three metres tall and with that she vanished into thin air.

Giving himself time to recover from this distraction, Woggle reconsidered his challenge while remembering, success is more important than time. Looking around at his surroundings, Woggle suddenly saw directly above what should be called daylight; should be, but in this hostile place, he was really uncertain. *But it's worth a go,* thought Woggle to himself. *If I can get up there, I might see more of the landscape. I might see the mountain I need to go beyond, in order to find the cave.* As he continued looking upwards, he was aware that what he was examining was something like an ancient chimney. He had a flash of inspiration; slowly, removing the box from his pouch and balancing it carefully across the rocks, he gently tapped the lid. As usual, it opened silently. Looking inside the empty see thru box, Woggle continued thinking, then reaching inside, he took out a bow and an arrow with a special steel crosshead on the one end and a long length of rope attached to the other end. 'Putting' the box back in his pouch and picking up the bow and arrow, Woggle settled himself firmly against the rock face. "Remember, success is more important than time," he whispered to himself. Then placing the arrow into position and pulling the bowstring back until it was taut and taking careful aim, Woggle steadied himself. The chimney was about 100 metres high with a small loophole at the top. He was just about to release the arrow when *roar* went the rock, heaving itself in a frantic, manic fashion. Woggle almost let the arrow fly.

As the rock sighed and started to settle down again, the front of the rock turned like a massive head towards Woggle and in a hoarse whisper said, "We want you to succeed and set us free," and with that, the rock settled in its place once more.

"What is the beast beneath my feet?" murmured Woggle. Settling back down in his position and regaining his composure, he once again took careful aim but this time with more grim determination.

Speaking slowly to himself he said, "Aim, steady now, hold it steady, now hold your nerve, now hold your breath and count to three: 1...2...3 and FIRE," letting the arrow go it sped upwards on a true course. Woggle waited and watched. The rope attached to the arrow kept unwinding, through the loophole went the arrow and out of sight.

Suddenly, there was a loud crack as the arrow found its mark, piercing a rock face and coming to a sudden stop as it anchored itself into the rock face. The rope stopped unwinding. *Robin Hood would be proud of that,* smiled Woggle to himself. Making certain the box was safe in his pouch, Woggle took hold of the rope and gave it a tug. "Hmmm that seems secure enough," he said to himself, "one more for good measure. Excellent." Feeling satisfied and very pleased with himself, he took hold of the rope with his paws and began the long climb. His advantage was being able to use his four paws on the rope. Onwards and upwards he went, but as he neared the top, he hesitated. Not knowing if the noise made by the arrow had aroused suspicion of his presence. Confident that all was safe, he finished the climb. As he made it out of the chimney, he began taking in his new surroundings. He was aware for the first time of the utter isolation of this desolate mountain range. Everything in every direction was dark grey. There were no flowers, no grass, no trees, no birds, not the sound of any animal, nothing except the howling wind. As Woggle looked all around him, he started focusing his attention on the far distance just to see if there was any change in the landscape. There wasn't, there was nothing. "Wait a minute, what's that way over there in the east?" he muttered quietly. It looked like an emerald shining out against the dark grey, which seems to be everywhere else, making it look out of place.

Suddenly, he realised that the dark grey mountain range was slowly engulfing everything, all except this emerald jewel, which was in danger of being swallowed up. As he continued staring at it, he realised it was The Land of Pleasant. Now he really knew why he had this commission. If he didn't get the secrets of his land back, they would become like this. His job was to save The Land of Pleasant.

What I must do now is get a message back to my friends, Oggle, Foggle, Boggle, Wise, and Brave. But how can I do that? thought Woggle. He had an idea. It was like someone switching the light on. "Inspirational," he whispered to himself, "That's inspirational." As he was reaching into his pouch for the Eveilebylno Box, the dark grey mountain began creaking and groaning as if its age was causing it pain. Spinning around, Woggle watched in horror as the mountain peak behind him started bending low in slow motion as if it was going fall on top of him. Woggle staggered back in amazement. Then in a hoarse whisper, just like the monstrous rock, it said, "Set us free from the Screaming Woman," and with that it slowly straightened up. The smelly damp air was instantly filled with a hideous scream, which filled the mountains. Woggle remained steady, even though his heart was pounding. He realised the sound was coming up through the chimney. Making certain the Eveilebylno Box was safe in his pouch, Woggle jumped to his feet, grabbing a boulder, which was nearby and using his incredible strength he lifted the boulder up, dropping it on top of the chimney stack, covering the hole completely.

I might have given the game away now, though Woggle, *well never mind, that can't be helped.* Resuming his interrupted task, he carefully took the box out of his pouch and with the black and silver spiral cane, he softly tapped the lid. The box opened silently; looking inside, Woggle started thinking, then reaching in he took out one at a time a few different items. The first was a large black envelope, on it written and underlined in silver was the word *Wise.* Next, he took out a few sheets of black parchment paper; written on this and again in silver was an account of all that had taken place. Placing these in the envelope, he placed them in the third item, a black pouch. Pulling the black drawstring tight and knotting it securely, he then rested the final item on a nearby large rock. Closing the box and carefully putting it back into his pouch, he turned his attention to his last item. He gently stroked its neck and tying the pouch around the neck of the big black bird of prey, he quietly whispered his instructions.

All Woggle had to do now was wait with the bird of prey until it was completely dark, then he would send the bird on its mission. Woggle sat and waited patiently, which is always a challenge when you prefer action to seemingly idleness.

While talking quietly to the bird, reassuring her of her mission and its importance, the big, black bird of prey's eyes gleamed with excitement. After what seemed like an age, the moment came, placing the bird on a large outcrop of rocks, Woggle checked once more, making certain the black pouch around its neck was totally secure. Then he sat down and waited for the bird to rise into the dark sky. It sat with its head moving from one side to the other, listening into the wind, which was howling more loudly than before. Listening and waiting. Suddenly, it sunk down onto its leg, then with a mighty heave, it lifted itself into the howling wind. Spreading its huge black wings it began to soar, riding the thermals, slowly climbing higher and higher in a spiral manner, hardly visible in the night sky as it circled in the wind. Woggle watched holding his breath, not daring to breathe. Up and up the bird kept climbing until it had risen higher than the howling wind. As Woggle continued gazing up into the dark sky, he was startled again by the Screaming Woman. This time she was standing further up a mountain about 100 metres away. "My word," murmured Woggle. "She is the most hideous thing I have ever seen. Thankfully the bird is well on its way by now."

At this point in the story, Brave paused and holding up a black pouch, he said, "It's because of this, we are able to give you a detailed account of all that Woggle went through. The big, black bird of prey arrived one morning, landing on that log just across from our tree. After we read his story, both the bird and the parchment disappeared, leaving us with just this black pouch. But now we must get on with his story."

Woggle was now able to get some rest, which he did for just a few hours. When he woke up, he was ravenous. *I wonder if this will work,* he thought and carefully reaching into his pouch, he pulled out the Eveilebylno Box. As he held the spiral cane, he noticed for the first time that the silver which was embossed into the black wasn't a pattern but writing. "I wonder what this says," he murmured, "first things first. I will study that later." Softly tapping the lid, the box quietly opened. Reaching inside, he took out a handful of mixed nuts—walnuts, Brazil nuts, acorns and monkey nuts. After eating these, he reached into the box again and took out a handful of mixed berries—blackberries, strawberries, blueberries, and raspberries. Feeling satisfied and well fed, he reached in one more time and took out his favourite drink—Woodland Surprise. "That's better," he said softly. Putting the box into his pouch, he turned his attention to the writing on the cane. It was difficult to decipher because it looked like one long word:

'This cane is called the cane of ytilibiderc.'

Finally, he worked it out. The Cane of Credibility. "Hmmm, that is interesting." Woggle noticed something else written around the one end of the cane. Again, it was all one word.

'Only in an emergency squeeze here.'

I must remember that, he thought. And he put the cane safely away. Contemplating his position, Woggle noticed a very narrow path going around the mountainside. *Right, I will follow that and see where it leads.* Making certain once again that the box and cane were safe and secure, he headed for the path. It was much narrower than he realised. To his left was a sheer drop, plunging down about 1,500 metres into total darkness. While on his right, the mountain ascended upwards and was totally vertical. The top of the mountain just disappeared out of sight. "This is the loneliest and most barren place I have ever been to," he said quietly.

Overhead, he heard the Screaming Woman shouting as if tormented. "None of you will ever be free. I have locked you up for ever. Forrrrr evvvvveeeeer," the words seemed to disappear as they trailed off into nothingness. The air around Woggle was thick, heavy, and icy cold, making breathing hard work. But he refused to stop, even though his pace was painfully slow because of the path he was on. Without any warning, the path up in front of him started writhing like a demented snake.

Woggle threw himself to the ground, lying frozen to the spot. "Don't move," he said to himself. "Just lie flat. As flat as you can, and wait patiently." As the path continued in this frantic motion, Woggle heard again the same hoarse whisper. "You must succeed, you will succeed. Keep going, the entrance to the cave is around the next bend and above your head," and with that the path settled down.

Chapter 5
Into the Cave

As he lay on the path, giving it a little more time to remain settled, Woggle heard the path whisper again with its hoarse voice. "Be careful when you enter the cave." Remaining still a little longer was what Woggle needed. It gave him time to think. *Right, I must press on. The cave is not too far ahead.* But the bend in the path went on and on and on into growing darkness. The heaviness in the air was getting more intense and oppressive with every step he took. His surroundings hadn't changed; the drop into the dark abyss was just as terrifying. The dark grey, slimy sheer cliff face kept rising upwards and disappearing into the dark grey clouds. Without warning, the path started rising, and falling beneath Woggle's feet. Instantly, Woggle threw himself to the ground again. As he lay there, the path whispered in its hoarse voice. "Don't give up, you are almost there, watch out for the zig-zag overhanging rock. Once you've passed it safely, look up." Instantly the path was totally still. The wind was howling more loudly than normal. Making his way cautiously around this continuous bend, Woggle was taken by surprise by a very low hanging rock, which was blocking most of the narrow path, half a step further and he would have been pushed over the edge of the cliff and into the dark abyss by its sharp pointed end which was jutting out. He breathed a huge sigh of relief as he realised how close he had come to his own destruction and an awful end to his commission.

Once again, Woggle composed himself. His heart was pounding. "I have been in some tight spots in my time, but this takes the biscuit," Woggle whispered. Like a sixth sense, Woggle knew he was being watched. He didn't know who by and he didn't know where from. He just knew something else was watching him. He also knew he couldn't stay where he was. He had to move on. His sixth sense helped him again. *I must climb around that rock,* he thought, *that's what's watching me.* Lying flat, he slowly wriggled backwards along the path. Looking carefully at the rock face, he worked out how to tackle this latest challenge. The slippery, slimy rock face was far more challenging than Woggle realised. Three times he slipped, almost losing his grip or his foothold. Once he actually fell; not too far fortunately, but when he did, he landed on his back on top of the zigzag rock. While getting his breath back, he was able to look more keenly at the rock face. As he scanned it carefully, he saw it. The entrance to the cave was directly above him, just 30 metres away. Beneath him the zigzag rock vibrated and a low rumbling noise came from deep within it; then in a hoarse whisper, it spoke slowly. "Be careful when you enter the cave. You will need your credibility." The rumbling and vibrating stopped.

"Thank you," whispered Woggle as he slowly rolled himself onto his belly and stood up on his hind legs. *Now for the cave,* he thought.

He was just about to resume his climb when he heard a soft noise behind him; looking over his shoulder he had the shock of his life. Sitting motionless was the big, black bird of prey, its black eyes twinkling brightly. Woggle sat down in front of the bird and gently stroked its neck, then he carefully removed the Eveilebylno Box from his pouch. Tapping the lid with the spiral cane, the box opened silently. Woggle thought for a moment and reaching inside took out a few pages of black parchment paper and carefully wrote another message in silver writing. Next, he took out another black envelope and a black pouch, putting the parchment carefully into the envelope and then the envelope into the pouch. Finally, he tied the pouch to the bird's strong neck. By now, Woggle was hungry again, so reaching into the box he took out some almond nuts, fresh berries and Woodland Surprise. The bird of prey put its head inquisitively on one side. Woggle smiled and gave the bird some nuts and berries. Without warning the bird launched itself off the zigzag rock and instantly disappeared.

Brave paused, holding the second black pouch in his hand. "It came in this, just the same as before, it is amazing really. But at least we know a little of what is going on. But I must continue with the story."

After the bird had gone, Woggle closed the box and put it safely back in his pouch along with the cane. Feeling refreshed from his unexpected rest and snack, he got ready for his climb to the mouth of the cave. As he reached up, getting a firm hold on the slimy rock face, the wind increased in its speed and pressure, howling with more ferocity. It was like a pack of wolves preparing for a hunt. As it died down slightly, the Screaming Woman could be heard. She sounded to Woggle like someone hysterical. Suddenly, the scream changed into a howling moan. *She is becoming my worst nightmare,* he thought. Then focusing his attention again, he began climbing. It was easier than he expected, and finally, he was able to have his first cautious peep into the cave. The smell was absolutely awful, like the death of 100 rotting corpses. It was so bad, it knocked Woggle backwards and almost back down the cliff. Summoning up his courage and taking a deep breath, Woggle crept slowly in the cave. The floor was covered in thick slime. The smell was disgusting. Now, Pleasantonians have excellent night vision, which is really useful in dark caves. As Woggle slowly stood upright in the cave, the slime around his legs began swirling like a whirlpool. Faster and faster. Woggle was knocked off his feet and onto his back and began spinning around and around the cave faster and faster in this whirlpool of slime. Without warning, Woggle was sucked into a tunnel at frantic speed, round one sharp bend after another. There seemed to be no end to this. *I must be in the heart of the mountain.* In a state of panic, Woggle had a brain wave. *The Cane of Credibility,* he thought. Using all his powers of concentration, while still being thrown around at great speed in this tunnel, Woggle took the spiral cane out of his pouch; gripping the end tightly he became aware that it was firmly fixed in his hand. Then reaching behind him, not knowing what he was pointing at, he squeezed the end. Like a coiled spring, the cane straightened out, giving a loud *BANG!!!* Like a rifle shot. The cane fired a thin strong wire rope that shot back up the tunnel, coiling itself around rock. Suddenly, Woggle came to an abrupt stop, then while still holding the cane, the wire began retracting into it, pulling Woggle with it. Slowly and patiently, Woggle gripped the cane. Up until now, Woggle had forgotten about the smell and the slime, which once again was filling his nostrils. Finally, he came to rest and unhooked the rest of the wire, which continued recoiling into the cane. Once this was achieved, the cane curled back into its spiral form again. Woggle was feeling dazed and completely disoriented. From the moment he entered the cave until now, he had been in a right spin. He managed to pull himself up on to the rock, the thin wire rope had been wrapped around. He was puffing and panting and desperately trying to calm himself down when he noticed above him in a crevice on the opposite wall, a large iron box. He forgot his weary dizziness. He forgot the smell and the slime. He forgot that he was trapped in the middle of the Naddibrof Mountains. In his burst of excitement, he almost forgot 'success is more important than time'.

Remembering this principle, he sat for a long time in the darkness of this damp, slimy, smelly, silent tunnel. He was aware that down here he couldn't hear the wind howling, but he didn't know if he was safe from the Screaming Woman. What should he do? What could be done about his escape? As he looked around him, he noticed carved into the roof of the tunnel these words: 'Welcome to the Caves of Riapsid'. *Wait a minute,* thought Woggle, *the secret must be in the phrase.* He reread it, only this time more slowly.

Welcome to the Caves of Riapsid. He paused again, pondering over the short sentence, quietly whispering to himself the word caves. "Now that gives me hope," he said with grim determination. "The best way to go must be down." By now, Woggle was just a little damp. Not totally dry but better than he was from his slimy slide. A plan was coming together in his head. "Hmmm," he murmured with a sense of deep satisfaction. "It's definitely worth a try." Taking the Eveilebylno Box out of his pouch and tapping the corner of the lid softly with the black spiral cane, it slowly and quietly opened. Staring into it, he thought for a very long time. *It must be sturdy and it must be bendable, it must be very strong and very robust. It will need a rope and some anchor points like eyelets to pass the rope through.* Making certain the Eveilebylno Box was stable whilst giving him room to manoeuvre, he reached in with both paws. Gripping firmly, Woggle lifted it up and out of the box, then placing it across the tunnel so he wouldn't lose it and making certain it was secure, he closed the box and put it back into his pouch. "Well that's step one," he said softly, "now for step two." He straddled the floor of the tunnel in order to get the best position for balancing his weight and made every effort not to get into the slimy sludge stuff again. Next, he fastened the rope, one end to the inflatable craft and the other with a slipknot to the rock, which had saved him a little earlier. Sitting himself in the inflatable craft, he took out the Cane of Credibility. As he gripped the cane, he had the same sensation as before. It was as if it became an extension to his arm. Taking very careful aim, he pointed the cane at the iron box above him and squeezed the end of the cane. *Wwwhhhooooossshhhhh,* out from the end of the cane came a metal hand like a grab. It secured itself around the iron box. Woggle could feel it as if he were actually grasping it. Next, he lifted it from its hiding place. It felt incredibly light.

Then lowering it into his inflatable craft, he secured it in the stern with another length of rope. The black cane returned to its spiral shape again, and Woggle put it safely into his pouch. Sitting just forward of mid-way, Woggle took hold of the loose end of the rope, which was securing the inflatable to the rock and gave it a sharp pull. The slipknot came undone, the inflatable was free and Woggle and the iron box were gaining speed more quickly than he anticipated. Plunging downward, faster and faster, firstly around one bend, then around another, twisting, jerking, onwards and ever downwards. Constantly gaining speed, Woggle was hanging on for his life. The slippery, slimy, sludge made the little inflatable gain more speed. A slight rise on the floor of the tunnel and the inflatable took off, and for almost 100 metres it was airborne. "Wow," cried Woggle, "I'm flying." As he hit the sludge and the floor, he was sprayed with the awful smelly stuff. Somewhere way behind him and back up the tunnel, he heard her screaming, "Ooooohhhhh nnnnnooooo. It's gone, my iron box has been stolen."

On and on and on, he continued on his downward flight. "Where is this going to end up," wondered Woggle to himself as he clung on to the sides of his inflatable. Without warning, the angle of descent was almost vertical. After free falling for what seemed like an eternity, he bottomed out at an incredible speed, bursting out of the bottom of the mountain onto a wasteland of small sharp rocks and jagged boulders.

Boom! Bang! *Hhhhhiiiiisssssss*. The inflatable punctured, the air in it came rushing out as it escaped, coming to a sudden stop. Woggle was elated. "Made it!" he exclaimed in his excited state. Turning around he looked at the iron box. "I've no time to lose, because I don't know how much time I have," saying this he took the black cane out of his pocket. Gripping it tightly, Woggle rammed the end of it into the lock in the door; as he did, it uncurled, straightening instantly, squeezing as he had done before. From inside the lock, smoke started pouring out and after a few minutes the lock disintegrated and the door eased slightly on its hinges. Putting the cane back into his pouch, Woggle forced the door open. Inside was a canister with this inscription: 'The Secrets of The Land of Pleasant'. Alongside this was a single sheet of paper with some instructions headed: 'How to Dispel the Screaming Woman Forever'. He read it quickly, then looking up as he pondered the problem, he noticed sitting on a rock a short distance away was the big, black bird of prey. It spread its wings and flew across to where Woggle was sitting. Woggle spoke to the bird, not expecting to have a conversation with it. "How is it you keep coming back, I thought I was only allowed to use things once from the box."

Without any hesitation, the bird answered simply. "You set me free. So I am totally free. I'm free to fly away and I'm free to stay and help. Either way I get to do what I was born to do and that is flying. But this way is the best. Fly and help. Help and fly. It's very simple really."

Woggle carefully pulled the box out of his pouch. Tapping it and reaching inside, he took out another black pouch, a few sheets of black paper with his latest adventure written on it in silver and an envelope. Carefully, he placed his story and the instructions concerning the Screaming Woman into the envelope, then placing these and the canister into the black pouch and tying tight, he then gently secured it around the bird's neck. The bird hopped onto a nearby rock with its head on one side, listening, watching, and waiting. Next, it turned and looked at Woggle, then it looked at the river. Suddenly, Woggle was aware that he was at a different part of the river. It was much, much wider here. It was so wide you couldn't see the opposite bank. "What a problem to be faced with." The bird looked at him again then at the river and spreading its wings wide and pushing up on its strong legs, she rose silently into the air. Only this time it didn't soar upwards but out towards the river. It was a screaming head wind that was howling now. Undeterred, the big bird flew straight at it, occasionally flapping its great wings. As it got a long way out of the river, it turned sharp left, keeping its distance above the surface of the water the same. Just two metres, that was all. Woggle watched and realised the bird was showing him the way to go. Reopening the Eveilebylno Box again, he thought to himself, *I need another one-man canoe with a longer, bigger paddle.*

Reaching inside, he carefully took out what he needed. As he carefully put the box away, he murmured to himself, "This box has been amazing." Carefully, he carried the canoe to an ideal place for climbing in. As he prepared to push off from the shore, he heard the hideous Screaming Woman again. "Right," said Woggle. "Let's execute the last part of this adventure."

Chapter 6
Trapped

"Quickly, Wise, come quickly," cried Boggle. "That big black bird of prey is here again." Wise came down the garden path through the hedge. Boggle was standing a little way off. This time the bird was standing still in the soft green grass. Wise came up, followed closely by Foggle, Brave, and me. Wise carefully took the heavy pouch from around the bird's neck and opened it. "There's more in here this time," he declared. Taking the canister out of the pouch, his hands started trembling with excitement. "I know what this is, this holds the secrets to The Land of Pleasant."

"Wow," they all gasped in unison.

Next, Wise read Woggle's adventure to everyone. "He's been in some scrapes in his time, but this beats them all," said Foggle. As Wise started to read the other paper, his face became grim and very grave.

"What's up?" I asked.

"I now know why you're here," replied Wise. "Now, listen all of you and don't interrupt me whatever you do," said Wise cautiously. All at once, everyone started asking him questions. "STOP. No questions. All will be answered as I explain what we have to do. This piece of paper gives us the steps for dealing with the Screaming Woman forever."

"Not the Screaming Woman," we all shouted together.

"Silence," commanded Brave. "We must all listen to Wise."

"Thank you, Brave. Right, this is what we must do," continued Wise. Then turning to me he asked, "Will you take the Mirror of Hturt out of your inside pocket, please." Slowly and carefully, I obeyed my friend. Continuing he asked, "Will you go into our home and bring out the full length mirror that's in the hallway. It's called the Mirror of Ecitsuj." I jumped up, slipped through the hedge, running up the garden path and into the house. Through the little kitchen and into the hallway, I carefully lifted it off the wall and carried it back to my friends.

"What's next, Wise?" I asked.

"Just to the right of the Willow Tree, we must stand these on end, and each mirror must face the other creating an eternal reflection. Then we wait."

"What are we waiting for?" asked Foggle.

"We wait for Woggle and hopefully he will get here before the Screaming Woman," answered Wise.

"What if—"

"Stop. No more questions, we've got work to do," interrupted Brave. "No what ifs, or supposing," Brave concluded. "We have work to do. Woggle needs our support right now." Then turning to me, he said, "Will you bring the mirrors near to the Willow Tree?"

"Of course," I replied picking them both up. The small troop headed to the spot to the right of the Willow Tree. While all this was going on, the big, black bird of prey sat silently watching everything from a branch near the top of the willow tree.

Meanwhile, Woggle was paddling upstream and against the current. He thought he was doing okay but because of the way the river was flowing, his progress was quite slow.

"You won't get away frommmmm meeeee," screeched a voice from somewhere behind him.

Gritting his teeth and talking through them at the same time, Woggle said in a determined voice, "If you want me, you will have to catch me," and throwing himself onto his knees, he began paddling for all he was worth. "Come on, Woggle, dig deep, you haven't come this far to lose out now," he encouraged himself. Again, he heard her screaming and screeching. *She really wants revenge,* he thought. "Don't give in, don't slow down. Success is more important than time. Hmmm, right now I'm not certain but it doesn't matter. My friends are depending on me and right now I'm depending on them," he kept repeating words of encouragement over and over again to himself. This way, he was blocking out her screams and threats while strengthening himself at the same time. All of a sudden, there was another screeching sound. Non-threatening but screeching right behind him. A quick glance over his shoulder and he saw her. The big, black bird of prey. She had put herself between Woggle and the Screaming Woman, shielding Woggle from her and creating a distraction at the same time. As Woggle rounded the bend in the river, he could hear some cheering and shouting.

He heard his name being called out. His friends were there urging him on. "You can do it," they shouted. "Not far to go now."

Woggle could feel his shoulders aching. His muscles felt as if they were on fire. His lungs, he thought, were about to burst. On and on, he kept paddling. Again, he spoke through his firmly set jaws and gritted teeth. "It will be worth it all, when this fight is over. Talk about true grit," he muttered. "John Wayne would be proud of me."

Finally, he saw the spot on the riverbank where he needed to be, just left of the Willow tree. "Hold your nerve. It's not over yet." His chest heaved, gasping for air as he encouraged himself again. Holding the right paddle firmly in the water, he made a sharp turn without losing any speed, now with the canoe pointing at the riverbank. He braced himself for a final burst of energy. "I'm almost there," he muttered, "Just a hundred metres… 90, 80. Come on, you can do it." Then he shouted to his friends on the shore to stand clear because Woggle had to entice the Screaming Woman to stand between the two mirrors. Scattering left and right, his friends did as he shouted. As they watched him approaching the shoreline at an incredible pace, the big bird of prey swooped upwards, climbing higher and higher in a great big arch until she was behind the Screaming Woman. Woggle's canoe came racing in towards the riverbank and up the small beach. Leaping out of the canoe, his aching legs almost gave way under him. Finally, he was standing between the two mirrors waiting, gasping for breath, but the battle wasn't over yet. The Screaming Woman seeing Woggle exhausted came diving out of the sky at him, her dark grey cloak streaming out behind her. The hood was completely off her head revealing her ugly bony face, with her sunken cheeks and hooked nose. Her grey hair was flying wildly in the wind.

The bird of prey was right behind her, chasing her as she reached out with her long skinny arms and long bony fingers to grab him and imprison him.

As Woggle leapt out from between the mirrors, the big bird of prey landed itself in the grass and the Screaming Woman was caught between the two mirrors, as she looked in horror at her ugly reflection, an anti-cyclone started swirling around her. The group were all rooted to the spot where they stood watching this scene unfold before their very eyes. Faster and faster the wind spun around, the Screaming Woman spinning with it, nothing she could do would help her. Faster and faster she spun around as the wind increased its speed. Her screaming and screeching was something never witnessed before in The Land of Pleasant. It was hideous. Again, the wind increased in speed. Faster and faster she spun around until she was nothing more than a dark grey blur.

Then very suddenly and unexpectedly, the wind began sucking her slowly, screaming and screeching into the Mirror of Ecitsuj and finally disappearing, her hideous screams becoming fainter as she vanished down into the corridor of eternal endlessness, never to trouble any one ever again. Finally, the Screaming Woman was gone.

All at once, calm and peace returned to the riverbank and as they stood in silence, Boggle pointed way down the river; they all looked and could see part of the Naddibrof Mountains. They were coming alive, in fact all over the mountains everything which was trapped started to escape or wake up. As the little group watched, they saw trees and bushes spring up, green grass and purple moss and heather was covering the rocks. Birds began singing and butterflies and honeybees were enjoying the warm sunshine and above the tree line, pristine white snow-capped the mountain peaks.

Then Foggle spoke up, "We don't often have opportunities here in Pleasant to say something is unpleasant but today I'm making an exception. Would Woggle the Wanderer please go and have a bath because you stink."

Woggle burst out laughing. "I do smell awful, the slime in that place was disgusting," and as a round of applause was given, as appreciation for his victory, he went and sorted himself out.

"What a great Pleasantonian he is," said Brave. And we all agreed.

Chapter 7
Homeward Bound

I yawned and stretched my legs out in front me. Looking at my friends I said, "I'm very proud of you guys. Your courage, faithfulness and friendship are awesome, and I would love to stay a little longer and listen to your story all over again, Woggle, but I must get back home."

"You must leave the way you came," said Wise.

"Well, I was hoping you could tell me the time of the next train."

"Don't worry about the train times, that's not important. What's important is leaving the way you came. You must stand with your back to the station nameplate, then look in the mirror.

We said our fond farewells, and I picked up my bags and headed for the station. As I wandered down the platform towards the sign, I reflected on my time with my friends and all that had taken place. Reaching the sign, I stood once again with my back to it and putting my bags down I reached into my inside pocket and carefully took out the mirror; then holding it up, I looked into it and smiled as I read 'WELCOMETOTHELANDOFPLEASANT', and what a welcome it had been. Carefully I 'put' the mirror back into my inside pocket, where it fitted snuggly. As I bent down to pick up my bags, I heard a loud hissing noise. Looking up quickly, I was pleasantly surprised to see a train standing at the station with a carriage door open.

I made my way on to the train and walking down the corridor, I slid open the door of the first compartment and putting my bags in the overhead rack, I settled into my seat breathing a deep sigh of satisfaction.

I was woken out of my sleep with a buzzing noise and the voice of the train driver. "This train will terminate at the next station stop which is Newcastle. Would all passengers please take all their belongings with them and please mind the gap when leaving the train. Thank you for traveling with North East Rail. We hope you had a pleasant trip and we look forward to you travelling with us again soon." Newcastle, almost home. What an eventful few days.

Another voice disturbed my thoughts. "All tickets and passes, please. Tickets and passes." I took my ticket out of my lapel pocket and showed it to the man in the uniform. "Your training went well in Penzance and the truth is they've invited you back again next year sir, well done," he said in a quiet but cheerful voice. As I looked up into his face, he smiled knowingly, in a familiar sort of way. As we looked deeply into each other's eyes, he smiled again that non-ghostly smile and vanished.

We were now passing Birtley. Yes, it had been eventful few days... And leaning back in my seat and smiling to myself, I said, "At least, I know the truth; well of course I did, I'd looked in the mirror."

Volume 3
Snake Attack

Chapter 1
Lofty

It was a very wet Saturday morning. By wet, I mean it was pouring down, tropical rain, it was raining cats and dogs. The sky was black, and it looked like it was in for the day. We were sat up in bed having an early morning cuppa, it was almost five past seven. "I'm glad I managed to cut the grass yesterday," I said to my wife.

"You and your striped grass, what are you like? What plans do you have for this morning while I'm in work?" she answered.

"I'm going into the attic, I have some boxes up there that are full of old assembly props and they need a good sorting out. Today is the ideal day for this job," I replied. And so at ten to nine, I opened the trapdoor, lowered the ladders, switched the lights on and climbed into the attic. The attic is divided into half, the storage part being the bigger half. I climbed through on my hands and knees, across the boards, and made my way to where these boxes are kept. They are easy to find because they have a green and white wavy pattern all over them. I pulled the first box out of its place and making myself comfortable, began untying the string that kept the lid on.

While I was doing this, I heard a noise coming from a dark corner of the attic. I turned my head quickly, expecting to see a furry creature like a mouse or something similar. Nothing. Maybe I disturbed another box and it was settling down. I returned to my task and as I was starting my first rummage, and I do like a good rummage, I heard it again, only this time it was louder and a lot nearer. Again, I turned my head quickly and had the shock of my life. Sitting on the suitcases was The See Thru Man, dressed exactly the same way as last time, on his face was that same non-ghostly but knowing smile. "What are you...how did you...?" I stammered in disbelief.

"There is no cause for alarm," he said calmly.

"No cause for alarm," I spluttered. "You're not the one being scared to death. How did you get here? What do you want?" I asked.

"Calm down, there's no cause for alarm. There's someone here I want you to meet," he replied quietly.

"Meet me here?" I stared around me. My attic is not high enough to stand up in. The slope or pitch of the roof won't allow you to. And between him, The See Thru Man and me, there wasn't much room left for anyone else.

"Yes, that's right. I've asked him to be here now, you see I own this loft but he lives in it." I was feeling very confused. I looked down while scratching my head. "Here he comes," replied my visitor.

I turned around quickly so I was facing the wall which separates my home from my next-door neighbour. The See Thru Man chuckled and said, "Not there, here." I turned back and there he was. He was the tallest, thinnest man I had ever seen. I wouldn't call him slim, he was skinny, like a stick, with eyes that twinkled, and an infectious grin to match, and he was standing about three metres tall. It was at this point I realised he was standing upright and I was still sitting on the boards on the attic floor. Then I got another shock. I wasn't in my attic but in someone else's. While I was trying to take this in, The See Thru Man spoke, "Let me introduce you to Lofty; he will assist you in the first part of your journey, leaving you only when you're in familiar surroundings."

"Wait a minute," I said without conviction, "How did I get here? And what place is this?"

"This is my loft, it's where I live," replied the tall stranger, "and you arrived here the moment you turned around."

"I didn't," I answered. I was looking around the loft; it was huge. Incredibly high, very wide and long, with corridors going in different directions, and The See Thru Man was sitting on a very big old sea chest looking very familiar. I started asking questions again, which isn't always a good thing to do because they are often ignored.

"Who owns the house?" I asked.

"What house?" replied Lofty and The See Thru Man in unison.

"The house beneath this loft. Lofts have houses," I replied. "They don't simply hang in the air."

"Unless they are created by The See Thru Man," answered Lofty with a grin, "you will be amazed at what he owns."

"Right then," cut in The See Thru Man, "no more questions because I'm not giving answers today and besides, you have an important task to fulfil for me today." And with that he started walking down a corridor. At the bottom of the corridor was a door, beyond the door was a very bright glow, which could be seen around the edge of the closed door.

Chapter 2
Flying

As The See Thru Man placed his hand on the door handle, he hesitated and looking over his right shoulder towards us, he said, "After Lofty has left you and not before, check inside your pocket." Then he quickly and noiselessly opened the door and disappeared. As he did, the loft was flooded with this incredible glow and a blast of cool air. Instantly, we were flying through the air at an incredible speed. It took my breath away. I was hanging on to Lofty for dear life. "Let me go," he shouted over his shoulder. "You will be fine."

Very tentatively, I let go and discovered to my amazement, he was right. I looked down towards the ground and we were flying over the airport, heading out towards the heart of Northumberland. At this moment in time, I had no idea where we were going, but the countryside below was whizzing past at a frantic pace. Without warning, we turned sharply to the left. Not 180 degrees but almost. After several miles, we made another left turn, not quite as sharp as the last one. Then off to my right, I could just make out the Enyt River as it twisted and turned on its course through the countryside. Swooping down low, Lofty headed for the river. Flying about five metres above the surface of the water, we followed its course down the Enyt Valley.

We had slowed down by now. How we did that I'm not certain but we had, we were gently gliding through the air, following the river as it flowed ever onwards towards the sea. We were still in the small hours; early morning was a few hours away and the night sky was still a deep velvet black. There was a little cloud cover and a few stars twinkling in the dark sky. Lofty pointed to his left; as I looked where he was pointing, I could make out the statue of the Ogre, a lasting reminder of a previous adventure. Without warning, Lofty climbed very high in the night sky, pausing in the air in a standing up position over a small hill known to the locals as Repcy Tip. I joined him, feeling rather strange by these recent odd events. He placed his two hands on my shoulders and said, "Point your toes downwards, keep your arms tight against your sides and hold on, we are going in."

Chapter 3
Palace Gardens

Instantly, we fell from the sky like two pillars of concrete. I was too terrified to look down, anticipating the worst as the ground came rushing up to meet us. Without warning, we were on a very pleasant green lawn surrounded by well-kept flowerbeds and a huge variety of trees, all different shapes and sizes but none of them looking out of place. Beyond this was a magnificent palace, with tall rounded towers and lovely arched windows. While I was taking all this in, I heard "*Shhhhh*" being whispered in my ear by Lofty. There was no need to tell me, I was too breathless to speak. Giving me time to recover, he pointed towards a very attractive tree, but a second glance told me there was something definitely wrong with it. "That tree has been poisoned; some time ago it was a very pleasant tree, delightful to look at, it looked good to eat too but no one ever tried until recently, and it was the Queen, who took a small sample of its delightful looking fruit, and since that time she has been poisoned and at death's door, and a strange transformation has taken place over most inhabitants of The Land of Pleasant."

"Can you tell me anymore?" I asked

"Only that the great Donacada Tree Snake is to blame. It has sunk its huge teeth into the roots of the tree and poisoned it. No more questions, I must leave you now. Go to your friends, they are waiting for you. Woggle has all the answers to all your questions. Oh, and don't go past the tree, go the long way around. And one last thing, don't forget to check inside your inside pocket." And with that he was gone. I sat very still and extremely quiet for a very long time. It was no good going over these recent events, it just wouldn't help. I looked first at the palace; it was grand, like something out of a fairy tale. A bit like Castle Coch in South Wales except the walls sparkled in the sunshine a deep rich pink-blue colour. It had seven tall towers. Six were around the outside walls and the seventh, the tallest, appeared to be in the centre of a splendid courtyard. Focusing on the courtyard, I saw someone I recognised from an earlier adventure. My heart leapt excitedly; it was Woggle the Wanderer. He looked incredibly serious and thoughtful as he paced around in a big circle. I sat still and watched him, not wanting to disturb his train of thought. While this was happening, I kept looking at the tall centre tower, something wasn't right with it. The windows all looked the same, same shape, same style, same everything, but something was wrong. I carefully looked at the six other towers. These were all splendidly elegant and identical to the seventh tower but shorter, so what was wrong? I was puzzled because I couldn't put my finger on it, and I knew it was staring me in the face. Just then, a shadow was cast over me.

Looking up, I was surprised to see Woggle standing there.

I had been so engrossed that I hadn't noticed him coming across. "Am I pleased to see you," he said pleasantly but with a hint of sadness. "Come on, we need to get you to Wise and the gang, they are expecting you."

Jumping to my feet from my semi-secluded spot, I said, "I'm ready when you are, Woggle, so lead on, my friend."

He took the long way around the gardens, pointing out interesting things about the palace: The Grand Hall, The Grand Ballroom, The King's Library, The Queen's Music Chamber. Four of the towers were named after points on the compass; the North Tower, South Tower and so on. The other two towers of the remaining six towers were simply called The King's Tower and The Queen's Tower, but Woggle never mentioned the tower in the centre of the courtyard. I thought that was strange but decided to say nothing for now. We stayed close to the high stonewall, which marked the boundary of the palace gardens, using the line of trees to give us cover. High up amongst the leaves and branches of the poisoned tree, the huge head of the ugly Donacada Snake moved slightly as it looked in our direction, its long black tongue flicking in and out quickly with a malicious smile on its evil face. Woggle kept leading the way until the poisoned tree was out of sight. We were passing a huge tree with a very straight trunk when he paused. He indicated for me to press its great trunk; to my surprise it was incredibly soft, almost sponge like. While I was making my examination, I heard a soft noise behind me; turning around I was amazed to see a narrow opening in the wall. Woggle urged me to follow him, as I entered the wall it closed silently behind me. We were standing at the top of a very steep stone staircase. Woggle took a flaming torch from off the wall, and we slowly and silently descended the staircase. I wasn't certain what to expect when we reached the bottom, which took a lot longer than anticipated, not because we were slow but because there was almost 600 steps to go down. Finally, at long last, we reached the bottom. Here we were faced with several tunnels, all marked individually; they were NT, ST, ET, WT, KT, QT, IT. I had quickly worked out what each set of letters stood for. NT: North Tower, and so on, but what was IT. Without saying a word, Woggle headed down the tunnel marked IT. Every so often, lights which were sunk into the tunnel walls gave us a soft yellow light on the tunnel floor. We walked through this tunnel for almost a mile, without any variation at all, on and on with soft noiseless tread we went; eventually we came to another staircase. We paused at the bottom of the stairs for several moments when Woggle grinned and pointed upwards. My eyes popped out of my head.

This staircase seemed to disappear into darkness.

Chapter 4
Meeting the Queen

Without saying a word, Woggle began climbing quickly; I thought to myself, *There's no way I'm going to keep up with him,* and I didn't. Eventually, and gasping for breath, I stood next to Woggle on a short stone landing at the end of which was a huge solid wooden door. On the door was an interesting design made from silver studs. Woggle ran his paws over the studs. Without warning, the door silently opened, as we stepped into a brightly lit corridor, the door closed softly behind us. "Where are we?" I whispered softly in Woggle's ear. Without answering, Woggle walked quickly along the corridor that ran in a continual upward spiral. Every so often, there were small windows in the wall looking out over the palace gardens. Each window was set at a different angle, which meant you never looked out horizontally, which gave interesting views. Onwards and upwards we went.

The corridor never changed. Woggle paused and spoke, "We are in the Imperial Tower. The Queen is in a stateroom at the top of this tower, it's the only room here. It was used by special guests, giving them the opportunity to enjoy the views of The Land of Pleasant. But since the Queen has eaten and been poisoned, she has spent her days in this tower. It's a personal quarantine for the sake of her people and their protection, and if we can't help her, she could die."

We were now standing outside a very large and impressive wooden door, with spectacular carvings telling the history of the country. It included faces of past and present visitors and friends. To my astonishment, I recognised my own face carved into the door. *What a privilege,* I thought. I was snapped out of pondering by Woggle. "We are being called in," he said quietly. As we opened the door, I had a sharp intake of breath, the room was huge, and very tastefully yet delicately decorated. Propped up on a large four-poster bed, which was covered in pink silk sheets was the Queen. Like all Stabmows, she was striped but as to be expected she was in different shades of pink. As we approached the side of the bed, I detected a strange unpleasant smell. Woggle glanced in my direction and whispered, "That's a result of the poison."

"Your Majesty, may I present to you our very noble friend. We simply call him the Man from the Other Side, who, as you know, has helped us on a number of occasions. In particular, the solidifying of the Ogre from Gulberia and the eternal imprisonment of the Screaming Woman." Mustering up her strength, she slowly raised herself up, then very gently offered me her right paw.

I took it tenderly in my right hand and bowed slightly, "I'm at your service, Ma'am, to restore you and The Land of Pleasant."

We were asked to be seated, and for some time we retold the adventures we had been involved in.

As we stood to leave, reassuring Her Majesty of our determination, she murmured to Woggle, "At the end of this, we must give him a suitable name." And with that she fell asleep, totally exhausted. We left quietly going back the way we came until we were at the door in the garden wall. He signalled to me to be silent, then very cautiously and slowly, as if taking nothing for granted, opened the concealed door and slowly peered into the garden.

Chapter 5
Trapped

The hair on his neck stood up straight and he silently reclosed the concealed door. "Snake" was all he said in a hoarse whisper. "It's in the palace gardens." Pulling the door, Woggle pointed to what looked like an ordinary stone in the wall and motioned me to rub it. He did the same thing to another stone further along the wall the other way. Then whispering, he said, "These are one-way windows; we can see into the garden without being seen." As I peered out into the garden, I was horrified at the enormity of this creature. It was over a metre in diameter and about 15 metres long. Its head was colossal, with its ugly mouth opened slightly and its long, black forked tongue flicking quickly in and out. The body of this monster was dark green with a pale yellow open diamond pattern, giving the creature a more sinister look.

My pulse was racing and my heart pounding as I asked in a hushed whisper, "What are we going to do?" Woggle didn't answer, he just watched the snake in total silence.

Then looking straight at me, he said, "Did The See Thru Man give you any instructions?"

"He did. He said when you get to The Land of Pleasant, check your inside pocket."

"Have you done that yet?" asked Woggle urgently.

"Well, no I haven't had much time and I'd forgotten, to be honest with you." All this time, Woggle was gazing through the one-way window.

"Good," he replied. "Back to the tower, we've got work to do," and with that he took off like a rat up a drainpipe. It wasn't long before we were at the foot of the stairs. Without stopping for air or anything, Woggle was racing up the steps, his long soft body stretching out fully as he raced for the top, six steps at time. Spurred on by the urgency, I found fresh strength and stamina, and was hot on his heels. We reached the top in record time. Pausing briefly, then quickly running his paws over the silver studs in the door, he opened it again and once more we stepped into the spiral corridor. Hesitating, Woggle indicated for me to rub a certain part of the wall again. These one-way windows gave remarkable visibility, a bit like a magnifying glass. From this viewpoint, we could see the huge snake making its way through the garden, heading towards the outside of the Imperial Tower. "We've got a little time but not much," said Woggle. "First things first, what's in your inside pocket?" I suddenly realised when I went into my attic I had an old shirt, an old pair of jeans and an old jumper on. No inside pocket. As I went on to explain this to Woggle, I discovered I was wearing a padded bomber jacket, which was black and red reversible, black jogging bottoms and black trainers. Snapping out of my dazed daydream, I undid the zip half way and slid my hand carefully into the inside pocket. I moved my hand deeper into the pocket; nothing, nothing at all.

Woggle looked at me with a twinkle in his big round eyes and said, "It's empty, right?" He could see the disappointment on my face. "We have a phrase here in Pleasant that goes like this: '*Rednaw traeh eht sekam derrefed epoh a*', which means if you lose your ability to focus, then we will lose the battle against the Donacada. Now you must focus; when Brave told us about his fight with the Donacada, how did he paralyse it?"

I thought for a moment, then said, "He rammed and wedged a piece of wood into its open mouth."

"So, what we need right now," interrupted Woggle, "is something similar, not wood but metal."

"I know what we need, it's a short length of silver steel about 65 millimetres in diameter and about 90 centimetres in length. That will never rot. Would it help if both ends were sharpened to a point?"

"Now you're thinking right, so when you're ready, take your time and remember the principle of the mirror."

I thought for a moment and murmured quietly to myself, "Put the mirror, put, don't struggle, put." Breathing easily while thinking about what I wanted, I slowly put my hand into my inside pocket and slowly drew out one item; a short bar of silver steel, 65 millimetres in diameter and 90 centimetres long, pointed at both ends. "That is amazing," I said as I handed it to Woggle.

Unfortunately though, in his paws this bar kept sliding. Woggle was unable to grip it tight enough for what we wanted it for. "You will have to do it," he said, "You have the right grip for this task."

Chapter 6
Defeated

I looked carefully at the bar of steel in my hand. Gripping it in the middle and holding it upright, I could see how effective it could be if I was successful, but if I failed it would be the end of everyone here and The Land of Pleasant. All we could do was wait. Woggle and I kept looking out into the palace gardens, watching the Donacada as it slithered slowly between the trees, then slowly, almost thoughtfully, it moved over the lawn between the flower beds and shrubs and eventually past the tress to the outer perimeter wall. Here it hesitated. There was no hurry in this beast, it just lifted its massive head slightly and with its beady eyes followed the line of the wall. After several minutes, it buried itself in the grass and circumnavigated the wall. We watched and waited as the snake continued on its slow journey, its long black tongue constantly flicking in and out. Seeing this monster fully stretched out was hideous. I wouldn't want to get caught by it. While we watched, I kept rehearsing in my mind what I had to do. It seemed simple enough in theory; just wait for the right moment when the snake's mouth was wide open and its head was in striking distance, I must thrust this steel bar into its mouth, wedging it open. What could go wrong? *Plenty,* I thought.

Timing, speed, accuracy, fear, lack of courage, or stage fright; what could go wrong?

Focus on the task in hand and those who are dependent upon you. Better to try and fail than not try at all.

So, I kept focussed, but suddenly my arms felt like lead, they were just too heavy for the task. I need a distraction of some sort. It was at that point I remembered my inside pocket. *Hmmm,* I thought, *what could we need that I could take out of my pocket that would help us?* Woggle was still at his window watching the snake as it continued slithering slowly around the wall. It was about a hundred metres away from our secret doorway. As he watched and waited, Woggle was running his paws over the walls of the corridor; I had no idea what he was looking for, the snake was about 40 metres away. Still Woggle kept smoothing his paws over the wall, 25 metres to go. Woggle didn't flinch, he kept watching and he kept running his paws over the wall. Ten metres to go. "Found it," whispered Woggle. Suddenly, my mind was alive like it was operating in overdrive. The Mirror of Hturt, I wonder if that will help. It will, I'm sure it will do the trick. I was convinced, so slowly I put my hand into my inside pocket and slowly pulled it out. It was still the same size as the first time I used it. Taking it out carefully, I placed it upright against the wall, opposite the doorway leading from the stairway.

I looked back at Woggle and out of my window.

The head of the snake was level with the doorway, which was ajar.

The snake appeared to ignore it when Woggle gently rubbed the stone and the door moved slightly. Immediately, the snake's massive head turned and disappeared through the opening, its massive body slowly following. When the snake had completely disappeared, Woggle rubbed his paw over the stone again and the secret door closed tightly, and the wall looked complete once again.

Woggle's face was grim as he turned and faced me. "It won't be long, if he follows our scent, then it should be with us soon." Then he saw the mirror against the wall and smiled. The smile spread wide across his round face. "I like your thinking," he said, "this should buy us a few seconds. The first thing the snake will see will be its own reflection, which he won't be expecting." We continued the waiting game, making certain that when the door opened it would conceal us. The seconds ticked slowly by as we waited patiently, not knowing where the snake was. Woggle crept nearer the door, which was closed but not locked. Nothing, not a sound could be heard. We knew it was inside the wall. We knew it would follow our scent. Woggle paused, looking at the door, then at the wall surrounding it. I could see something had caught his attention. He quickly examined the wall next to the door's opening edge. Gently pressing a stone in the wall produced a soft click. "And now we have double doors," said Woggle, delighted.

"Quickly now, let's move the mirror so it's centre to the doors. Excellent, we can both sit opposite sides of the doors and when the snake pushes through, we will both be concealed but we will be able to see him first. Can you put your hand back into your pocket and bring out another steel bar but this time one with a paw grip in the middle?" Slowly and deliberately, I put my hand once again into my inside pocket and slowly removed the steel bar. "Excellent," whispered Woggle excitedly.

"Now, we take up our positions and wait." Once again, the seconds ticked slowly by. We both were kneeling on one knee, looking intently at the mirror. Suddenly, I saw Woggle tense, his round ears stiffened, his fur started to bristle and stand on end. He caught me watching his reflection, and he nodded knowingly. I couldn't hear anything except the pounding of my heart in my ears. But I was fully aware that Woggle had and that was enough for me. We continued waiting in silence, staring at the reflection of the door in the mirror. Without any warning, he was there in a cross-legged sitting position with that none-ghostly smile on his face. I was about to look directly at the door when I noticed Woggle was grinning from ear to ear. He was still wearing the same outfit: the tall black hat, the long black frock coat and black trousers and the worn but highly polished black boots, and yes while he was sitting 'in the mirror', he was still see-thru.

We resumed our vigil of staring at the door in the mirror. Fortunately, we could see through The See Thru Man; it took just a moment to get used to it, but I did. Then I heard it for myself, a soft slithering sound. Where on the long staircase this creature was, I couldn't tell, all we could do was wait in a state of alert readiness. Watching and waiting. Nothing more complicated just watching, waiting, and listening: *ssslither, ssslllither, sssllliiittther*.

It was a hideous sound. The See Thru Man sat motionless with a long bony finger resting on his lips, indicating for us to be very quiet. Woggle and I remained poised as the moment drew closer. Would we be successful? We knew we only had a few seconds to execute our plan. And still we waited. There were moments when the slithering stopped. Was the snake deliberately taking its time? We couldn't tell. All we could do was watch, wait, and listen. I wondered how big its head would be close up. Would my nerve hold? I hoped so. Would the doors open slowly? I hoped so. All these unanswered questions were going through my mind. BANG!!! Without warning, the double doors burst open. Good grief his head was huge and ugly and was swaying slightly in the air; then its massive mouth gapped open as it looked at its own reflection in the mirror. Springing to our feet and coming out of hiding, we came around the doors with steel rods at the ready, and in one lightening smooth movement, we rammed the rods upright, wedging them into its cavernous mouth and forcing its gaping jaws to remain permanently open. Success. Instantly, we jumped backwards and watched as the snake's head slowly swayed as it became like a rag doll, collapsing, totally paralysed. We sunk to our knees relieved, then turning to look at The See Thru Man, we discovered he had vanished along with the mirror.

Chapter 7
Mission Accomplished

"That was a lot better than planned," panted Woggle, "You did remarkably well."

"Thanks. I think we make a good team," I replied, still getting my breath back.

"Good," smiled Woggle fully composed. "Great is the word we are looking for."

"Awesome, outstanding, truly wonderful," came a weak and unexpected voice. We turned and looked up because we were still on our knees, into the face of the Queen, who was looking radiantly relieved despite her weak state of health. Then seeing the full size of the snake almost fainted, Woggle was at her side steadying her. Recovering quickly, she said with a faint smile, "You will have to move it, it can't possibly stay there." We bowed slightly, then at her request I rose to my feet.

"We will see to it straight away, Ma'am," said Woggle.

"If Your Majesty would like to watch," I said, "we will show you. You will then be able to rest and relax properly." I could feel Woggle's amazed stare. He would rather solve the problem without an audience.

"What do you plan on doing with this monster?" asked the Queen to Woggle.

Coming quickly to his rescue, I said, "I have the right tools for the task right here." And very slowly, I put my hand into my inside pocket and took out a steel strongbox. It was 30 centimetres long, 20 centimetres wide and 25 centimetres deep, with a triple-hinged lid and four strong locks, one at each end and two at the front. The Queen and Woggle stared. "It won't fit in that," they said in unison. I smiled and put my hand back into my inside pocket and slowly pulled out a large pair of tweezers.

Again, they spoke in unison. "What good are they?" Without saying a word, I put my hand slowly into my inside pocket a third time. This time I slowly pulled out a powerful pair of binoculars. At this point, they both burst out laughing.

"What an interesting concoction," remarked the Queen. "But I don't see how they are any help in our quest at all."

"Allow me to demonstrate," I replied calmly. Placing the binoculars to Woggle's eyes the wrong way around and giving him time to focus them, he caught a glimpse of what I was trying to achieve. Woggle gently passed them to the Queen so she could examine the snake through them. The Queen caught her breath and quickly removed the binoculars from her eyes. Looking at the snake, she was disappointed to see it at its true size. While they had been busy doing this, I had carefully taken two more pairs of binoculars out of my inside pocket; at this the Queen gave an interestingly knowing royal smile but said nothing.

"Ma'am," asked Woggle politely, "are you feeling well, you have had a lot of excitement in the last hour?"

"Never better, my good and noble Woggle," replied the Queen without hesitation. "But let's get this ghastly beast locked away forever."

"Right then, Woggle my friend, listen carefully, we must both use the binoculars with one hand each at the same time, with my other hand I will hold the strongbox open, and if you use the tweezers with your spare paw, you will discover that you can pick up the snake and coil him into the strongbox, I will close the lid and if Your Majesty would please snap shut the four locks, that will complete the task." Woggle looked doubtful but obliged. We took up our positions. Binoculars at our eyes, I had the strongbox open and ready in my left hand. Woggle had the tweezers ready in his right paw and Her Majesty ready with the fours locks nearby. Nobody said a word. Woggle slowly reached out with the tweezers while focusing on the snake through the binoculars. Sliding the bottom jaw of the tweezers underneath the length of the snake's body, then squeezing them closed, he carefully and slowly lifted the snake off the ground, bringing it clear of the doorway and bringing it towards me. I lowered the strongbox so Woggle wouldn't have to lift the creature higher than necessary. We held our breath; we didn't want to disturb the steel rods that would be fatal. Over the box Woggle brought this monster, lowering it carefully into the box.

"We are almost there, keep your nerve," I whispered encouragingly. Slowly, Woggle removed the tweezers. I closed the lid quietly; slamming could ruin everything and that would be dreadful.

Swiftly and elegantly, the Queen secured the first lock, quickly followed by the other three. Now, finally, we could breathe more easily.

The Queen was the first to speak, "I am amazed, where did you learn to do that?" she asked.

"In Africa, it was how I caught an elephant. But on that occasion I used a matchbox to put it in," I explained with a smile.

She looked at me and shook her head slowly. "But I now know what I'm going to call you," she replied softly. "But you will have to wait a little longer. Now you boys must bury that box and go back to the tree, your friends are waiting for you, and I have had enough excitement for one day, I am going for my afternoon siesta. Thank you so very much." And with that she turned and made her way back to her room.

Picking up the box which the Queen had put down, we headed through the doors, closing them securely behind us we descended the long staircase. As we stood at the bottom of the staircase, Woggle hesitated, "I've just had a thought. How do you fancy a slight detour? It will be very beneficial, especially for the strongbox."

"I'm with you, my friend, lead on," I said. We hurried back down the tunnel towards the first stairwell, holding the strongbox securely. At the stairs, Woggle headed straight down the tunnel marked KT. I had no idea where he was going. After about 500 metres or so, we came to a fork in the tunnel. Taking the left fork, which was smaller and much narrower, Woggle scampered along. I was forced into a stooped position, which made progress slow and keeping up with Woggle impossible. The tunnel was dark and damp with a strange atmosphere, weird rather than uncanny, not eerie, just not pleasant. The tunnel was running steadily downwards. The further we went, the darker it became, and the darker it became, the more unpleasant was the atmosphere and the air we were breathing. The tunnel finally levelled out.

"We are almost there," said Woggle as we rounded a bend in the tunnel. Woggle paused and began searching the floor of the tunnel.

"What are you looking for, Woggle?" I asked.

"The entrance to the Tip Sselmottob," he replied.

"The what?" I asked.

"It's an ancient shaft where we throw stuff that's nasty and disruptive. As you know, this is The Land of Pleasant; not perfect, but pleasant. And to keep it that way, this is how we throw anything which threatens that. This strongbox needs to be thrown in here. It's such a long time since it was last used, I almost forgot about it." Continuing to brush the cold, damp dust to the edge of the tunnel finally revealed a trap door. Releasing the concealed ring in the centre of the trapdoor proved to be more challenging than anticipated. No matter what we did we couldn't release the ring, it was totally jammed in place. It was for all the world like it had solidified into the trapdoor.

Woggle continued, persevering in his endeavour to open the concealed entrance.

Finally, he was forced to rest. Kneeling up straight, he continued staring at the ring, wondering why he was failing in his quest. Suddenly, he slapped his paw against his forehead and said, "Come on, Woggle, put the light on." Then resuming his position, he placed his left paw on top of his right paw which he placed on top of the ring. This was done in one smooth movement; pressing down on the ring, he slowly turned it anti-clockwise. "Be ready to drop the box in quickly. We don't want to remove the lid more than we have to. Besides, the smell will be awful," said Woggle. There was a soft clicking noise followed by a faint whirring sound. I held the strongbox close to the floor, ready to slide it in as soon as the gap was big enough. But I wasn't prepared for the stench. As Woggle slowly completed this action, part of the trapdoor lifted slightly. *Whooooosh*, a bad odour rushed out, knocking me backwards with incredible force. I slammed into the wall of the tunnel about 15 metres away from where I was kneeling. The flat of my back hit the wall of the tunnel with such force that all the breath in me came rushing out in a series of loud agonising groans.

"The strongbox," I gasped and then passed out. A little while later, I started coming around. Slowly at first. I didn't know where I was or what I was doing. As I began focussing on my surroundings, I saw a very round happy face looking down on me. Woggle was gently bringing me back to my senses.

As I looked at him, one word crossed his lips, "Success."

Gradually, I came to my senses. "That smell and the gush of stale air was disgusting, Woggle, it took me completely by surprise." It was then that his word success seemed to register in my brain, it happened just as I was saying, "But what happened to the strongbox?" I had visions of it hitting the wall with incredible force, the lid flying open, the snake thrown out, the steel rods being flung free and the snake returning to its normal ferocious ugly self.

Woggle rested his paw reassuringly on my arm and said, "We have succeeded. Before you were thrown backwards, I had my paw at the ready and was holding the strongbox tightly when you had the full force of the blast. When you were thrown backwards, you left the box in my hand, and I threw it into the Tip Sselmottob and quickly closed and resealed the trapdoor, which means the first part of our mission is a totally success."

"The first part?" I said.

"Yes," replied Woggle. "Now we must get to the tree because it needs treating and the fruit needs rescuing, then we need to revisit the Queen. Besides, the gang is waiting for us at the tree, and Wise should know what to do." We made our way back to the stairway which would lead us back to the secret doorway in the garden wall. But at the bottom of the stairway Woggle hurried past.

Chapter 8
The Poisoned Root

I spoke up and Woggle simply shook his head and said, "I have an idea." We came to a fork in the tunnel. Without any hesitation, Woggle took the left tunnel. This was very small, narrow, and with a low roof. Woggle was forced into going very slow, which meant my pace was slower still. I was crawling on my hands and knees. On and on we went. This tunnel was darker than the other narrow tunnel. Without warning, we were greeted by an awful smell, and Woggle said over his shoulder, "We're almost there." The tunnel was getting narrower all round; shoulders were touching both walls, and my head was banging against the roof of the tunnel. My knees were red raw from crawling but still we pressed on. Woggle paused, making certain I was okay.

"Where are we going and what are we looking for?" I asked.

"It's a bit of a long shot, but this tunnel should lead us underneath the tree where we might be able to see the damage to its roots," answered Woggle. Without saying anything else, Woggle turned and continued scampering along the tunnel. Suddenly, the tunnel veered to the left and downwards where we came to an abrupt stop in what looked like a huge underground cavern with no way out except by the route we arrived. The stench was disgusting, like bad ammonia mingled with stale vomit. "A torch would be handy," said Woggle.

"Will one like this do?" I said as I withdrew my hand from my inside pocket.

Woggle smiled and said, "I like your style." I switched it on, flooding the cavern with a bright white light. As I shone it at the roof, we saw the reason for the stench. The poisoned root was sagging through the roof of the cavern and was slowly leaking its poison onto the cavern floor.

Woggle's ears were erect as he detected a faint sound. "Voices," he whispered looking at me. We stood in silence for several minutes as he listened. Slowly, a smile spread across his round face as he said, "Wise and the gang are above us."

"How far above us are they?" I asked.

"Too far to be of use at the moment; right now, we need to focus on the task down here," replied Woggle.

"Firstly," I said, "we should wear these," and taking out of my inside pocket I held up two protective suits, complete with full facial hoods and protective goggles. Woggle stared in disbelief. "We don't know what we are dealing with," I said, "and we need to be safe and uncontaminated when we get back into the garden."

"Awesome, let's get to work," replied Woggle with fresh determination.

And so, clad in our new clothing, we began by looking intently at the root; either side of the sagging section looked reasonably healthy. "We need a closer look to examine it properly," I remarked. Woggle looked at the walls and started climbing them, by the time he got close to the poisoned root, he was at the wrong angle to inspect it properly.

"What you need, Woggle, is one of these," I said as I put my hand into my inside pocket.

"One of what?" he replied.

Slowly and carefully, I took out of my inside pocket a set of stepladders. Woggle's eyes were like saucers. I opened them, making certain they were safe to climb. I went up them and helped Woggle onto the top platform step. From this vantage point, we could examine the poisoned root. Woggle had a brainwave, "If we cut the root about halfway into the good part of the root there and again there," said Woggle pointing to where the root was undamaged either side of the poisoned section, "we will be able to carry the poisoned root to the incinerator and burn it up; this way we can save the tree, rescue the Queen and prevent another disaster from happening."

"All that sounds good, but I am concerned about one thing," I replied.

"What's that?" asked Woggle with a puzzled look on his pleasant round face.

"How are we going to achieve that?"

"Stabmows have very strong teeth. If you steady the root by there," said Woggle pointing to the good part of the root, "I will bite through by here." Working quickly, he made short work of his task. "Brilliant, keep hold of that end with your left hand and reach across to this point here with your right hand. That's it, just stretch a little

107

further." I couldn't quite make it. My arm was ten centimetres too short.

"Hang on a moment," I said, "I've got an idea."

Slowly, I put my hand into my inside pocket and slowly I withdrew it. My hand was empty. Woggle stared in disbelief.

Undeterred, I reached out once again and discovered I was able to reach the right spot of the root to support it for Woggle. Once again his eyes were like saucers, and for a few seconds he didn't move. Then grinning from ear to ear he set about once again using his sharp teeth and in no time at all we had the poisoned root in our hands. Carefully, we climbed off the ladder and once again we stood on the floor on the cavern. "The palace incinerator is too far away," said Woggle, "if we attempt to carry this back up the tunnel and on to stairway, which leads to the secret door in the garden wall, I think it will burst and that will be disastrous." We pondered the problem for some time when Woggle finally spoke up. "This branch is about 14 centimetres in diameter right and it's not dried out, so it should smoulder if we could get it alight."

Using the torch we made a thorough search of the cavern. Finally, in the furthest, farthest, deepest, darkest corner of the cavern, we found some rotting root remains. Gathering them up, we carefully covered the poisoned section of the root, which was now lying on the cavern floor. Woggle hesitated and standing up straight, stared upwards, then climbing the ladder he listened intently, his head on one side.

"What is it, Woggle, what are you listening to?" I enquired.

"There's a lot of singing and celebrating going on in the garden. The tree has started looking healthy again and the Queen has made a full recovery."

"That's fantastic news; let's get this fire going and go and join them," I replied. Taking a box of safety matches from inside pocket, we knelt down, and after several attempts, we lit the rubble, which smouldered nicely, slowly burning into the poisoned root.

"I think we should hang around a bit longer," said Woggle, "I want to give a full and completed account to the King and Queen when we resurface." So we squatted down and waited. The smoke made my eyes water. I wanted to cough but managed to fight off the urge. The poisoned root was hissing as the heat from the smouldering dead roots did their work. We kept our mouths closed and noses covered. There was no wind or draft in this cavern so the smoke ascended slowly towards the roof.

Hissing, squeezing and slowly bubbling, the heat kept doing its work. Eventually, the noise subsided. Woggle didn't move, not a muscle or a whisker. He just sat and stared. The smouldering continued but now there was no noise. The smoke swirled slowly and silently towards the roof but never going all the way. Gradually, the smoke became less and less. "Almost done," murmured Woggle, "I'm waiting for the heat to cleanse the floor where the poison seeped out and to make certain that all we are left with are two pieces of good wood free of poison and not a trace of it anywhere." We continued waiting.

Little by little and moment by moment, the rising smoke became less and less, and the smouldering gradually decreased. Finally, all we were left with was a dark burnt stain on the floor and two healthy ends from the poisoned root that were slightly charred. Satisfied that our mission was complete, Woggle picked up the remaining ends. "I'll carry one of those," I said, and we left the cavern, heading back up the tunnel towards the stone staircase.

Chapter 9
Naming and Knighthood

The return journey was over in no time at all. The ascent up the stairs was the same, quick and without any problems. As Woggle ran his hands over the surface of the wall to open the door, he looked at me grinning as he said, "That was another fine adventure we have enjoyed together." As the door opened slowly into the palace gardens, a huge cheer went up from the crowd that had gathered. The cheering was suddenly replaced with hysterical laughing; at first, we wondered why everyone was laughing so much. Suddenly we realised, we were still wearing our protective clothing; we looked like a pair of aliens. Quickly, we got rid of them with the help of a palace official, who hurriedly took them to the incinerator. Looking at the crowd of smiling faces which had gathered, we easily spotted our friends Oggle, Foggle, Boggle, Wise and Brave. The King Suoegaruoc III called everyone to order.

"Before we dine, I want to hear what these two brave individuals have achieved for my Queen, every Pleasantonian, and The Land of Pleasant itself. Everything we know and love would be ruined beyond recognition without their determination. And so on behalf of myself, my Queen and everyone here in Pleasant, thank you very much. And now we want to hear your story, so please step forward and tell us everything."

Amidst the cheering, whistling and loud applause, Woggle and I stepped forward. "As a Stabmow and Pleasantonian, I think it only right and fitting that I should explain in detail everything that we have gone through during these last few hours." Woggle took his time, going through the story step by step including the instruction from The See Thru Man about my inside pocket. Amidst *gasps* and *ahhhs* and other such noises, Woggle gave a detailed account leaving nothing out. "And so, we present to you the remaining two pieces which were either side of the poisoned root. And if you look firstly at the tree," concluded Woggle, "and then at our wonderful Queen Gnorts II, you will understand how successful our mission has been." Huge applause erupted as the crowd looked at the tree then at the Queen; she was radiant. A hush fell over the crowd as the Queen stepped forward looking splendid in her full-length royal pale pink gown with hundreds of sequins giving it that extra sparkle, and a silver tiara in-laid with diamonds on her royal head.

Then turning towards Woggle, the Queen announced in her most royal voice, "Would Woggle the Wanderer step forward, please." As Woggle stepped forward to face his Queen, she turned to a Paige, who was standing just behind her, holding a large royal red cushion with an ancient sword resting on it. The Queen lifted the sword off the cushion, the Paige placed it on the floor in front of her.

Looking directly at Woggle, who was standing in front of the Queen, she graciously asked him to kneel on the cushion. Continuing to speak, she said, "In the company of the noble citizens of The Land of Pleasant and in the presence of His Majesty King Suoegaruoc III, it gives me great pleasure to dub thee," at this point the Queen, using the sword, lightly touched Woggle first on the right shoulder then lifting the sword over his head, she lightly touched him on his left shoulder. This action was done three times as she continued speaking, "Sir Woggle the Wanderer, The First Knight of The Land of Pleasant. Arise, Sir Woggle." At this point, the crowd went wild. The cheering, whistling, hand clapping and foot stamping lasted for many minutes. Eventually, Queen Gnorts II raised her right hand for silence; as the crowd became calm, she called me to stand near her. "It has been my privilege to meet you. We are all so very pleased that you were willing to come to our rescue once again. It is not, however, our custom to give those from the other side accolades such as knighthoods, even though I feel you deserve one. What I will do for you today is to give you, as promised, a name suitable and fitting for you in the light of the many tasks you have successfully performed on this mission. I, therefore, name you as a Fellow of The Land of Pleasant, and from this day forward and for as long as you visit and help us, you shall be known as Pockets, the Man from the Other Side."

Once again, a huge cheer of gratitude filled the air. As the noise subsided, the King in a loud commanding but joyful voice gave an order. "In honour of Sir Woggle and his brave companion, Pockets the Brave, let the banquet begin." Another cheer went up from the crowd. As we made our way towards the banqueting tables with its banners blowing in the breeze, I noticed it was only the centre banner which had an inscription on it. In Rorrim, it read 'Sih Rennab

Revo me si Evol'. On our way through the palace garden, I heard Wise speaking to the Queen about the tree, now it was restored and looking very healthy.

I heard him say, "Well, Ma'am, The Great Mungawumba Tree is a living picture, and it is more splendid than ever."

"Indeed it is, my noble Wise, indeed it is."

As we reached The Royal Banquet, we were joined by Oggle, Foggle, Boggle, and Brave. Brave spoke first. "Tell me, Pockets, what do you think will happen in your next adventure in The Land of Pleasant." I was about to answer him when I looked up and discovered my attic was incredibly tidy and organised. I climbed out of it and closed it up.

A little later on, while having lunch with my wife, she asked me, "What was the nickname you had when you worked at Cashmores?" I smiled and gave her the answer while thinking to myself, *What an amazing adventure that was and all before midday.*

Volume 4
The Flying Slimeyosaurus

Chapter 1
Another Monday Morning

It was just another Monday morning, the time was 7:45. I was on a Metro on my way to work; I'm based at a school in Gateshead. The train had just crossed the River Tyne and had entered the tunnel that would bring us to Gateshead Interchange. Just before arriving at the platform and still in the tunnel, the Metro stopped; the tunnel is completely dark. I looked up for a moment from my iPhone; I was checking my early morning emails. The carriage lights caused the windows to act as a mirror, causing me to see myself looking back at myself. Returning to my emails, I was interrupted as the driver made an announcement, "I apologise for the delay but the train ahead of us is going slow due to low adhesions on the line."

"Low adhesions," said a voice opposite me chuckling. I took no notice. "That simply means there are leaves on the track," said the voice again. This time I looked up; my eyes nearly came out of my head, sitting opposite me was The See Thru Man. I was about to speak when I realised his bony index finger, which is also see thru, was resting vertically across the centre of his mouth, indicating for me to be quiet while he continued speaking, "You can see and hear me but they can't."

I looked quickly around and realised the carriage was full. Of course it was full; it was now just 7:50. Passengers were going to work, dropping children off at playgroups and at grandparents, young people were going to college and school.

The See Thru Man was sitting next to an old lady, who smiled kindly at me and said, "I don't like these cold winter mornings. I would much rather be at home by the fire enjoying a nice cup of tea and reading my magazine."

The See Thru Man spoke up. "Follow me," he said, and with that he stood up and walked down the carriage.

As I stood to follow him, the little old lady asked, "Don't you want to stay and chat?"

"I would love too," I replied, "but I'm just stretching my legs for a moment while we have stopped."

Walking through the crowded carriage while keeping an eye on The See Thru Man, some passengers complained even and I apologised and politely said, "Excuse me please." It was really awkward, I could see him, but they could only see me.

Wouldn't it be easier if they could see him as well, I thought. The See Thru Man hesitated, waiting for me to catch up.

Chapter 2
Underground

We were standing at a set of double doors, the kind which close automatically on trains like this one. "When the train starts moving, don't hesitate, just walk through the doors as if they are open, you will be fine," he instructed. *Walk through the doors,* I thought to myself, *I must be having a bad hair-do day or something.* The Metro was still in the tunnel. The windows were still acting like mirrors. Once again, I could see myself but not my normal reflection in the glass. In fact, as I looked at my reflection, I realised it was also see thru. *How amazing is that!* I thought. The train gave a slight jerk as it started moving; I looked up, The See Thru Man was outside beckoning me to him. The train moved a little faster. I held my breath, closed my eyes and stepped towards the doors. Without any warning, I was standing next to The See Thru Man, but we weren't standing on anything solid. Taking me by the elbow, we turned around and walked through the old stone tunnel wall and kept on walking through solid mass as if this was the normal thing to do. There was no such thing as an obstacle. We just kept on walking. The See Thru Man was holding my right elbow in his left hand as we walked in a dead straight line without speaking. Not a word was uttered. For one thing, I didn't dare open my mouth. I was afraid I might swallow something like a piece of masonry or an old decaying tree root or some creepy crawly thing, which lives in the deep dark forgotten soil. The See Thru Man broke the silence. "In The Land of Pleasant, in their native tongue Rorrim, they have these sayings: '*Dekoorc edam dog tahw thgiarts ekam nac ohw.*' And, '*Thgiarts shtap ym sekam eh,*' which simply means: when we do what is right no matter what stands in the way, our path will always run true, like the first rays of sunshine on a new day."

"That's worth knowing," I replied, "but where are we going?"

"All in good time," he replied as we continued on our underground journey. We were deep underground, in a forgotten world without daylight, any sense of direction, no landmarks, nothing, just walking through tunnels, ancient foundations, tons of rubble, tree roots and a host of other stuff, which was buried and out of sight to human eyes and still no conversation happened between us. This gave me time to think a little about The See Thru Man. He always looked familiar but I couldn't put my finger on why or who. He always appeared to be dressed the same, a tall black top hat, a long black Victorian frock coat, black trousers and worn but highly polished black boots. The same non-ghostly smile, and see thru. Not transparent, just see thru. *Why was he familiar,* I wondered. I couldn't put my finger on it. *Never mind, maybe one day I will bring it back to my memory, but for now I need to focus on our journey.* How long or far we had walked, I had no idea. And where we were in relationship to Gateshead Interchange, I couldn't tell. We just kept on walking. Suddenly I heard The See Thru Man singing a little song; he had a deep bass voice, which was very pleasant. Listening carefully and after a little while, I could make out the words clearly.

"My boots just keep on walking.
It's what they do each day.
My boots just keep on walking.
They lead me in the way.
My boots just keep on going.
Doing what is best.
My boots just keep on walking.
They're full of zeal and zest."

Looking at me out of the corner of his eye and smiling that non-ghostly smile. It's called not ghostly because he is see thru but he's not spooky. "I gave my boots a name a long time ago, in Rorrim they are called Boots of Ecaep, which is quite profound really," he said still smiling. Then he added, "You're not very talkative this morning, is everything all right?"

"All right," I spluttered, "this is the third time we've met and every time it's different, I suppose I should be used to it by now, but this is totally bizarre."

"You think this is bizarre, you ain't seen nothing yet," he grinned. By now, we were in some underground chamber. It wasn't huge, but it was damp and chilly, I shivered.

"In a few minutes, you will be in The Land of Pleasant but not in a part you are familiar with. Now remember, in the land everything is pleasant but not perfect. Where you are going today is over the other side of 'Ycrep' hill, there's a small colony of

Stesomrams, they used to be friends with the Stabmows, but things went wrong some time ago. I need them to settle their differences because I need them for a bigger challenge." Then addressing me by the name, Queen Gnorts II gave me on my last adventure, he said, "When I leave you, Pockets, in a few moments, you must leave via that wall over there." I looked at the wall he was pointing at with his long bony, see thru index finger and shuddered. It was slimy, cold, damp and unwelcoming.

"What do you mean, leave via that wall over there?" I asked.

"Exactly that, as we have been doing all along, you leave via that wall and when you do, all will become clear. They are expecting you, you know," and with that comment he left. Disappeared, just like that, there one minute, gone the next.

Chapter 3
Thru the Wall

This underground chamber wasn't the place to stay. The atmosphere had an uneasiness about it. Slowly, my eyes grew accustomed to the light, which was taking longer than expected. But as they did, I realised I was in a vault, the ancient kind you find beneath ancient churches in old graveyards. To my left was a very old headstone on a tomb with a faded inscription, which I was just able to make out; it simply read: *T. S. T. M. Born on Sunday, 29th day of February, 1688 BC. Believed to have passed away. Date unknown.*

I went cold. I understood the initials. I just wondered why he left me here. I snapped out of my ponderings and remembered his final command, 'leave via that wall over there'. As I looked at it again, it was even less inviting, now my eyes were used to the darkness of this vault. The slimy wall looked much worse than when I first looked at it. And I had almost forgotten how we got this far, which seemed easier when following The See Thru Man, and less daunting. I reflected for a moment on my recent past experiences, the mirror in my inside pocket and the importance of the word 'put'; then there was taking items out of my pocket. On both occasions, it was always without struggling and today was no different, we had walked through all sorts of things but that was with him. Now I had to do it on my own.

What if I couldn't? What would happen to me? Would I be trapped? No one would know where I was. I started to panic; my unanswered questions were crowding in on me, I felt as if I was suffocating. With a huge amount of self-control and determination I brought myself under control. There was nothing else for it, I had to walk towards the wall and hope for the best. I braced myself, took a deep breath and walked at the wall. The slime stank. It was so bad it almost knocked me off my feet. I recoiled holding my mouth, expecting to be sick. I longed for fresh air. I paused for a few moments, thinking about it, going over in my mind once again our journey to this point. "We didn't walk at anything, we walked as if obstacles didn't exist," I said out loud. *Hmmm, I wonder let's give it another go*; so, with a little more confidence and determination, I walked towards the wall. The same thing happened again; at the last second I was overcome by the evil smell. Six attempts later and I was still in this dreadful place. Once again, I reflected on the journey that got me here; once again I thought about the absolute simplicity of it, we just walked as if obstacles did not exist. "BINGO! I've got it," I said out loud. And with that resolve, I walked to the furthest point away from the slimy wall and with eyes wide open I strode towards it, undeterred. When I reached the wall, I didn't walk through it as I'd expected, no, the wall just dissolved, and I found myself standing in a pleasant sunlit meadow. The shock took me by surprise. I wasn't certain what to expect but it wasn't pleasant, fresh air and a pleasant meadow. I turned around to look at the wall I was behind a moment ago; there was nothing just a row of trees lining the edge of a small wood. *Oh well,* I thought to myself, *all's well that ends well,* except this wasn't really the end.

Chapter 4
Fresh Ground

"You made it," said a voice. I spun around not knowing what to expect. Leaning against a tree in a very casual manner was The See Thru Man.

"Where did you come from?" I spluttered.

He just smiled and replied, "Follow me, we've got people to meet, places to visit and things to do." And with that he walked off taking very long strides. I rushed after him wondering where we were going. We crossed the meadow at a rapid pace and went through a small wood. While we were going through the wood, I had a strange sensation, the kind of feeling you get when you are being watched but didn't know who by or where they were hiding. I kept looking around me while keeping a close eye on The See Thru Man.

"Have you spotted them yet then?" he asked smiling.

"Spotted who?" I asked, trying to act innocent.

"You keep glancing around you as if you think you're being followed or watched," came his reply.

"I feel as if the trees have eyes, that's all, it's just a strange sensation I keep having."

"I'm pleased to hear that," came his answer, "because on this adventure you will need your sixth sense more than ever."

My sixth sense, that's a laugh. Mine has never been that good, it will need to improve drastically to be of any use, I thought to myself. "It will," said The See Thru Man, and before I had chance to answer, he continued, "You will find your sixth sense rising to new heights on this adventure," he concluded.

As we came to the end of the meadow, I could see a small hill off to our right. "The other side of that hill is where your friends live, but at the foot of the hill is a small hamlet where your new task will start from," said The See Thru Man and with that he vanished.

Chapter 5
Sixth Sense!

I remained still for a few moments taking in my new surroundings. The hill in the near distance I recognised but the small hamlet was totally new to me, a small group of about 18 or so small log cabins. These were randomly dotted about, facing away from the small hill.

It was while I was taking all this in, I got my first surprise. I distinctly heard a noise and it was definitely behind me and to my left. I wanted to spin around and look in its direction, but I refused and kept looking in the direction of the hamlet. I kept looking because my eyesight was acting strange; everything in my vision was very sharp and crystal clear. The settlement as the crow flies is approximately one mile away, yet it was as if I was within 50 metres of it or using powerful binoculars. Slowly, I turned my head to my left, then focusing on the furthest point, I studied the horizon, again everything came into sharp focus. Every branch and every twig were easily defined, but when I looked without concentrating, my eyesight was normal. Then I thought about my sense of smell. Wondering if it had changed, I closed my eyes and slowly breathed in through my nose. At first, there was no difference, then suddenly I caught a full on fresh smell, very pleasant, full of different fragrances. I was transfixed like someone in a trance.

Without warning, this first smell was overpowered by a thick sickly smell, then thump, wallop and I was flat on my face, pinned to the ground. "So much for a sixth sense," I sighed, "but when you're down, there's only one direction you can go and that's up." I raised my head slightly to see a huge shadow passing overhead, and I was surrounded by at least a dozen bodies. The creature pinning me down stood up and apologised, I was helped to my feet by him; looking around I was instantly aware that these Pleasantonians were very similar to my friends the Stabmows except their fur was plain-coloured not striped, they were slightly t0aller, slimmer and with a more serious expression on their round faces.

Chapter 6
The Flying Slimeyosaurus

I stood up and looked towards the sky as the thing that caused the huge shadow was slowly disappearing. "What is that thing?" I exclaimed.

"It's called The Flying Slimeyosaurus and it's originally from the Dartknoy Wilderness of Gulberia. It is massive, its dark brown body is covered in huge ugly scales, and its four legs have big feet with three claw toes like talons. The hind legs are huge while the front legs are slightly shorter and slimmer and not so muscular. Its neck is long and sinewy and like its body, covered in ugly scales. Its tail is about four metres long, ending in a sharp arrow point, and it's not just used for balance in flight but as a whip; the beast can coil up its tail then unleash it at will on whatever it chooses. It has a huge head with massive jaws and two rows of razor-sharp teeth. Narrow evil orange eyes and a hideous jet-black nose with two great nostrils, which constantly flap in and out with every breath it takes. Its ears are always erect and if you keep watching, you will notice that it oozes a horrible greenish and dull brown slimy substance from underneath its scales. Its leathery wings, each three metres long, have a separate claw protruding out from half way along and in total length from nose tip to tail point, it's about 18 metres long," concluded the creature standing next to me. "Why it's here, why it is intimidating us, we have no idea."

Chapter 7
The Angry Stesomram

Surrounded by these inhabitants of The Land of Pleasant, we made our way towards their homes. As we drew nearer, I could see a large number of them busy working clearing up the slime. The mess and the smell was disgusting. Firstly, it wasn't easy to clean and secondly, the stench made it difficult to get close enough to make the cleaning operation worthwhile.

Without warning, the leader got everyone's attention by sending out an ear piercing, high-pitched shrill whistle. Those who were busy cleaning up the slime stopped what they were doing and made their way to the centre of the settlement, others who were in their doorways came out and joined us, whilst a few stragglers, who were further away at the foot of the hill, joined us a little later. The crowd was about 50 strong, a buzz of voices rose in a great crescendo; it was obvious by the way they were jabbering and looking at me and pointing at me with their paws that I was the centre of attention. Their leader raised his hand and silenced the crowd, then he spoke, "We have with us today a visitor from the other side; I think it is probably right to say that The See Thru Man has sent him. Why, I don't know. In a moment, I will ask him to speak to us and tell us how he arrived and why he is here. Please be patient and listen carefully to all he has to say. I will ask our visitor to introduce himself."

He sat down, and as I started speaking, a stern looking Stesomram started shouting from the back of the small crowd, "We don't need your sort here trying to help us, we can manage on our own, we don't want outsiders here poking their noses into our business." I paused, waiting to see if the crowd would respond. Nothing, so I continued giving a brief account of my first three visits and adventures in The Land of Pleasant. I suddenly realised I hadn't given my name. Giving an account of the end of the last adventure, I concluded with, "It was at the end of the ceremony that Woggle the Wanderer received from Queen Gnorts II his Knighthood and I was given the name Pockets. I was given this name because I simply followed the instructions given to me by The See Thru Man. And so, from that day forward, here in The Land of Pleasant, I have been known as Pockets."

From the middle of the crowd applause starting rippling through. Most of the crowd cheered and clapped but the stern member at the back of the crowd shouted out again, "It doesn't matter who you are, or who named you, we still don't want your kind here." While he was shouting out, I remembered my new ability with my senses and focusing my attention on him, I looked more closely at him.

His right ear had been torn or chewed away in a fight. His jet-black fur looked threadbare and in his mouth, he had more gaps than teeth, his teeth were decaying yellow and black. As I continued looking, he became more and more agitated. It was at this point, I got a real shock. It was as if the curtain of his soul was pulled back, and I could see right into his inner being. In Rorrim, this is called an '*Egdelewonk fo drow*'. "What are you staring at?" he shrieked.

"If you're so smart, let's see you do one of your clever things right now," a deathly hush fell upon the crowd. I was undeterred.

Looking straight at this angry character and speaking in a steady clear voice, I said, "For the past six years, you have been spying on the Stabmows, you have taken up this way of life because your wife is fed up with your bitterness and argumentative ways, which has driven a wedge between the two of you. Your three children, Yltneg, Yltfos, and Ylrednet, are tired of the way you treat their mother, and they are growing more and more afraid of you with every passing day. And on top of that, deep in your inner most being, you are resentful of your leader and jealous of Sir Woggle the Wanderer. How am I doing so far? Would you like me to share any more of your hidden secrets?"

The Stesomram was rooted to the spot, not certain if he should retaliate or run. "Who told you all of that?" he blurted out.

"Nobody here told me. I've only just arrived, it was simply revealed to me when I looked at you and listened to you," I replied.

Then very quietly and sincerely, the angry stesomram Zebaj asked, "Can we have a private chat later?"

"Of course, we can, I will come to your place a little later," I answered. A huge round of applause ascended amid shrieks, cheers and whistling while his wife and family, standing next to him, were all tearful or crying with relief as if a major breakthrough had just happened.

Chapter 8
One-to-One

The leader came and standing next to me made this announcement to the assembled crowd. "As your Chieftain, I not only welcome our visitor, but I recommend that we firstly listen carefully to all he says, secondly, we take his counsel seriously and thirdly, we act upon his recommendations even if they are painful." This time the only citizen cheering was the stern faced creature at the back of the crowd, whose facial expressions had softened a little.

"Before I invite our visitor to speak to us again, I think it only right that I apologise for my rudeness in not giving some formal introductions; I am the Chieftain of this clan and my full name is…*RRRRrrrrroooaaaarrrrr*…without warning, the sky went totally black as the huge Slimeyosaurus flew slowly overhead, making a deafening noise and dropping great big dollops of slimy sludge everywhere. Instantly, everyone dived for cover. Fortunately, no one or anything was caught in this dreadful deluge. As the creature slowly and ungraciously disappeared, everyone returned from their hiding places and reassembled. "As I was saying before our rude interruption, my full name is Baron von Fulycrem the Third, but I am usually known as the Baron, and we are ready to listen to all you have to say." Once again, I stood to my feet and addressed the crowd.

I explained in detail the events which brought me here but not the resting place of The See Thru Man. Finally, I gave them the message he had given me about my mission. "This is what The See Thru Man said to me, 'There's a small colony of Stesomrams, they used to be friends with the Stabmows but things went wrong some time ago. I need them to settle their differences because I need them all for a bigger challenge.'"

"For me to help you," I continued, "I need you to be absolutely honest and willing to make the first move."

"Why us?" shouted out a youngster from the second row.

"That's a fair comment, why us?" shouted others.

I waited for silence then slowly added, "Why not, The See Thru Man believes you are capable of making the first move and besides, you are the ones under threat from the ugly Slimeyosaurus. But I believe this thing is not the real problem. First, we must talk through what's gone wrong and what we can do to put it right," a hush lay heavy in the air.

No one spoke for several minutes, so I continued, "My recommendation is that the Baron sends an envoy to the Stabmows and brings, Wise, Brave and Sir Woggle the Wanderer, Oggle, Foggle and Boggle here, then with a small select group of the Baron's choice, we sit down and talk this through and find a proper solution."

The Baron gave his seal of approval and sent three of his most loyal and trusted citizens, Gninnuc, Tsafdaets, and Ytfarc, to go to the Stabmows. "Tell them their friend is here."

They left straightaway and early the following morning returned with the Stabmows. While the three Stesomrams were on their way to meet the Stabmows, I was taken by the Baron to meet with the angry Stesomram and his family. They entered through the neglected front door of a dilapidated dwelling, the smell was awful. At this point, the Baron left them. The wife and mother apologised for the state of their home. All the window frames were rotten, and many of them were just open empty spaces. There was no furniture of any sort. So we sat on the dirty floor. For some time, we sat in silence, the family looking at their father to speak first. The wife stared at the floor. The silence was embarrassing. Eventually, he spoke. His voice crackled and choked, as if he struggled to regain his old aggression but it was no use, he was broken and embarrassed. "My name is Zebaj, and I have become a pain to my family, my neighbours, my countrymen and my King and Queen. Many years ago, I thought I was related to the Stabmows. I discovered this was impossible because none of them are married. I also found out to my shame that while I am a Stesomram, I am an orphan, the only orphan in The Land of Pleasant. I allowed myself to become bitter, cruel and jealous.

"It's these three things which have driven me to spying on the Stabmows and to ill-treating my wife and to intimidating my children. It wasn't instant, it all happened over a long period of time; the more embittered I became the greater the jealousy. The greater the jealousy, the more I spied. The more I spied, the more intense my cruelty became. It was a vicious circle and I was in a mess." As I listened intently, Zebaj's wife and children wept. It was a pitiful sight. Zebaj continued by asking his wife and children to forgive him. They all responded favourably. He realised this was only the beginning, but at least it was a small but significant step in the right direction.

"And finally, whatever help I can be to rid us of this monster then I'm available, count me in any time." With this final comment, Zebaj looked totally worn out, and right where he sat, he fell asleep.

I remained where I was for a short while longer as the family slowly gathered themselves together. The mother spoke first, "My name is Dimit and I've never been strong enough to stand up to him but today I feel as if we have a fresh start, thank you."

Chapter 9
Thrown Together

As I walked out into the fresh air towards the Baron's house, I heard a buzz of commotion. Lots of voices but not all pleasant. Some arguing, some sounding pleased, some grumbling and others just asking questions. "Look out," bellowed the Baron. Suddenly, the Slimeyosaurus was swooping out of the sky, swaying from side to side in a frantic rocking motion as if it was out of control. Everyone dived for cover as the monster plummeted to the earth. Instantly, a loud screeching and screaming was heard. Without instruction, everyone jumped out of hiding to see this creature trying to gain height, while in the claws of its wings it clutched two Stesomrams. The concerned family members were shouting in horror. Sir Woggle and Brave were on the run chasing the Slimeyosaurus, closer and closer they got. Inch by inch they were gaining on it as the monster failed to gain height. Its great tail was hanging just about a metre or so off the ground. Without slowing down, Woggle and Brave kept racing after it, gaining on it with every stride. The tail was now in reach after just a few more strides. Woggle reached out his right paw and grabbed the tail, making certain he dug his claws in deeply. Brave grabbed Woggle's left paw in his right. Suddenly, Brave heard someone shouting at him, "Give me your left paw."

Brave did so as he quickly glanced over his shoulder catching a glimpse of the Baron. "Hang on tight," roared the Baron and with his spare paw he grabbed the trunk of a tree they were passing. A huge struggle began. The three Pleasantonians were using their combined effort, strength and determination. The monster was still flapping its great leathery wings and its captors were thrown up and down as they remained clamped in its claws. Six more individuals arrived to lend a helping paw and hand, including me, they were Zebaj, Wise, Foggle, Oggle, and Boggle. Two groups of three positioned themselves under each wing claw. Both groups shouting words of encouragement.

Sir Woggle hollered loudly, "Get ready for a shaking," and with that he started wagging the tail of the Slimeyosaurus violently. Up and down. Up and down. The beast let out an agonising wail, and bending its massive head downwards, it tried without success to bite at the six helpers on the ground. Next, it twisted its massive body backwards trying to bite Woggle, but it was of no use. Suddenly, it released its prisoners who were caught safely as its tail snapped off. The impact of this sent Woggle and Brave careering backwards into the Baron. The three of them ended up in a great heap while the creature was catapulted unsteadily away.

The three scrambled to their feet and stood looking at one another. Baron was looking at Brave and Sir Woggle with them looking back at him.

Brave slowly and cautiously extended his paw to the Baron and said, "You came to our aide not just to rescue your own, didn't you?"

"That is very true," replied the Baron. "We've had a very eventful day, your friend Pockets is quite a character and he's been brought here for a special task from The See Thru Man, which involves all of us and some imminent—" *CCCcccccccrrrrraaaaassshhh.* We had forgotten about the Slimeyosaurus. It failed to fly and gain height, and instead, it crashed into a small hill on the other side of a little wood. We set off at a quick trot with the Baron leading the way. As we arrived at the other side of the wood, the Baron held up his right paw, warning the group to be cautious. We were at the top of a steep cliff, which went down for about a hundred metres into a narrow gorge, the opposite side was rough gravel and jagged stones and rocks making the cliff face almost impossible to climb. The monster clung on where it had crashed. There it lay in its own slime, which was oozing out from its body as it gripped anything it could on the cliff face to stop it from slithering down into the narrow gorge. Woggle spoke first. "I've encountered these things before on my wanderings, its tail will grow again, it takes about three days and it will be stronger than the last one. The slime will eventually stop and dry up. When that happens, it will fly again and be more aggressive than before, it won't spread slime, but it might breathe fire. All we've done today is buy ourselves some time, not much just three days maximum."

"Right," I said, "we need to get back because we have things to discuss and ground to gain." With that we left the edge of the narrow gorge and headed back to the Baron's house and the rest of the

Stesomrams. On the way back, Zebaj spoke to me and the Baron. "It felt so good to be involved in helping others, thank you."

The Baron looked at him and then at me and smilingly said, "And there's more of that to come."

The Baron sent word summoning everyone to an urgent meeting. No excuses were acceptable, everyone was to attend. The Baron had supper organised; a community supper because it was getting late.

Chapter 10
Honesty and a Pleasant Surprise

The Baron arranged a single row of log seats for Sir Woggle and the five Stabmows, his special envoy Gninnuc, Tsafdaets, and Ytfarc, a chair for himself, and one for me. In the front row was Zebaj, Dimit, and their girls; Yltfos, Yltneg and Ylrednet. They were all looking very sombre but relieved. The Baron opened the meeting by thanking everyone for their promptness and for the willingness of the Stabmows to attend and for the incredible work of those involved in rescuing the two captives who were a little sore and badly shaken up but nothing more serious. Again, he handed the meeting over to me.

"Once again, thank you for your welcome. Thank you for your willingness to cooperate and it is so good to see my friends again. Before we consider the immediate problem, we must look at the root cause which is why in this wonderful Land of Pleasant, two close groups have fallen out and have failed to settle their differences." Instantly, uproar and pandemonium broke out with angry comments being hurled around like, "but you don't understand" and "your great grandfather started this by doing…" and "It wasn't him, it was your old uncle Salis—"

"Enough," roared the Baron. "None of you are right. There are only two people who know the truth and that is me and…" The Baron paused for a long time.

Everyone was silent, watching, waiting, and wondering what would happen next. The Baron finally spoke again, repeating himself, "there are only two of us here, who know the truth and that is me and…"

Before he could finish the sentence, someone else spoke up, "And me."

The Baron turned and looked full in the face of Sir Woggle and in a much calmer voice spoke again to the crowd. "For too long now, there has been strife and unrest between our two groups. The truth was never told and because of this, rumour, speculation, and unrest between us has spread, causing strife and family feuds to ruin us. Today we, Woggle and I, want to make a fresh start so that peace and tranquillity, unity, and harmony will be restored again."

Interrupting this speech, Woggle spoke up, "This fault is all mine and it's only right I tell you what happened. Many years ago, when we were much younger, we were on an adventure together in the Dartknoy Wilderness of Gulberia. We were searching for the Slimeyosaurus, believed to be extinct, until that is the people of Gulberia spotted two of them flying in the skies over the Dartknoy Wilderness. They told us about them when we were on a different mission. So we decided to return and investigate. It was on that actual trip that things went wrong. I was busy kneeing on the edge of a cliff in the wilderness looking for a way into their lair, when without warning, I was hanging over the edge of the cliff gripping a rock for dear life.

"My mistake was this: I thought the Baron had deliberately pushed me over the edge as if he were trying to finish me off. I now know he was saving my life not pushing me to my death. One of these creatures came diving at me out of the sky. The Baron dived at me and suspended me over the edge of the cliff. Believing me to be safe, the Baron went on to pursue the creature which almost finished me off. I climbed to safety but in my anger, ignorance, and hot-headedness, I left him in the wilderness and made my way back home, which is a dreadful thing to do. And since then I failed to right the wrongs. Tonight, I not only ask every Stesomram to forgive me but the Baron as well."

Then turning to face the Baron for the first time since giving this account, Sir Woggle said seriously, "I wronged you many years ago. You saved my life when I thought you were going to k—" most of the crowd began shouting again as with one voice: "If", "What about", "But", "Rubbish", and "That's not true".

"Enough," roared the Baron. "As I said a few moments ago, there were only two of us on that expedition and that was myself and…"

"That's not true," shouted someone from the front row. For the second time, the Baron was interrupted. But this time the interruption had a profound effect and an instant silence descended. The Baron and Sir Woggle stared in shocked dumbstruck silence.

Slowly, the speaker on the front row stood up and climbed onto the low platform; it was Zebaj.

Finally, he spoke, "Some of you may remember that when the Baron and Woggle went on their adventure, I went missing.

Actually, I followed them and witnessed everything that took place as Sir Woggle has explained, and everything he has told us all tonight is true. But because I was jealous and Sir Woggle was angry, I spread malicious rumours, and whenever I got the chance, I just added fuel to the smouldering fire, and today it is I who needs your forgiveness because the disunity and disharmony has been my doing. Well, I have confessed all, and I feel better now it's in the open, if you choose not to forgive me, I won't hold it against you, but now I have my home to put in order because it is a disgrace. Thank you," and with final comment Zebaj left the meeting, his wife, and daughters running after him. As they got closer to their home, they were alarmed because all the lights were on. The lights hadn't worked in years, then they heard someone singing in a deep baritone voice. They couldn't make out the words at first but it sounded like someone was having a good time.

"Ship shape and Pleasant fashion.
That's the way it's done, it's done.
Spit and polish and elbow grease.
Work is so much fun, so much fun.
Throw out the old, bring in the new.
With a spin and a twirl. It's all brand new."

The family stood still, frozen to the spot and listened. Zebaj started running, the rest of the family followed quickly behind him. As he neared his home, he heard a voice saying, "Come on, Lofty, it's time we left, we've done a good job." Zebaj and his family were rooted to the spot just outside their home, witnessing a strange phenomenon; a whirlwind was rising up through the roof, in the whirlwind they saw two figures. The one was see thru and the other was incredibly tall. As they watched this spectacular sight, the two men in the whirlwind gave a brief wave to the watching family and disappeared, spinning in the whirlwind. Zebaj and his family rushed to their front door and suddenly stopped, the front door was brand new, all the window frames had been renewed and fitted with glass. Tentatively. They went inside, there was no bad smell, but every room in this small dwelling had been transformed from top to bottom. Dimit was the first to speak, "It's as if our home has been reborn."

"And that's just how I feel," replied Zebaj. Meanwhile, a crowd had gathered outside their home; seeing the strange whirlwind they rushed to the house expecting to find devastation, instead they were greeted with an incredible surprise, the house was brand new, inside and out, and brightly painted as well. Zebaj and his family were wandering about as if in a dream.

The Baron arrived, out of curiosity. No one, never mind a crowd, had gathered outside this dwelling for a very long time. Zebaj came out to meet the Baron, who threw a great big hairy arm around his shoulder as he asked, "Did you hear anything, or see anything?"

Zebaj told the Baron everything. He smiled and said calmly, "That's The See Thru Man and Lofty."

"Wow," was all they could say. As the crowd went their separate ways, Zebaj and his family went back inside their new home.

"What's this?" asked Dimit holding up a golden envelope with the following message on it: 'F.A.O. The Baron, Sir Woggle, and Pockets'.

"I'd better deliver it straightaway," replied Zebaj.

"You are not going anywhere dressed like that. Before you do anything else, you are going to shower or bath and sort your fur coat out first."

"But…" protested Zebaj.

"Go," replied Dimit firmly. And take a good hot bath is what he did. When he reappeared from the bathroom, he looked, smelled, and felt better than he had done for a long time. His chewed right ear, terrible teeth, and matted coat were completely restored. His daughters squealed in delight and rushed up to their daddy and gave him a big huggel. In case you are wondering, a huggel is a combination of a hug and a cuddle.

"Now it's down to business," said Zebaj, and with that he left with the golden letter in hand. He returned two hours later, satisfied he had done the job justice.

Chapter 11
A Council of War

The Baron summoned all the Stabmows, his special envoy Gninnuc, Tsafdaets, Ytfarc, and me to an urgent meeting in his underground chamber. The chamber was oval shaped, the walls richly covered in oak and beech tree bark. The only furniture in the chamber was an oak oval table and 11 chairs. The lighting was produced by 16x6 candlestick holders. When everyone was seated around the table, the Baron began, explaining about the golden envelope, which was passed around for everyone to examine and finally handed back to the Baron, who then gave a brief account of the transformation of Zebaj, his family and home, and how they witnessed the whirlwind whisking away The See Thru Man and Lofty. "And so to close this account, it is only right and proper to let you know that at Dimit's firm request, Zebaj had his first bath in about six years, although sometimes I thought it was much longer," finished the Baron and with that he carefully opened the golden envelope, inside was what appeared to be a blank piece of gold paper. As the small group watched, the Baron turned the paper over and then back again, raising his eyebrows he passed the paper to Ytfarc, who was sitting to his right, in turn everyone examined the golden sheet until it came back to the Baron who was re-examining the envelope.

Everyone except Boggle was frowning and making comments like 'Is this some sort of joke', 'is The See Thru Man having a laugh' and so, finally, Wise turned to Boggle and asked, "What are you grinning about, Boggle?"

"If my good friend, the Baron, will pass the golden letter to me, I will show what's written on it," replied Boggle. The Baron obliged. Boggle took the golden page and started examining it more closely. "They don't call me Boggle for nothing," he murmured with a grin. Then standing up he walked to a nearby candle and held the letter close to the naked flame. All eyes were on Boggle as they held their breath wondering what he was doing. Patiently, he slowly and carefully warmed the letter. When he was satisfied that this task was complete, he passed the golden sheet back to the Baron and returned to his seat. The Baron thanked Boggle and read what was on the sheet. "'These instructions come from my own hand. A big thank you to Boggle for quickly solving the simple mystery. It was necessary to use invisible ink to demonstrate the importance of the naked flame in the rescue plan. You must follow these instructions implicitly for the successful deliverance of The Land of Pleasant from the Slimeyosaurus.' That's the introduction," said the Baron. "I will now read the instructions and we must all listen carefully.

1) You must have two straight rows of flaming torches, at least 500 metres long and ten metres apart.
2) The finishing line must be 50 metres beyond the point where Pockets entered The Land of Pleasant on this trip.
3) Ten metres beyond the finishing you will need a filled water butt.
4) Entice the beast by using either one of you sitting around the table or Zebaj. My preference for this task is Zebaj.
5) The torchbearer must run between the two rows of flaming torches, racing across the finishing line and extinguishing the torch in the water.
6) Standing either side of the finishing line must be the Baron and Sir Woggle the Wanderer, and you must use these.

"Use what?" remarked the Baron, there was nothing on the page or in the envelope. The Baron stared at the golden sheet for several moments, as he stared at it, as if through the page, two objects appeared floating in air, rising out of the sheet of gold, "I'll go to the foot of our stairs," exclaimed the Baron, "that is extraordinary." Everyone around the table saw what was taking place.

"You must take hold of them," exclaimed Wise, "they are called The Keys of The Modgnik, and I can tell you what you and Woggle must do with them at the finishing line," concluded Wise excitedly.

"Thank you, Wise. We will listen to you a little later but first let me finish with the instructions, now where was I, oh yes at the end of point six. The final point, point seven says,

7) Do not be afraid. Just remember, timing is everything and one final point, listen to the wise counsel from Wise. P.S, don't worry about closing the hole. Your very special friend, TSTM.

"That's all the instructions, does anyone have anything to say?" concluded the Baron.

Wise spoke up, "The instructions are straightforward, but they will require cooperation from everyone, every willing individual must cooperate with a good attitude, and a genuine willingness, because this is more about restored unity amongst us than it is about victory over this creature. If we have success without unity, our problems will return and be far worse than anything we have experienced. The first thing to be done is to explain to everyone the need for unity and their cooperation in this present task. It is my recommendation that the Baron and Pockets meet with everyone, explaining in detail everything which needs to be achieved.

"If no one has any questions, I will explain how these work." Wise paused, giving everyone gathered a chance to take in all he had shared. Nobody spoke. Continuing, he said, "The keys you have been given will only work at the required spot and they must be used in unison, which is why your restored unity is crucial." Then moving next to the Baron, Wise said, "If you hold the keys up please, I can explain how they are used." The Baron did as Wise asked. "You will observe that the keys are identical, circular in shape with a hook on the outer rim, and directly opposite it and fitted onto the inner rim of the ring is a holding plate, this plate has four slots, one slot for each finger. This is how you should hold them." Wise gave a brief demonstration, "The purpose for the hook is to," Wise paused, "you see the veil of sight is very thin and the purpose of these keys is to unlock an opening in the veil big enough for the Slimeyosaurus to disappear into. We need the two keys because the opening must be made while keeping Woggle and the Baron at either side of the entrance of the opening. Now, if Woggle will join me, I will demonstrate exactly what must happen." Woggle joined the Baron with Wise, "Imagine you are at the chosen spot, Woggle you are right handed so you need this one and the Baron you need this one, they are similar but not identical, the difference is in the hook at the end. Now remember, the veil of sight is very thin. At the right moment, you must have your hooks touching at the apex of what will become your half of a semi-circle, and your hooks must meet forming a complete circle. As you make this circle, you must stay as far away from the circle as possible because when the circle is complete, it opens away to the underworld and the creature will disappear forever.

"The noise will be deafening and the hole will seal itself. My advice to you both is:

1) Go with Pockets to the designated area, so you will know your positions when the time is right.
2) In secret, practise, the bigger the circle the greater the success.
3) Don't tell anyone outside of this chamber about these keys.
4) Be responsible for your own key.

Now we should make plans and preparations for the showdown."

Chapter 12
A Nasty Surprise

As the group left the chamber, they were greeted with loud screaming and shouting. Total panic and terror was everywhere. The Slimeyosaurus had returned. In a frantic haphazard way, it was breathing fire everywhere and causing pandemonium. "We must buy ourselves time," shouted Wise, "can the Baron and Woggle repeat today with the beast what they did earlier."

The Baron spoke first, "I'm up for a challenge and I must protect my Stesomrams."

"I'm with you on this," replied Sir Woggle, "and so are the rest of us. Let's get going."

On the way, the Baron warned us that this would be more challenging. While we were on our way, the screaming and crying was more intense. Trees were on fire, some homes were burning. Zebaj had organised the locals into small groups; they were trying to bring the blaze under control, some had already been destroyed. Grabbing a piece of flaming timber, the Baron called to Zebaj to join him, replacing him with Oggle; then giving him the burning timber, he instructed him to wave it frantically in the air to attract the attention of the beast. "When you have his attention, run like the wind in that direction and in a straight line. Whatever you do, do not look over your shoulder and don't forget, run like the wind. We will be right behind you. Have you got that?"

"I have," and with that Zebaj was off to the centre of the small hamlet. The Baron and the rest of the group headed further down the track and concealed themselves in the undergrowth. Zebaj was dancing around in the centre of the hamlet looking like he'd lost his marbles. Dimit came rushing up to him wanting to know why he was making a fool of himself. Without stopping, Zebaj tried explaining he was obeying orders. Suddenly, there was deafening *wwwhhhooooshing* sound, Zebaj threw himself on top of his wife, flattening her into the ground. The fiery Slimeyosaurus just missed them. "Run for cover," shouted Zebaj as he dragged Dimit to her feet and forcing her to run into hiding. Then he resumed his position and his frantic dancing. The beast was hovering high in the sky, watching the frantic actions. Without warning, it dived at Zebaj. Dimit and her daughters held their breath and watched and waited. Zebaj took off like a rocket, running in a straight line, whatever was in his way he jumped, mounds of earth, tree stumps, logs, everything. He raced through bushes and shrubs, nothing was too great or too awkward.

As he sprinted on, he could feel the hot breath of the Slimeyosaurus on his back.

Without looking over his shoulder, he kept running. The Slimeyosaurus had climbed back into the sky getting ready for another dive at him. Somewhere behind him, Zebaj heard the Baron shout, "After it, Zebaj needs our help." The shout gave Zebaj encouragement, and encouragement gave him strength and power, and strength and power gave him more stamina and speed. Once he raced, not stopping for anything, as sure-footed as a mountain lion.

The Slimeyosaurus was swooping in again, diving at a frantic pace. "Faster guys faster," bellowed the Baron. The Slimeyosaurus was flying parallel to the ground about 20 metres clear of it and about 100 metres behind, Zebaj frantically chasing him as he waved the flaming torch above his head. The Slimeyosaurus was gaining on Zebaj but the Baron and co were losing ground.

"Come on," roared Sir Woggle, "we mustn't lose pace now." Zebaj heard the shout from Woggle and realised the desperate state of his situation. Instantly, he had a plan, he didn't have time to formulate it or consider its consequences, he just operated on instinct.

Stopping dead in his tracks, he turned and made an angry face at the beast while waving the flaming torch. It was so sudden and unexpected that for a few seconds the beast slowed. Without losing a moment but taking full advantage, Zebaj was off again; full speed. He was just a blur on the landscape. The effect was perfect. "Get ready to hang on," shouted the Baron and he grabbed the creature's tail with his right paw sinking his claws in deeply. The Slimeyosaurus let out a blood-curdling roar. The Baron reached backwards with his left paw, Brave caught him, each paw gripped the other's forearm. This sequence carried on down the line until it came to Sir Woggle the Wanderer. The chain was complete.

"Get ready to break," roared Sir Woggle as he threw his left arm and paw around the trunk of a great Mungawumba tree. The beast trying to escape kept the line of Pleasantonians tight, which was to their advantage.

"Hang on," yelled the Baron, "I'm going to start shaking," and with that he began heaving the creature up and down. Everyone gripped each other as the Baron set about the task. The beast flapped its leathery wings but to no avail. Up and down, up and down, up and down. Without stopping for breath, the Baron kept the shaking going and the group hung on with Sir Woggle doing a fantastic job as an anchorman.

Meanwhile, Zebaj, realising he was surplus to requirements for now, had quickly climbed a nearby tree and was able to witness the full effect.

The beast continued, letting out its agonising roar as the Baron continued shaking the beast. Without warning, there was a very loud crack! Like a rifle going off. The little group were flung backwards as the creature shot forward like a stone fired from a powerful catapult. As it went flying forward at an incredible speed, the small band gathered themselves up, quickly congratulated each other and set off following the creature to discover where it would end up. Zebaj shinned down the tree, headed to where the group were shaking the beast by the tail and picked it up where it had snapped off and headed for home, going via the Baron's place first. Back in the woods, the small troop rushed on trying to catch up with the creature that was propelled through the air at a frantic speed. *TTTTThhhhhuuuuudddDDD, WWWooo lllPPP*. This was followed by a deep rumbling and grating sound. At this, the Baron spoke up, "It's paid off, let's check it out just to be satisfied." They arrived at the scene. The creature had again collided with a small rock face about 250 metres high and slid helplessly down into the narrow gorge, where it lay wedged. We were all delighted and exhausted, as we turned to make our way back to the hamlet.

I spoke, "It's good that it's trapped but how much time do we have? And what will it be like when it's fully recovered?"

Woggle answered the questions, "We have a maximum of three days, and when it's recovered, it delivers fire and slime. The only advantage we have is that it lacks accuracy and cunning."

"Which must mean it has poor eyesight. If it could see properly, then surely its path of destruction would be far worse," I observed.

"That's exactly right," answered the Baron joining in the conversation, "that's why we need two rows of flaming torches and Zebaj with a flaming torch and why we needed him today with one because it will always focus on the fiery torch," remarked the Baron in conclusion. We hurried on arriving back at the hamlet where Oggle was still busy. All the fires were out, some locals were busy repairing homes and helping families who were dealing with fire damage. Another group was laughing, something had amused them. Wise asked what they were laughing at.

"We are laughing at Oggle, he's been doing this impersonation of Pockets," replied a member of the group. Then he shouted to Oggle, "Do your Pockets impression for us again, Oggle."

With an infectious grin, Oggle shouted to everyone, "Pay attention please, I need your cooperation and what I would like you to do—" before Oggle could finish, everyone was in fits of laughter once more.

Chapter 13
Deception Defeated

The Baron called everyone together and explained everything what had happened, but he deliberately didn't say anything about the keys. Everybody was put into small working groups. Each group had a leader, a gatherer of brushwood, a binder to tie it all together and a planter. The planter would bring the brush wood torch to Wise and Boggle, who would mark out the exact length and width of the strip once I had marked the finishing line. "It is essential that the finishing line is marked first, don't ask me why, we haven't the time for details and full explanations right now. Without further ado, let's get cracking, we have a beast to finish off. Oggle, Foggle, and Boggle along with Ytfarc, Gninnuc, and Tsafdaets will supervise the groups and the quality of the torches. They must be perfect," concluded the Baron.

Wise, Brave, the Baron, Sir Woggle, and I headed for the edge of the woods. Nothing stood out as a reminder to me. I paced back and forth looking for clues, which would help me but there was nothing.

"It must be nearby because the other side of the wood is where Wise and the gang live." I paused my thinking, searching my memory for some indication but it was no use.

"How did you get here?" asked Wise. I told them about walking through the wall covered in slime and how it eventually dissolved and how I found myself in a meadow with the wood behind me. While I was explaining the events, I remembered my sixth sense, so staring ahead, I started listening intently, I wasn't certain what I was listening to or for, but suddenly, I could hear these awful sounds of screaming and wailing, like creatures in torment. Slowly, I walked forward, the noise became less, walking back and left the noise was more intense. Continuing on this course, I looked up and realised I was near the tree The See Thru Man was leaning against when I arrived earlier. I smiled to myself, then as I slowly walked a few more paces, I said, "It was right here. Definitely at this spot."

"Now then," said Wise, "we need a finishing line 50 metres beyond this point, then a filled water butt ten metres beyond the line, not forgetting that the Baron and Woggle must be either side of the finishing line." A ten-metre finishing line was marked and a spot allocated for the water butt.

Brave spoke up, "If it helps, I'll get the water butt sorted out."

"Thank you, Brave," replied Wise gratefully, "that will be excellent."

Brave hesitated and replied, "I'll involve Zebaj. I can prepare him for the flight of his life." And with that comment, Brave disappeared.

"Right then, Wise, I think we'd better mark out the lines. If you do the one and I do the other, that will make it quicker, but we need something to mark both edges and to get the width right," I said after a pause.

"It's all sorted," replied Wise grinning, "we can use this," and with that he walked across to the tree The See Thru Man leaned against and from around the trunk he unravelled two long lengths of twine, and very quickly he had removed a long, reasonably straight thin branch.

"This will do for the width," Wise said to me over his shoulder. But I wasn't listening to Wise, I was staring into the middle distance with the look of concentration on my face. Carrying my new bundle of equipment over my shoulder and the measuring rod in my right paw, Wise rushed over to me, "What's up, why that intense look on your face?"

"Listen, can you hear that?" I asked.

"Hear what?" asked Wise.

"We must get a move on, the beast is trying to climb up the hillside, I can hear it clutching and struggling up the gravel slope." With no time to lose, we marked out the run. With the job done, we headed to the hamlet. Here it was a hive of activity. All the torches were finished and ready to put firmly into the ground marking out the full length of the run. Brave joined us with Zebaj having put the full water butt in place. Zebaj was bristling with excitement. It was a long time since friends and family had seen him like this. Sir Woggle and the Baron arrived, I went and spoke to the Baron explaining the noise I had heard and what it meant. With that news, the Baron took charge. He walked briskly amongst the busy throng assessing quickly their progress, then very quickly he called order, giving a brief update and the urgency of the moment. Next, he rearranged the working groups bringing it down to one group who were to finish off the torches, everyone else was involved in erecting the torches along the chosen route. Quickly and efficiently this was done and completed as the working group brought the remainder of the torches along. Lining either side of the route to the finishing line were 250 torches, each one had to be lit.

Wise spoke up, "We don't have a moment to lose, with your permission, Baron, I think it would be best now if everyone takes up their position by hiding amongst the trees and bushes. I believe it would be best if Ytfarc and Gninnuc start here and light each torch. Zebaj and Brave should walk down to centre of this route to the point where Zebaj can see and be seen by the flaming, flying Slimeyosaurus. When Zebaj can clearly see the creature, he must light the torch and start waving it, the beast will prepare itself for flight, this can be sped up by Zebaj as he starts to run the chosen route, but for the creature it will be flying the gauntlet."

"Right," said the Baron, "let the battle commence. Everyone with a specific role to play take up your positions, everyone else may line the route but you must stay well back." Suddenly, through the crowd came Dimit and her daughters Yltfos, Yltneg, and Ylrednet. They embraced Zebaj and wished him every success.

Dimit said as encouragingly as possible, "If anything goes wrong and you are not successful, we are very proud of you. Thank you," and with that they withdrew and joined the crowd who were hiding amongst the trees and bushes. Zebaj felt ten feet tall and more determined to succeed.

Brave and Zebaj arrived at the starting place. Looking across at the rough cliff face, they were shocked and stood rooted to the spot. The Slimeyosaurus was perched on top of the cliff, poised, gloating, and peering, watchfully waiting. Every scale on its massive, ugly body oozed slime, and from its mouth and great big nostrils came fire and smoke. Brave and Zebaj crouched down, hiding themselves on the edge of the ravine.

"We must wait a few minutes longer for Ytfarc and Gninnuc to arrive," whispered Brave. "They will light your torch and leave you. When we are concealed, then you must get the creature's attention and start the run of your life. How are you feeling?" asked Brave.

"Nervously excited," answered Zebaj. Just then, they heard a crackling and a rushing, rustling sound behind them. Turning cautiously, they saw Ytfarc and Gninnuc coming down the line. They were running at a steady pace either side of the route and as they were running, they quickly lit each brushwood torch with their own. They kept in unison for the full length of the track. As they approached Brave and Zebaj, Zebaj held out his torch to be lit but before they did, his three comrades gave him a big bear hug and said, "On behalf of everyone including the Baron, Sir Woggle, and all the Stabmows, your wife and girls, Pockets, and especially your King and Queen, we thank you for your bravery, courage, and willingness. We all wish you every success, and even though we will be in hiding, we will be with you as we cheer you on."

RRRrroooaaarrr, the air was suddenly filled with a hideous angry sound. The four friends spun around, the creature was raising itself up ready to launch into flight.

"We must be off," said Brave.

"Follow us," replied Ytfarc, "we know a better way."

"Don't start running, Zebaj, until it's airborne," added Gninnuc, and with that Ytfarc led the way. They disappeared into a large bush, at the centre of this was an entrance to an underground tunnel. As they entered it, Brave was aware that he was between Ytfarc and Gninnuc. A noise above caught his attention, and Brave knew the entrance had closed behind them; for some strange reason he felt suspicious. The tunnel was just wide enough for a single file. Ytfarc looked over his shoulder without saying anything but the glint in his eyes, which was evil, said it all. Brave kept running as if everything was fine. Meanwhile, Zebaj was staring at the creature as it continued squatting on the clifftop, those horrible orange eyes were gloating, staring directly at him, "Be patient, Zebaj, don't hurry this moment," he muttered to himself.

Near the finishing line, I spoke quietly to Wise, "What's that sound I can hear, it seems to be coming from underground."

Wise listened keenly but heard nothing. "It's not close," I said but there's something going on underground."

After a long pause, Wise spoke slowly, "I wonder where Brave and the other two are? They should be back by now."

"There it is again and this time there're voices, they are still a long way off and they are definitely underground."

Back at the starting line, Zebaj was still staring at the beast as it remained hunched up on its hind legs. Deep inside the creature's belly, a rumbling sound was getting louder, and more slime was oozing out from its ugly scales and thick dark grey smoke was billowing out of its nostrils. Its huge leathery wings were twitching and their claws kept opening and closing in a menacing manner.

A whispering was going around those in hiding, wondering how long Zebaj was going to be and what was keeping him. Oggle, Foggle, and Boggle encouraged everyone to be patient and quiet.

Meanwhile, underground, Brave and the two Stesomrams were still dashing through the twisting, turning tunnel. Brave suddenly shouted, "Where are we going?"

There was a long silence then Gninnuc shouted back his reply, "Not we but you, Brave, you." Ytfarc suddenly stopped. In the tunnel, they were at the top of a very, very long steep incline.

"This is where we part company, Brave," remarked Gninnuc. "It's been good knowing you, but get ready for the last ride of your life." Brave said nothing but every fur on his muscular body bristled. Ytfarc lifted his right paw to the side of the tunnel and pulled a lever; at the bottom of the slope a small opening appeared which seemed to be an entrance into a flaming pit, like a bubbling volcano. Brave was ready. The noise and the heat, which came out from it was intense. Gninnuc grabbed Brave from behind, Ytfarc also made a dive at him but Brave wasn't going down without a fight. For many minutes they wrestled. At times, Brave thought they might get the upper hand. In the midst of the fighting, they called him names and insulted him, but Brave kept a cool head and his mouth shut. Suddenly, he got the upper hand. Like lightning, he caught each of them behind their heads and banging them together with such force knocked them unconscious. Then, as quick as a flash, and before they had time to recover, he tied them together like a big furry ball, and bowled them down the slope towards the pit. Bouncing from one side of the tunnel to the other, they rolled and spun in a frantic manner, going faster and faster as they hurtled on towards the flames that were to engulf them. There was no way they could slow down, there was nothing to stop them. Closer and closer they sped on to their destruction. Still they remained entwined, unaware of the fate that was waiting for them. Onwards and downwards they spun without any awareness.

Brave stood watching and waiting, at the last minute he reached for the lever, pulling it back he closed the entrance locking it in place. *Wallop!* With incredible force and speed the furry ball hit the closed door and instantly disentangled as they were bounced backwards coming to rest sprawling on the floor of the tunnel. Brave turned and made his back along the tunnel. "Two wrongs don't make a right," he murmured. They might have been Gninnuc and Ytfarc but unless you're brave, you haven't got anything.

"Something is definitely going on beneath our feet," I whispered to Wise. "I've been sensing some strange goings on and now everything is very quiet, I don't like it one bit."

"All will be revealed soon," answered Wise.

Chapter 14
Run for Your Life

Zebaj was still staring at the Slimeyosaurus, watching its every movement, every twitch of every muscle. He was unaware of what had taken place underground. Without warning, the beast breathed, belched and snorted out fire and smoke. "It's trying to intimidate me, and I won't be intimidated," said Zebaj to himself. "I will, however, take the initiative and fight fire with fire," and with that defiant decision, he started waving the flaming torch at the beast, tormenting it, aggravating it. The beast could take no more, it rose on its hind legs and letting out a deafening roar launched itself into flight. Zebaj started running. Not too fast at first. The sun was behind him, which allowed him to see the shadow of beast. Zebaj could feel flames on his heals; now it was time to run faster. This was one activity he excelled in, he was the fastest in The Land of Pleasant. He was running like the wind. The beast's shadow was huge but unsteady as it came after him. Zebaj didn't slow down, he kept sprinting with the torch held high and the flames from it streaming backwards. The torches lining the route burned ever brighter as he raced on. The Slimeyosaurus kept spilling slime and breathing fire as it flew after him in its erratic state. Without slowing down, Zebaj looked ahead, the finishing line was about 350 metres way, he kept sprinting on and the beast kept chasing him, and the stench from the slime was awful.

Again Zebaj felt the scorching heat on his back as the creature breathed out more fire. Zebaj glimpsed his wife and daughters in the crowd. Just then, Wise inspired everyone to cheer him on, and a huge cry went up from the crowd. Deep inside Zebaj felt a burst of encouragement, which gave him extra speed and strength in his legs, and he sprinted on gaining ground on the Slimeyosaurus, which continued roaring, breathing fire and smoke and oozing slime from every ugly scale on its ugly body. There were a hundred metres to the finishing line. Pain in his side suddenly gripped him, causing him to stumble. The beast seized the opportunity, came swooping in low, casting a long ugly and unsteady shadow over its victim. "Fight the pain, Zebaj," he shouted encouragingly to himself. "Fight the pain."

With 70 metres to go, the Baron roared encouragement to everyone, "Cheer him on, he needs your encouragement." The blast from the Baron's shout was so great that it caught in the wings of the beast slowing it down. In response, a huge encouraging cry went up from the spectators. Again, Zebaj found new strength and stamina, fighting through the pain he found fresh speed. Twenty metres to the finishing line, 30 metres to the big water butt. The Slimeyosaurus was hot on his heels. The crowd of spectators urged him. Dimit, Yltfos, Yltneg, and Ylrednet were screaming for him at the tops of their voices, their lungs almost bursting.

The Baron and Sir Woggle increasing the volume by adding their booming voices in the cheering, three more voices of Brave, Ytfarc and Gninnuc were added, increasing the noise level. No one was prepared for what was about to happen as Zebaj had five metres to the finishing line. The loud cheering continued. The beast chased on relentlessly, breathing out fire and leaving a long trail of slime in its wake. The Baron and Sir Woggle raised the golden keys aloft so that they touched. The creature sent out a blast of flames at Zebaj which caught him, setting his back on fire. Those who saw it screamed in horror. Zebaj was undeterred. As he raced across the finishing line, the Baron and Sir Woggle each cut a huge arc in the air with their golden keys, making an entrance to another world. Meanwhile, Zebaj had thrown himself into the water butt to put out the flames, which were burning his back. As soon as the Baron and Woggle had made the opening, the crowd heard the most horrendous sounds, screaming of those in perpetual torment and a deafening sucking sound as the Slimeyosaurus was sucked in, bellowing, twisting, turning, and fighting against his ultimate end. Into this world of torment, agony, and constant unquenchable pain he was sucked, and the flames from the hundreds of torches were sucked in with him. Every piece of slime was sucked off the ground from every tree, bush, shrub, and home, and slammed into the body of the beast as it tried in vain to clutch at the air to claw its way from the screaming, the torment, and the intense heat of this inferno. But it was all useless. Into this hole it was slowly dragged, kicking, and bellowing as it went, with all the slime and disunity, with every gram of mistrust, discord, and unpleasantness, until the Land of Pleasant was restored.

As the Slimeyosaurus finally vanished along with all its ugliness, a statement written in gold around the top of the entrance for all to read appeared. '*Ycrem evah lliw I mohw no Ycrem evah lliw I*'. Without any warning, the entrance to this other world closed and everything returned to normal. Well almost everything, Zebaj was soaked right through but unharmed apart from a nasty scar on his back. The Baron put his big hairy arm around Woggle's shoulder and remarked quietly, "The veil of sight is very thin."

As Zebaj climbed out of the water butt, the Baron and Sir Woggle were running up to him. They lifted him out and placed him on their shoulders, amidst the cheers from the crowd. His wife and three girls couldn't hold their excitement and admiration in any longer, they burst through the crowd, rushing up to him with loud shouts of praise and admiration. Without warning, they started a procession which everyone else joined in.

The crowd headed for their little hamlet. The Baron declared the celebrations were on him. On the way, Ytfarc and Gninnuc spoke in depth to Brave, thanking him for not committing them to eternal torment. Forgiveness and reconciliation flowed. They ended by agreeing to change their names and to leave their old ways of behaving behind them. As the celebrations got underway with music and feasting and dancing, I felt an odd juddering, as if the ground beneath my feet was shaking.

Chapter 15
Back Where We Started

The Metro jerked into action and I walked back through the crowded carriage, discovering my seat opposite the little old lady was still vacant. "I'm so glad you've come back," she said with a twinkle in her eyes. "I do like an early morning chat. How did you get on with The See Thru Man, he's an interesting character, isn't he?"

My mouth dropped open like I was catching flies. "You know him?" I spluttered.

"Know him? I should think so, we've been married since 985 BC."

Volume 5
Wizard Wonky

Chapter 1
Fog

The dark grey, damp, chilly November fog swirled around me. The temperature was just above freezing. The fog was so dense, visibility was reduced to about a metre. The bus I had been on had broken down so rather than wait in the cold bus for the relief bus to arrive, I decided to walk home through the fog, it would take about 15 minutes and no more.

This fog is that thick, I thought to myself, *you can't see your hand behind your back, it's like old-fashioned pea soup.* The effect the fog had on my surroundings was strange—eerie and still. No birds were singing. There was no wind blowing litter along the pavement or through the bare trees. The only sounds I could hear were my shoes on the footpath crunching small stones beneath my feet and even that seemed to be distant. The fog was so thick that I struggled to stay focused. *You could quite easily get lost in this,* I thought. I looked at my watch, it was 21:21. Speaking out loud to myself, "That can't be right, I've only just got off the bus and then it was 16:16." Standing still I checked my watch again, 23:23. "That's odd," I murmured. "I wonder what's going on." I walked slowly forward, pausing to check my watch for the third time, 02:02. "I'll take it to little jewellers in the market on Saturday," I decided as I continued walking into the fog. Without warning, I walked into the back of another man; a tall man in a tall black hat. "I'm sorry," I spluttered, "I didn't see you through the fog."

"That's alright," replied the stranger cheerfully. "I've been waiting for you. And I didn't want anyone to know."

"Wait a minute," I asked, "how could anyone know, you can't see anything in this fog."

"Precisely," he smiled, "I created the fog to conceal us but now I need to introduce you to your old friend."

"My old friend? But I'm going home; in fact, I should be there by now, but I'm totally confused. Who are you anyway?"

With a toothless grin, he answered, "Me friends call me Misty, because I create lots of it. You think this is thick. You haven't seen anything yet."

"I can't see anything full stop. So, you're Misty and you are going to introduce me to an old friend and where did you get that tall black hat?" I spluttered again without stopping for breath. As I asked, I realised, and before Misty could answer, I continued, "So where is The See Thru Man then?"

"You won't see him just yet. I've just borrowed his hat. Now if you walk that way," said Misty pointing in a diagonal direction, "you will find an old friend in need of help."

"If you know he needs help, why don't you help him?" I responded.

"Because I create fog and lots of it, but I can't undo knots," Misty replied. I went to answer but Misty had disappeared.

Chapter 2
Knots and Lots of Them

I should have been panic-stricken but this time I wasn't; not yet anyway. "I've been in this predicament before," I murmured. "All I have to do is walk in a diagonal direction over there; right then, best foot forward." And with that confident comment, I walked into the mist. The moment I took the first step the damp, grey, dense fog swirled around me and rolled upwards, like someone rolling up an old dust sheet and it disappeared; 'there it was gone.'

I blinked and looked around me. I was standing in a green meadow with lots of unusual looking wild flowers, a woodland was across to my right, birds were singing, somewhere further away, and I could hear a babbling brook as it gurgled merrily on its way. "Pleasant, very pleasant," I murmured, "not perfect, but pleasant." This area was familiar but new to me. As I walked forward, I found myself tangled up in a spider's web, making me step back in total surprise. Wiping my face, I said, "How come I didn't see that there?" It was huge, totally blocking my path. As I stared at the web, I expected to see a huge hairy spider in the centre, but there wasn't. Instead the web was filled with thousands of little spiders slightly bigger than money spiders, all of them busy making this huge web. I was spellbound and totally engrossed. I was brought abruptly out of my mesmerised state by a voice calling for help.

"I'm over here, can anyone hear me?"

"I can hear you," I shouted back, "but where are you?"

"Over here, I'm trapped behind this bush." As I tried to walk past the spiders' web, another one was instantly thrown up in front of me and again it was instantly full of these tiny busy spiders. I went the opposite way and as soon as I passed the first web, another web was thrown up in front of me. Once again, it was full of these spiders, all busy spinning the web and making it stronger. Again, the voice shouted for help and again I made several attempts to get past the webs to help the person in distress. Every attempt I made ended with the same result. I was about to shout for help but realised that if help came, their predicament might be the same as the trapped individual. After a short period of going back and forth trying to find a way past them and getting nowhere, and by now there was about 50 big webs blocking my path, I slowly and thoughtfully paced from one end of the row to the other. Something was odd, something wasn't quite right. Every time I attempted to get to the end of the spider web line, another one was thrown up, blocking my path. The number of webs had increased to about 65. I suddenly realised, it was only the last web which had the multitude of spiders. Going back to the centre web, I picked up a small branch, which was lying in the grass and without hesitating struck the web in a swift downward motion and the web disintegrated. Keeping a firm grip on the branch, I turned full circle, all the other webs were still complete with the spiders busy in the last one. In one swift motion, I completed my task. Walking away, I called out again, "Where are you?"

"I'm over here, Pockets," came the reply. I walked in the direction of the voice but found no one.

"Where are you?" I shouted again.

"Over here," came the reply.

"Who am I looking for?" I replied, walking once again in the direction of the voice.

"It's Zebaj," came the reply.

"Zebaj, hang in there, I'll get to you soon," but when I got to where I thought Zebaj should have been, he wasn't there. I called again, "Zebaj, where are you?"

And again he replied, "Over here."

Before I rushed off in the sound of his voice, I asked, "Zebaj, can you describe your surroundings for me?"

"I'll do my best. Firstly, I'm in some kind of hollow at the bottom of a bank, the hollow is a large shell-like cave, which means that when I call you, I must sound as if I'm somewhere else; covering both ends of this cave are huge spiders webs with thousands of tiny spiders, and they are tying me in knots with their web."

"Can you give me any more clues," I called, "like, how did you get there? Did anything specific happen to you? You know, something which will give me a clue."

"I entered the wood, went around the Great Mungawumba Tree and wham. I was sliding down a bank caught in this web. The more I struggled, the more entangled I became so right now I'm trying to lie still," answered Zebaj.

"That's helpful," I shouted in reply. "Hang in there, I'm on my way," and with that I made my way into the wood. Now the Great Mungawumba Tree isn't easy to hide. It's huge; it's the biggest tree in The Land of Pleasant. Deeper into the wood I went. Without warning, I crashed into an invisible barrier, which bounced me backwards, knocking me off my feet. After several unsuccessful attempts, I contemplated the problem, while sitting on the woodland floor I could see where I wanted to be, but I couldn't get there. "Odd, very odd," I murmured quietly. Then very slowly I crawled forward. When I reached the spot, I discovered that while I could see further into the wood, my way was blocked by what was an invisible force field. Standing up slowly, I began to feel my way along this invisible barrier, having moved along the invisible wall in both directions for almost an hour, I was about to give up when I heard a deep, hollow chuckling sound; looking around quickly I spotted a large tree shaking and chuckling at the same time. "Let me guess," I said. "You are a Nugumba tree."

"That's right, and you should learn a famous phrase we have here in The Land of Pleasant, which in Rorrim is: *Wodniw a snepo semitemos eh rood a sesolc dog nehw*," answered the tree. "And furthermore, if you want to get over the invisible barrier, then you need my help," continued the tree, "so if you reach up to my lowest branch, I will get you where you need to be." I looked up at the Nugumba tree; all its branches were way too high. I walked around the tree several times, staring up at its lofty branches. Every so often I would hear Zebaj calling me and at each call his voice seemed to come from a different direction. As I stood still staring up into the tree, I remembered, 'this is The Land of Pleasant' and with that I stood on tiptoe and stretched up as high as possible, which was still about three metres too short, but as I stretched upwards, the Nugumba tree bowed at its trunk and bent its branches down low to where I was standing. As I climbed onto a branch, the tree said, "Hang on tight, we are going to the top and when you get there, look to the west and wave with both arms."

"Why?" I shouted, as the tree branch carried me to the top.

"Because your friends will see you, even though you can't see them." Balancing myself, I turned west and waved. In the distance, Boggle was busy outside his tree repairing an old palmtop, which he still used. As he straightened himself up, something in the distance caught his attention; focusing his eyesight, he saw me waving frantically.

"Hey, guys, come here quickly, Pockets needs us. He's at the top of the Nugumba Tree." Oggle, Foggle, Brave, and Wise came out of their home and looked in the direction Boggle was pointing in.

"Quick," said Wise, "we need to go and find out what's going on and why he's arrived today." In no time at all, they were ready and on their way.

Chapter 3
Wizard Wonky

Meanwhile, Zebaj was still trapped in the web from the small spiders who were busy wrapping him up, and I was perched at the top of the Nugumba tree, which was giving me more instructions. "When I bend and raise this branch, be ready to leap high into the air as if you are jumping off a springboard," encouraged the tree. As I steadied myself for my leap into the unknown, I suddenly heard voices behind me. Spinning around and almost losing my balance, I was amazed to see my friends, Oggle, Foggle, Boggle, and Wise perched on the same branch.

"Good to see you guys again. Where are Woggle and Brave?" I asked, delighted to see my friends again.

"Woggle is on his way to Gulberia on a new mission and Brave is on the other side of this invisible barrier," answered Wise. "Don't ask how because we don't know. Right then guys, are we ready to leap?" I didn't ask any questions, I just got ready for a leap into the unknown.

As we were about to leap, we heard a sinister cackle of a laugh followed by an evil sounding voice, "You will never clear it, it's much higher than you think, and your friend has given up his struggle against the spiders and their wonder web." Oggle had been secretively looking around trying to pinpoint exactly where the voice was coming from.

Suddenly, Oggle located him, and whispering softly, he said, "He's hiding amongst the foliage about 50 metres away, at ground level."

"Who is?" whispered Boggle in reply.

"It's the wizard of Rodne, but we usually call him Wizard Wonky."

"Why is that?" I joined in.

"Because of the way he walks," smiled Foggle.

At that moment, the Nugumba Tree joined in the conversation, "While you've been talking, I have been slowly growing," it whispered, "and if you hang on, I will keep growing until I am high enough for you to get over the invisible force field," he continued. We did, and the tree continued growing; eventually, it was over 200 metres high and the ground was a long way down. "Get ready for the leap of your life," whispered the Tree, "and when I count to three, leap." There was a long pause, which seemed to last for ever. "Ready. One, two, three," and we leapt. What a strange sensation. As we launched ourselves forwards and upwards, the Nugumba Tree catapulted us faster, further and higher.

Suddenly, Wise shouted, "We've made it." We were hurtling, feet first, at a frantic speed through the branches of other trees in the wood. We didn't have time to think about avoiding anything.

"Turn sharp left," shouted a voice; recognising it, we instinctively obeyed, and without warning, landed into a huge mound of grass like a haystack.

Catching our breath and struggling out, we were greeted by Brave's grinning face. "What's taken you so long?" he said. Wise gave him the update, especially about Wizard Wonky.

"He's a sly, devious old fox," said Brave, "but while I've been waiting for you, I've been busy finding Zebaj and the trail to Wizard Wonky's place, but first let's set Zebaj free, he's in a cave not far into Prickle Wood; then we need to get through Prickle Wood to Wizard Wonky's cave."

"How do you know that?" asked Wise.

"I've been in Prickle Wood before and it plays havoc with your fur coat. More of that later, it's this way to Zebaj," and through the undergrowth went Brave leading the way. After almost an hour, we came to a clearing in the wood, in the centre of this was the Great Mungawumba Tree. Its massive trunk had a circumference of 30 metres. Its branches were like huge giant muscular arms with its fingers intertwining as the tree soared upwards to the sky. Its leaves are like those from a huge rhubarb plant, only 20 times bigger. Our small troop hesitated, gazing up in awe at the massive ancient tree.

"Come on," urged Brave, "we are on a mission, remember," and off he dashed. A short distance beyond the great tree, the ground fell away in a steep drop. "Slide," shouted Brave in command. Instinctively, we obeyed, and immediately, we were hurtling down the steep slope at breakneck speeds. We finally came to rest a short distance from a huge prickly bush. "Welcome to Prickle Wood," Brave said grimly, "this place is a nightmare."

"Why do you say that?" spoke up Foggle and Boggle together.

"Because there is no easy way in," replied Brave.

"But you have been here before, so how did you manage?" I asked.

"Many years ago, I found this place by accident, we always thought it was an imaginary wood, but while I was in pursuit of Wizard Rodne, I followed him to this place. Unfortunately, I was unable to penetrate very far into Prickle Wood because of the huge thorn bushes, which make up the wood. It took me three and half days to go about two and half metres."

Foggle spoke up, "With all of us attacking these thorn bushes, we should make better progress."

Boggle had been staring deep into the wood while Foggle was speaking, shaking his head and said, "It will take forever, and we would be too exhausted at the end of it to rescue Zebaj." There was a long silence as we all contemplated the challenge.

Wise finally broke the silence. "Brave, you said you found Prickle Wood when you were chasing Wizard Rodne. Well what happened to him? Where did he go?"

"Firstly, he's no ordinary wizard. Secondly, he created this wood for his own protection. Thirdly, I believe his cave is in the heart of this wood and fourthly, in the cave is where Zebaj is trapped."

"But he sounded so close when I first arrived," I interrupted.

"That's because of where he's trapped and who is responsible for taking him prisoner. Remember, this is the work of the wizard," answered Brave.

"Do you know anything else about him?" enquired Wise.

Brave thought for a few moments, reflecting on his previous adventures, finally he spoke. "Wizard Rodne can change his appearance in the twinkling of an eye. Traditionally, he is slightly taller than us but slightly shorter than Pockets. He usually wears a long blue cape covered in gold stars, on his head he wears a Merlin Hat, he has a long flowing white beard, and on his right side, he wears a golden sword called the Sword of Destruction; fortunately, he has never mastered its use."

"Why is the sword on his right side?" asked Boggle with a frustrated look upon his face.

"Because," answered Brave, "he is left-handed."

"Is anybody there?" called a voice. Suddenly, everyone remembered Zebaj.

"Hang in there, old buddy, we are working on a plan," shouted Wise.

"But how are we going to cut our way into Prickle Wood?" hissed Foggle quietly. We were all startled by a loud chuckling sound behind us.

Spinning around together, we saw sitting on the bough of a tree was The See Thru Man, he was laughing so much he looked quiet comical, while at the same time he was pointing with his long, bony, see thru finger at me and declaring, "You weren't called Pockets for nothing," and with that he gave a huge chuckle and disappeared, vanished, there one minute gone the next.

"He wasn't hanging about," declared Oggle.

"But what was that about?" asked Foggle, staring at me.

"I've no idea," I replied, equally confused.

After a few moments of confused silence, Wise spoke up. "The See Thru Man was here helping us," said Wise.

"But how?" we asked in unison.

"Think about it for a moment, he said 'you weren't called Pockets for nothing', which means the secret to our success lies not with you, Pockets, but in one of them," concluded Wise.

"By jingo," shouted Foggle, "that's how it's always worked for you, you simply reach into your inside pocket and take out what you need at that moment in time. It's awesome." Sudden excitement encircled the group, but I remained silent and thoughtful.

Brave spoke first, "What's wrong, Pockets, you seem troubled?"

"I'm a little perplexed," I replied, "my pockets are not prefilled with the right objects at the start of an adventure, otherwise, I wouldn't be able to move. It's a matter of choice: choosing before taking. Now, if I chose chainsaws, they would be very effective but very noisy and the element of surprise would be lost. If I chose fire, the risk would be too great; we would all be at risk, Zebaj would be at risk and the wizard would know we were on our way. If I decide to use axes and machetes, they would be effective but once again too noisy. What we need is something silently effective."

Chapter 4
The Right Tools for the Job

Once again, I was lost in my own thoughts. No one spoke. Prickle Wood was deathly silent. The seconds ticked slowly by. The seconds became minutes. Slowly, a big smile crept over my face as I remained deep in thought. Then reaching deep into my inside pocket, I slowly withdrew; all eyes were focused on me, wondering what I was taking out, not one but six strange looking objects. Each one had a set of long extendable handles. These handles were joined together at the far end, where they crossed over and formed large cutting expandable jaws. "Wow," whispered the small group.

"How do they work?" asked Boggle with his eyes wide open.

"Let me show you but we might need these and these as well," and taking out of my pocket and placing on the ground, I put six pairs of gloves and three coils of rope. "I figured these will be helpful," I said, picking up the gloves. "Those thorns look fierce, and the rope, we might have opportunities to set some interesting traps for Wizard Wonky. Now, let me show you how these work," and stepping closer to the first big bush in Prickly Wood, I released the small safety catch, and opening the jaws, I secured them around a nearby branch. Then closing the handles in a swift silent movement, the branch landed almost noiselessly on the ground.

Fresh excitement penetrated the group, then with one voice, the Stabmows cried, "Let me have a go. I'm first, I want that pair, I should be the first to try."

"Silence," I shouted, raising my voice above the din, then calmly I placed them in a semicircle, giving them all one pair each and said firmly, "These are not toys, please don't use them for any other purpose. Now watch and copy." Slowly and deliberately, I went through each stage. How to enlarge the jaws, how to lengthen the handles, how to grip and cut. "These are versatile enough for what we want, strong enough for all we need and silent enough to create an element of surprise, if required. Now let's start cutting."

167

"I would like to suggest," said Foggle, "that we start with a concealed entrance then make a tunnel which is wide enough for two of us and a little higher than Pockets; so if you guys are willing, three of us could gnaw part of the way through some of these branches then the other three could intertwine them tightly so that it closes behind us as we tunnel into Prickle Wood." Everyone agreed that this was a splendid idea.

"Now you're thinking like a team as well as friends," I said. Half an hour later and the job was done.

"We need to cover our tracks," said Wise, and he began gathering up the clippings which lay scattered on the ground.

"Now then, if I take a length of rope and cut about this much off it, we can tie the entrance open with a slip knot and when we are far enough into the wood, we slip the knot and the entrance closes behind us," remarked Brave with a satisfied smile.

"I like your thinking," I remarked, "now we need to get on with the task in hand. If you don't mind, I will lead the way as I'm slightly taller, then if you guys work in pairs behind me, we will have the tunnel roughly the right width and height." Once again, everyone liked the suggestion and the task soon began taking shape.

After an hour or so, I hesitated and looked back at their handiwork, murmuring to myself I said, "Not perfect, but pleasant, very pleasant."

Wise heard me and said chuckling, "You are becoming more like one of us with every visit."

"This is thirsty work, does anyone have a drink with them?" asked Oggle, gasping for breath. Nobody answered, but very quietly I put my hand slowly into an inside pocket and slowly pulled out six bottles of morning dew and passed them around.

"How do you do that?" asked Boggle.

"I chose to believe in The See Thru Man and the gift he has invested in me, I've learned it is better to try and be wrong than not to try and discover much later that I was right, I hope that helps," I answered. I continued, "At first, I would struggle with it and I always got it wrong but when I simply trusted him, it always turned out right. Does that help?"

"Hmmm, I think so, am I right in thinking that because your gift is different to mine, that only means we are different and not that one of us is more favoured by The See Thru Man than the other."

"That is absolutely right," I responded.

At that moment, Foggle shouted out in horror, "Oh no, look everyone," he was pointing back down the tunnel. The branches that we had cut down and stacked on either side of the tunnel were sprouting rapidly and closing the tunnel behind us.

"What are we going to do?" gasped Foggle in despair.

"All our hard work was in vain."

"Don't panic," I said, "I've got an idea, which might just work."

Chapter 5
Salt Water

Once again, I reached slowly into my pocket and took out a large cylinder with a pump action spray gun attached to it. "Let me give this a go," and I began spraying the branch off cuts. Instantly, with a horrible hissing sound, the branches all began to shrivel and die.

"Will that work on the live stuff?" asked Wise.

"I'll give it a try."

"Look out, everyone, Pockets is going to spray these thorn bushes," shouted Wise.

"Wait a minute, why not spray at ground level, then the roots will get this stuff right into them," suggested Boggle. With that suggestion I aimed the sprayer at ground level and began. Within seconds, these huge thorn bushes were hissing loudly as they began shrivelling and dying and making our job a lot easier.

"What is that stuff?" asked Brave smiling.

I replied, "It's salt water."

"That's all, just salt water?" asked Brave.

"Just salt water. I remembered reading something similar in a book a long time ago, how salt water was the simple solution."

"Does it mean then that we no longer need these?" asked Brave holding up his cutting tool.

"We shouldn't get rid of them just yet," replied Wise. "We may still have a use for them."

"Exactly," I answered, "now let's press on with the task at hand."

For the following few hours, Prickle Wood continued to shrink as I continued spraying. "Can I have a go?" asked Boggle.

"I tell you what," I said and reaching slowly into my inside pocket, I took out six specially designed backpacks to put their cutting tools in and a cylinder and sprayer each.

"Now let's get this job done," I said.

The woodland air was soon filled with a constant hissing sound and a steam like vapour as with renewed energy, we set about the task of spraying everything in our path. In less than an hour, our task was almost complete, the bank which Zebaj had slid down was about 50 metres in front of us.

"We must be cautious right now," said Wise, "just in case there is a trap. I suggest that only two or three of us continue spraying." Everyone agreed. Suddenly, there was an ugly sucking, gurgling sound, as the ground where we were standing started to swallow us up. With a mad scrambling and leaping action, most of the group made it successful to dry ground; all except Brave, who was up to his chest in this horrible bog.

"You must stay calm, Brave, struggling will mean certain death," shouted Wise to his friend. Oggle and Boggle were on the opposite side of the bog. I was staring at where they were and where I was, Brave was directly in between us, the distance was about 20 metres. At this moment, I remembered the mirror and the original instructions.

"Do something," called Brave, "I'm sinking."

"Hang on," I yelled and slowly I reached into my pocket once again. "It never ceases to amaze me," I said smiling to myself as I very deliberately pulled out a very, very long ladder, which more than spanned the bog. Shouting to Foggle to grab the other end, they brought the ladder up to Brave.

"Grab hold of it," they shouted together. Just as Brave caught hold of the side of the ladder, he hollered a second time.

"Something is wrapping itself around my legs and is slowly working its way up my body."

"I know what that is and how we must kill it," shouted Oggle. "I've read about it in one of my books, it's called the giant Regnoc Eel. It slowly crushes its victim to death."

"Thanks, Oggle," interrupted Brave, "that's just what I need to hear right now."

"And the only way to kill it," continued Oggle, "is to cut or chop its head off."

Wise spoke up firmly bringing order to the group, "Pockets and Foggle will man opposite ends of the ladder, keeping it firm and steady, Oggle and Boggle will crawl along the ladder towards Brave each from opposite ends and armed with one of these cutting tools. The jaws are adjusted and fully open to their widest point when needed. You must make certain that when you strike, it is with maximum effect. Any questions?"

"Just one point, this is going to be messy," concluded Oggle, "and I mean messy."

"Right," said Wise, "let's get a move on." The two Stabmows climbed onto opposite ends of the ladder. Foggle and I took up their positions and held the ladder securely. Brave was gripping the ladder with all his strength, as the giant eel continued winding its great long body around him. As it did, it also continued pulling him downwards inch by inch into the swamp. Oggle and Boggle crept along the ladder, trying to move in unison so that their movements would not cause the ladder to flip over. Foggle and I were keeping their ends of the ladder as stable as possible on the uneven ground. Wise was giving encouragement first to Brave to hold on and hang in there because Brave was slowly being dragged into the swamp, as the giant eel was wrapping itself around him. He was now up to his shoulders.

"Keep going, guys," shouted Wise, "not much further to go, and keep your end steady, Pockets, hold your end firm." Brave was now struggling to keep his chin above the swamp. The eel was wrapping itself around his chest. With a violent heave, Brave raised his head up just enough to open his mouth wide and take in huge lungs full of air. Instantly, his head plunged beneath the surface and disappeared into the murky swamp.

"Come on, Boggle," cried Foggle from his end of the ladder, "he really needs us now." Suddenly, as they approached the middle of the ladder the huge head of the great, ugly Regnoc Eel rose above the surface of the swamp. As quick as lightening, Oggle clamped the jaws of the big cutting tool around the eel's neck and squeezed.

"Release the pressure slightly and then snap them shut," I shouted urgently. Oggle did. *SNAP* went the jaws, instantly the huge head was cut off and under pressure shot high into the air before finally plunging back into the swamp and sinking out of sight.

As it slowly disappeared beneath the surface, it made a horrible gurgling, sucking sound and Oggle murmured, "When it's you or us, then this phrase rings true: 'it's a self-preservation society'." The body of the eel vomited out an erratic flood of a greenish, black slimy sludge, as its body was constantly twitching and flapping around with diminishing nervous energy. Bursting up from beneath the surface of the swamp and gasping for air was Brave.

"We did it," he shouted deliriously. "I was counting on one of you guys to understand what I was up to."

"You mean to tell us that it was you that thrust its head above the surface," shouted the group, except for Oggle, who worked out what Brave was up too.

"They don't call you Brave for nothing," said Oggle with a big grin, "now let's get you onto the ladder and back on dry ground." It wasn't too long before they were back on dry ground and away from the swamp.

"Right," I said, "it's you three, especially Brave, we are going to shower." Before they had time to ask how, me, Wise, and Foggle swung our water cylinders into action spraying our three friends. After 15 minutes of fun, everyone was soaking wet. Without warning, we found ourselves sliding, rolling, spinning, and tumbling down a steep bank.

Chapter 6
Trapped

As we finally came to rest, we were brought back to our senses and the reason for our mission, as we heard a familiar voice calling, "And about time too, what's taken you so long?"

"Zebaj," the group shouted with one voice and turning to our left we saw our friend trapped in a hollow set back in the bank; it was cone shaped and looked like a small cave. Zebaj was bound up in silky spiders' webs from his feet to just below his chin, and the spiders were still busy. We rushed to help our friend, ripping the huge mass of spider threads from him. Just as we were finishing our task, there was a huge flash of lightening and a clap of thunder followed by a loud sinister laugh.

"Got you all in one go." We spun around and standing just outside the cave was the wizard of Rodne. His wizened, wrinkled, and very old face was filled with evil delight.

"Wizard Wonky," yelled Brave, "you won't get away with this."

"We will see about that," screamed the wizard. Wise slowly stepped forward and as was expected, the entrance was closed up with an invisible see thru barrier. "That's right," shouted Wizard Wonky, "you can see me, but you can't get me and without oxygen you will all suffocate," and slowly, after a long pause, he shouted, "DIE. And the Land of Pleasant will be mine, all mine."

From the back of the cave, Oggle whispered, "Don't move any of you, just keep me covered."

Without moving his lips, I replied, "What are up to?"

"I'm seeing if it's possible to find or to dig our way out."

Our group trapped in the cave were talking through our dilemma and possible solutions.

"Can we break through this barrier?" asked Foggle.

"How much air have we got and how long will it last?" I asked. The temperature in the cave was going up very quickly.

"We don't have time on our side," whispered Wise, "this is not good for us. We should sit down to talk through our plans." FLASH, BANG, CRASH was suddenly heard outside.

Wizard Wonky had waved his wizard's wand and instantly in front of the cave was a huge, hairy spider. Shouting with a gleeful evil voice, the wizard screamed, "I'm leaving him to guard you. And should you break the invisible force field, she will poison you and you will slowly die," and with that parting comment, he disappeared. The spider was ugly, fairly black with bright yellow spots; it was massive. Slowly, it looked at the group and made its way towards the mouth of the cavern; raising itself up on its back legs, it pressed its huge underbody against the invisible barrier.

Chapter 7
More Mess

The temperature in the cave was getting hotter by the second. I was deep in thought wondering if a way of escape or a solution could be found. Brave was becoming agitated by the minute through inactivity, seeing an enemy but unable to confront it in anyway. Foggle and Boggle were staring at Wise then at me and both were deep in thought, seemingly lost to the pressing need. The ugly, hairy spider now had its huge mouth wide open, displaying its rotten fangs as it tried intimidating our small group. Breathing was starting to get difficult as the oxygen in the cave was getting less and the temperature continued to climb. My pale cheeks were now beetroot in colour. The ugly spider kept on pressing its huge mouth against the invisible force field. Brave was struggling to maintain self-control. By now, everyone in the cave was led on the floor. Wise spoke in a hoarse, croaking whisper, "Where's Oggle?"

"I've no idea," replied Zebaj, speaking for the first time, "but I do know that this is all my fault."

"That's enough," whispered Brave, "this is not the time for guilt trips and pity parties."

Somewhere in the distance, as if from another world came a word of encouragement. "GUSHER," it was Oggle shouting out a warning; a blast of cold air filled the cave, instantly followed by a mighty rush of crystal-clear water. Into the cave Oggle blasted, the water smashing into the invisible force field, which was no match for it. The ugly spider with its huge mouth still wide open instantly consumed gallons of water. Oggle struck it smartly on its top jaw with both his feet. The spider was sent reeling backwards unable to react defensively, its huge body filled with too much water. We came bursting out of the cave, the cold water was incredibly refreshing, but there was no time to relish the moment, we were propelled through the water with such force it was staggering. Twisting, rolling, spinning, and tumbling, we continued, carried along by the sheer force and volume of the crystal-clear water.

Up in front of us, the spider, unable to close its mouth, was swelling to an enormous size. Its eyes were bulging in its sockets. Its mouth was stretched so wide that its ugly face was more hideous than ever, and its huge body was swollen to bursting point. As more water was constantly rushing into its mouth, everything about the creature became more and more distorted and disfigured. We burst through the surface in unison to witness the next event. *BOOM! BOOM!!* The spider's two ugly, gob-stopper eyes exploded like pistol shots. Realising what would happen next and gasping for air, Brave and Wise shouted at the same time, "Race for the rocks over there." Scrambling to drier, higher ground, our group collapsed in a heap and turned to watch where Oggle was pointing. The swollen, eyeless spider looked like a creature from outer space. Like a cannon going off, it finally exploded. *BOOM*, creating a tidal wave all around it. The exploding spider turned the water into a dark purple blackish colour.

"Lie flat on your faces," shouted Brave. Our group was brought sharply out of their transfixed stare by Brave's commanding voice to see a tidal wave rushing towards us. Instantly, we all rolled face down and gripped the rock as the wave struck and swept over us. For what seemed like forever, we hung on as the torrent of dark purple, blackish water thundered over us. An age passed before the torrent of water showed any signs of slowing down. Wise slowly lifted his head, the colour of the water was now a pale shade of pink. The crystal-clear water, which had forced us out of the cave was still flowing, diluting, transforming, and cleansing the dark water back to its purity once again. Wise never spoke, he just watched and waited. Brave slowly raised his head and looked around him, then turning over he sat up, and viewed the surroundings. In turn, we all did the same, by now the water was flowing calmly, sparkling, and crystal clear.

"Does anyone know where we are?" asked Zebaj.

"Never mind where we are for a moment," replied Brave, "what I want to know is what and where did Oggle go and get up to?"

Oggle grinned his biggest grin ever and said, "I'll tell you all about it after I have had a swim and have freshened up."

Chapter 8
The Rescue Plan

Without another word, Oggle launched himself high into the air as he dived into the water. "What a great idea," cried Zebaj. Brave and Oggle promptly followed. It wasn't long before everyone was doing the same thing.

Back on the rock, we settled down to listen to Oggle as he began telling his story. "It suddenly occurred to me that if you could keep me out of sight, I could start burrowing a way out. For the benefit of Pockets, you need to understand that when Stabmows go burrowing or tunnelling, they don't kick out behind them huge mounds of earth. They don't, that's just the way it is. I figured that sooner or later I should get to the outside and this would bring fresh air into the cave and give us a way of escape. I figured Wizard Wonky wouldn't miss us if we left one by one. As I tunnelled my way along, the biggest obstacle was the roots from Prickle Wood, which kept snagging my fur. After ages of burrowing upwards and not knowing where I was, I suddenly heard the sound of running water. I headed towards it, hoping I could get to the riverbank and not the riverbed. As I continued in my task, I was confronted by a large Mrowhtrae; they live underground. Most Pleasantonians believe they are fictitious. Well, let me tell you, he was more horrible in real life than any so-called mythical images. His eyesight is poor, his sense of smell is awesome, its face seems to be all mouth full of sharp teeth and it has an identical head at both ends of its very long body. As I was burrowing along, it was there right in front of me, coming from the opposite direction. I didn't have time to think I just reacted, quickly clicking my left claws like this produces a flame, 'click' instantly a flame burst forth; the Mrowhtrae hates fire of any sort and so it retreated at such a rapid rate that it hit the inside of the river bank. At that moment, I heard the sound of rushing water and I just had enough time to roll on to my back and shout. The water filled my tunnel, hitting me in the back as I shouted 'Gusher'. I had no idea if you'd heard me or not, and I didn't know if my plan would work. The rushing swirling water propelled me back down the tunnel I had just made. I didn't realise how long the tunnel was, but after what seemed like an absolute age of plummeting downwards, I re-entered the cave with such violent force that the barrier along with the spider was blasted away and you guys with it; the rest of the story you know," concluded Oggle.

"Well, I'm delighted that we have all—"

"It's no good reminiscing," said a voice behind us. We all spun around and there standing upright but not actually standing on anything was The See Thru Man.

"What are you…"

"How are you…"

"Why…"

As the confused chorus subsided, The See Thru Man said while still chuckling, "You look so secure on the rock but how are you going to get back to the mainland?" Our small group looked at one another without speaking.

Eventually, Brave broke the silence, "Now that's a good question," he said, "and right now, it's one I don't have an answer to."

"But I do, come on, it's time to leave, you have an unfinished task to complete," replied The See Thru Man. "You must stand in a straight line and place your right hand or paw on the shoulder of the person in front of you." Zebaj was directly behind The See Thru Man and Oggle was at the end of the line. Once the line was complete, a visible blue, electric energy of light and power surged through us and we were instantly flying over the surface of the river. It didn't take long before we were back in the wood near the Nugumba Tree.

"Don't forget," said The See Thru Man, "your next mission is dealing with Wizard Wonky. For victory to be effectively permanent, both him and his cave must be destroyed."

"Any clues as to where we can find the cave, please?" asked Wise.

"Keep your ears open and you'll have all the help you need," replied The See Thru Man and with that he was gone, just like that, there one moment, gone the next.

For a few moments, no one spoke a word but we all kept staring back in the direction of flight. Some of us were smiling, others looked perplexed while Brave stood rubbing his paws together, relishing the next part of this adventure, which was about to unfold.

Chapter 9
Wizard Wonky Again

A sudden chuckling sound, like someone enjoying a good joke quickly brought our group back to its senses. "What are you laughing at, Oggle?" asked Zebaj.

"I'm not laughing," replied Oggle, "I thought it was Wise."

"Me, I'm not laughing," responded Wise. "I thought it was Boggle."

"Does this look like my happy face, I'm just deep in thought wondering what we do next," replied Boggle. While these comments were flying around, the chuckling continued, Brave suddenly spun around.

The Nugumba Tree was shaking as it was chuckling. "What are you finding so funny?" demanded Brave of the tree.

"Friends and Pleasantonians, lend me your ears," replied the Nugumba Tree."

"What's wrong with your own?" asked Foggle.

"It's a phrase," said Wise, "and it means, give me your undivided attention, this is what The See Thru Man was on about; we will get help from the Nugumba Tree."

"Of course," smiled Brave as he joined in the conversation, "this is a seeing, hearing, bending, speaking tree."

"Right," interrupted Wise. "Gather around and pay attention everyone." Our small group sat in a semicircle a short way off from the base of the great tree and waited.

The Nugumba Tree bowed slightly and started. "It is a long time since I had a captive audience, so I ask you to be patient as I get my thoughts together. Right then, the thing you need to beware of is this; Wizard Wonky is brilliant in his foolishness and his foolishness is often brilliant by default, but to find him, you must follow the way of the wind."

"What is that supposed to mean?" demanded Foggle.

"*Ssshusssh*, Foggle, remember the advice from The See Thru Man. Keep your ears open, and you'll have all the help you need."

"All we need to do is remember the advice and put it into practice," answered Wise, "which was: keep your ears open and you'll have all the help you need. Now we've been told to follow the way of the wind, so what are we waiting for, let's get started."

"But which way is the wind blowing?" asked Oggle. We paused not knowing which direction we should be heading in. I licked my index finger and held it up.

"That way," I pointed and with that I set off expecting the others to follow.

"Hang on," shouted Brave, "how can you be so certain?"

"Trust me," I replied. They did and we set off in a single file not really certain what would happen next. After 30 minutes of following a gentle breeze, we came to a small clearing, which was made up of a small meadow with six young trees in the middle.

"Does anyone know where we are?" asked Zebaj. No, nobody did.

Oggle spoke next, "The breeze we were following has stopped so what do we do now?" Our small group looked at each other and before anyone had time to answer, the air in the small glade became very cold, the leaves on the trees started rustling and swaying frantically with increased force as an anticyclone of tremendous force filled the small meadow. Instantly, our group grabbed hold of each other and without warning, we were caught up into the swirling force of wind. Higher and higher we went at a dizzy speed, leaving the ground below us while spinning in an anti-clockwise fashion. Without warning, the anti-cyclone seemed to bend towards the right, so instead of climbing, we were propelled through the air parallel with the ground far below while still spinning anti-clockwise.

"Does anyone know where we are going?" yelled Zebaj.

"To the far side," shouted Brave.

"Where's the far side?" hollered Boggle.

"Not where but what, is what you should be asking," shouted Brave in reply, "and let me tell you," he continued, "it's an odd, desolate place, hostile, lonely and very cold." The anticyclone dipped sharply towards the ground and suddenly, on an area of fine black gravel we were skidding along, and as we finally came to rest, the wind ceased and everything was calm and still, for the moment at least.

Chapter 10
The Far Side

Surveying our new surroundings, our group wondered what would happen next. "This, gentlemen, is the far side," said Brave in a very grave voice, "I've never been here before, but I know from Sir Woggle that this is a very unusual place."

Behind them to the west about 100 metres away was a huge mound of what appeared to be black granite rock, beyond this a black cliff-face soaring several hundred metres up into the sky blocking out the rest of their view. To the east was deadwood. A vast area of tangled dead trees so closely knit together, it would be impossible to penetrate. To the north and south was Death Desert. A place where nothing lives; well, almost nothing. The ground beneath our feet began to tremble violently, in the distance a loud roar started, slowly filling the air. "What's that?" I asked.

"We have this phrase in Rorrim, '*Ruoved lliw ti esoht gnikees noil gniraor a ekil dnuora seog ti.*'" As the roaring continued, a black mound rose up silently like a huge black grotesque monster. Its head was massive. His eyes were a fiery red, his ears were totally spiky, as if they had dozens of rows of needles sticking out of them. Its mouth was enormous and filled with huge jagged teeth. The body of this beast was like that of an ancient dinosaur. And it had six enormous legs with 14 sets of claws on each foot.

"That's the Htomehebausorus and it's not interested in us. It's been roused by the distant roar. And I suggest," continued Brave, "that we remain very still because if we don't, they will be after us and not one another." As Brave finished off, the ground shook beneath us like a gigantic earthquake was about to erupt. Closer and closer came the noise and the rumbling sound. *THUD.* Rumble, shake, and violent quaking were felt and heard. *THUD.* Rumble, shake, and violent quaking. *THUD.* Rumble, shake, and violent quaking. Suddenly, the sky which was already a dark grey became as black as velvet and a beast of humongous size was seen on the edge of the black distant cliffs. *THUD* went its huge heavy feet in succession and the rumbling, shaking, and violent quaking of the ground continued beneath them.

"What is that thing?" asked Foggle in amazement. Before anyone had a chance to answer, it raised its massive head in the air, opened its cavernous mouth and let out a deafening roar. *RRRRRrrrrrrrrroooaaarrrrrr*. Our small group was momentarily paralysed with fear. Then it leapt high into the air, landing with a deafening crash at the foot of the cliff. In an instant, the beast was locked in a fierce battle. They had both risen on their hind legs and were charging headlong at one another, the thud of their feet on the ground, the clash of their great bodies as they continually collided with each other and constant roaring and growling filled the air with the most horrendous noise, sent tremors through the ground like that of a great earthquake. Minute by minute, blow by blow, the battle raged on as they fought for supremacy unaware that they were being watched by a small group of five Stabmows, one Stesomram, and another strange looking creature from 'the other side'. Foggle grabbed Wise by the arm and spoke in a hoarse whisper, "There's a breeze blowing, what we are meant to do now?"

"That's no breeze, that's a draught," answered Brave, "look." There was an urgency in his whisper. We turned our attention to where Brave was pointing; 200 metres away a crack appeared in the ground, which was creeping towards us, getting slowly wider as it was snaking its way closer and closer. The nearer it came, the greater the draught. As the fighting between these two beasts continued, the ground continued splitting open like a jagged crack in a huge ancient dinosaur shell. The splitting ground was getting closer and closer by the second, then for some unknown reason the crack split off into two different directions like it had a mind of its own. It went either side of our small group, right around us cutting through the ground without slowing down and about 20 metres beyond us, it came together again forming one crack. When it would stop nobody knew or cared because right now our small group was sitting on a large oval shaped piece of ugly ground, which was rocking very precariously beneath us as if it was pivoted on something very unstable. "Hang on," shouted Brave, "lie flat face down. We are going down." The two great beasts were still fighting each other totally unaware of the damage they were causing or the danger they were creating. Finally, the ground beneath our small group gave way and we were plunging downwards at a frantic, dizzy speed as we lay flat on this huge unpredictable disc. Where we were going, we couldn't tell. Breaking the silence, Brave hollered suddenly, "We are not falling, we are flying."

Wise shouted back in reply, "Remember the phrase 'follow the way of the wind'. Well, I think it's driving us, which is why we are not plunging downwards anymore." His comment gave us a little bit of confidence.

"Do you remember the phrase our King once had over the main gates into the palace," continued Wise: "*Kcor eht no ylmrif teef ruoy xif ytiruces dna ytefas ruoy rof*."

"What does that mean?" I yelled in reply.

"For your safety and security, fix your feet firmly on the rock," answered Foggle, who was closest to me.

"Brilliant," yelled Brave and with that he jumped to his feet and shouted, "Look guys, I'm air boarding." While all this was going on, the huge piece of rock was circling in the huge underground cavern we were in and slowly spiralling downwards at the same time. Brave's antics brought a slight distraction for a few moments; watching him balancing as we were hurtling through the air was quite a special moment. It wasn't that he was showing off, he just realised how safe he was.

Suddenly, Boggle shouted out, "Look out, tunnel ahead." Brave threw himself flat as the sides of our disc curled upwards with seconds to spare. Without slowing down, we shot into the tunnel, which spiralled upwards rotating us constantly through 360°. Round and round we spun as we spiralled upwards. It seemed never-ending as we continued spiralling.

"Daylight ahead," hollered Zebaj excitedly.

Chapter 11
Prickle Wood Again

Hanging on for dear life, we slowly looked up. Sure enough in the distance, at the far end of the underground rocky tunnel, which seemed to be a long way off was a patch of bright blue sky. The disc stopped spiralling and headed for the distant opening, going faster and faster as it went higher and higher, getting ever closer to the opening. The huge rough oval disc with its small group of adventurers burst out of the tunnel into the daylight. BOOM! The sound was deafening as we went through the sound barrier and up into the sky. The midday sun was behind us as we started to level off and slow down slightly. Foggle broke our silence as he pointed into the distance, "Look over there," he shouted.

"Over where?" our group answered in unison.

"Directly in front of us but at ground level," he replied, "it's Prickle Wood."

"Hang on, guys, we are going down," yelled Zebaj.

The obscure oval disc seemed to have a mind of its own as we swooped down towards the ground. The sides of the disc had flattened out helping us to skim through the air. We had slowed down but we were still travelling incredibly fast. And being much closer to the ground made it feel faster than we were actually flying. Prickly Wood was now about five and half miles away.

"Hang on tight. We are going in," shouted a voice, "and it's going to be rough." Our small group instantly threw ourselves flat on our faces.

Oggle spoke first, "Who shouted out the instruction?" he yelled, then half looking over his shoulder he got the shock of his life.

"You'll never guess who's really flying this thing," yelled Oggle again.

"What are you going on about, Oggle?" shouted Boggle and Foggle together.

"Look over your shoulder and you'll see for yourselves," answered Oggle.

We did and we too had the shock of our lives. There he was with his long, black coat flying in the wind. His old, black shiny boots pointing backwards and his tall, black hat tilting slightly backwards but firmly fixed to his head. And the biggest non-ghostly grin you have ever seen spread across his see thru face. It was The See Thru Man. There was no time for questions or answers. The huge rough disc was cutting through Prickly Wood, making a huge path like a landing strip. There were thorn branches flying everywhere. Suddenly, the disc was out of the wood and turning in a tight circle. The only ones enjoying this part of the adventure were me, Brave, and Zebaj.

"Hang on, we are going to be like a circular saw for a while," shouted The See Thru Man. And starting at the outer boundary of the wood, we started whizzing around in an ever-tightening circle. Once again, thorn branches were flying off everywhere. I was the only person not enjoying this now, I had a definite green colour about my cheeks. "We are nearly done, just a few more turns around the wood and then I'm finished," shouted The See Thru Man. With a few more completed spirals and each one getting tighter and tighter, the disc finally skidded and bumped along the ground, coming to rest in an obscure looking place. Our group slowly got to our feet; on this occasion, I was definitely last.

"Where did he go?" asked Oggle.

"Who?" enquired Wise.

"The See Thru Man," chorused Oggle, Foggle, and Boggle. "He was the one flying this lump of rock," they exclaimed.

"No wonder it was jet propelled," declared Brave. "That was some ride."

"It was," I added, "but no one will believe me when I get back home."

Suddenly, Zebaj shouted, "there's a note wedged in the base of this thing; it's from The See Thru Man. You read it, Wise, you're much better at this sort of thing than I am."

Wise took the note and quickly read it to himself, then gave a soft whistle as the instructions registered. "Well I never," he murmured to himself. Our group sat down on the huge disc and waited.

Finally, Wise spoke, "If everything goes according to plan, we should get rid of Wizard Wonky forever." Wise began to read. We sat with bated breath.

"'The Rock which you have travelled on, which has given you security and brought you through your recent adventure is called the

Gnilbmuts Rock. This is the only thing that will defeat Wizard Wonky. You must make certain he stands in the centre of it and he must be provoked into anger. When that happens, a deep dark mist will descend. The outer rim of the disc will fold upwards to a point cocooning him tightly in it. It will then start spinning at an incredible speed…that's it,'" concluded Wise. A long silence prevailed.

Finally, I remarked, "What an odd way to end the instructions, with an unfinished comment."

"That's because we wouldn't believe it even if he'd told us, which means we are left with an element of surprise," replied Wise.

"Firstly," said Brave, "I think we should discretely scout around the area. We need to find out where Wizard Wonky is, then plan a surprise attack which will cause him to stand on this slab."

"What kind of surprise do you have in mind?" asked Foggle with a puzzled look on his fury face.

"I've not thought that far ahead yet," replied Brave, "but I think we should go in pairs and Wise should be allowed some peace and quiet to think," continued Brave as he looked at his friend's thoughtful face. Wise looked up and nodded in agreement.

"Right then, this is what we will do. Zebaj and Pockets, you go to the north. Oggle and Foggle will go to the east and work southwards. Boggle and I will go west and work out to the south. We should meet up roughly in the same place," said Brave taking charge.

"Hang on," said Zebaj, "if Pockets and I go north, who will be going north to the east and north to the west?"

"You will," answered Brave with a grin.

"But why?" challenged Zebaj. We looked on in bewilderment.

"Because you are taller than us and Pockets has longer legs," chuckled Brave.

"We need to be back here in three hours." And with that parting comment, we split into pairs to begin our search.

Wise sat still deep in thought, the time ticking slowly by. In the trees, some birds were singing but, on this occasion, Wise didn't hear them. In front of him, a family of six fluffy Seloms were frolicking merrily, but Wise didn't notice them either. In fact, he didn't see or notice anything, he was totally absorbed in his own thoughts sitting in the centre of the rock. What Wise didn't know was while sitting here he was totally invisible. He could see everything but no one could see him.

Meanwhile, we, in our pairs, were slowly and discretely searching the area for any traces of Wizard Wonky. After three hours of searching and creeping in and out of different places, we made our way back to where we had parted company.

"We should keep our information to ourselves for now until we sit down with Wise, that way we only tell it once," said Brave as we walked back towards Wise.

"*Ssshhh*," said Boggle putting his paw to his mouth, then in a hushed whisper, he said, "Look, there's our piece of disc but where's Wise." Slowly and silently, they skirted around the huge disc looking for signs or clues, any form of evidence as to which direction he might have wandered off in. Zebaj stepped cautiously onto the rock. In doing so, two things happened; firstly, he found Wise, sitting where we had left him, deep in thought. Secondly, he was invisible to the gang.

How odd, he thought to himself and thirdly, we were looking for him but couldn't see him and he was in touching distance of them. Cautiously, Zebaj stepped off the rock, looking at himself as he did. It was weird because by doing this slowly he watched himself reappear.

"Where have you been?" asked Brave. "We have been looking for you, you shouldn't just disappear like that."

"Like what," replied Zebaj innocently. Then, without waiting for a reply, he continued, "or do you mean like this?" and while he was speaking he stepped back onto the rock and vanished.

"How did he do that?" asked Boggle.

"Do you mean this?" chuckled Zebaj as he reappeared before their very eyes.

"Come on, Brave, step on the rock and you will see what I mean." Brave did and to everyone's amazement, he vanished out of sight before our very eyes.

"Wow," shouted the group in unison as we followed Brave, "this rock is something special."

"Which means we must use it to our advantage," broke in Wise with a serious expression on his round, furry face.

"Now before we make any plans, tell me what you discovered on your spying mission," continued Brave.

"Why don't two of you go outside and stand at opposite ends of the rock and see if you can see each other," added Wise. So Zebaj and Brave did as Wise suggested, and to their amazement neither could see the other which was what Wise expected.

"Excellent. Just excellent. We must utilise it to our advantage," said Wise. "But before we finalise our plans, I need to hear how you guys got on exploring."

Brave and Boggle shared first, and Zebaj and me second but neither of us had anything of real value to share. The group sat in silence as we told our stories, Wise was looking more and more thoughtful. Finally, he turned to Oggle and Foggle, "Well boys, have you anything better to add?" asked Wise hopefully.

"Well," said Foggle, speaking first while looking and winking quickly at Oggle. "We wandered off not certain which specific direction to go in," continued Foggle.

At this point, Oggle chipped in, "What Foggle is saying is, there was no point in wandering aimlessly around, so we didn't wander anywhere."

"And feeling very exhausted, tired, and extremely thirsty, we found a small stream nearby, had a long cool drink, led down, and fell asleep. When we woke up, we were totally refreshed, and it was time to get back and that's about all that there is to tell," he concluded.

Wise is normally very patient but at this point he interrupted. "WHAT!?"

Brave was so angry, he had steam coming out of his ears. "I don't believe you guys," he roared. Zebaj had spotted a slight twinkle in Foggle's eye; he nudged me and whispered in my ear two words.

"What are you whispering, Zebaj?" interrupted Wise. Brave at this point was busy lecturing his two pals on their lack of commitment and totally missed Zebaj's reply.

"Wind-up, that's all I said to Pockets," answered Zebaj innocently. Wise just stared in disbelief, Oggle and Foggle burst out laughing, and it was some time before Wise and Brave managed to recompose themselves and bring order to the group.

"Right," said Wise finally with a sigh while shaking his head from side to side, "will you pair please tell us what you discovered?"

Foggle spoke first, "Just after we all separated, Oggle and I were faced with a slight challenge, we were confronted by four paths going off in different directions, we decided to explore two each but not going more than 200 metres down each one before returning to our starting point. Well, to cut a long story short, paths one and four re-joined, and eventually led us to the mouth of a cave. This cave is sunk into a hillside, which means it's very hard to find apart from a half hidden chimney, which at first glance looks like a molehill. We led on the grass by it and listened, and we could hear Wizard Wonky practising some magic spell and the smoke coming out of the chimney was definitely unpleasant."

Wise suddenly interrupted, "This is awesome. Well done, guys, now here's what I think we should do." We sat in silence with bated breath. "We make a smoke bomb, a very effective one. Brave can do that; drop it down the chimney, causing Wonky to panic and taking him by surprise, he will rush out of his cave."

At this point, Zebaj, who was totally engrossed, interrupted, "I will make certain that he only has one path to run down to get him here; I will do it by using the off cuts, which we created when we entered Prickle Wood."

"Brilliant," shouted the group in agreement. Is started chuckling; the group sat and stared at me wondering what was so funny.

"Are you going to tell us what you're laughing at?" asked a bemused Oggle.

"I've got this idea, which I think will add a touch of terror to the smoke bomb. Wizard Wonky doesn't know me, and he won't recognise the sound of my voice either, so just before the smoke bomb is dropped down the chimney, I will shout down it, he will wonder what's going on. Before he has a chance to pull himself together, we drop the smoke bomb down the chimney, his cave quickly fills with smoke, in blind panic he rushes out and down the path created by Zebaj."

"That's awesome," shouted Brave.

"What are you going to shout down the chimney?" asked Boggle, his eyes gleaming with delight.

"I know," interrupted Foggle. "It should be *Nisrap, Leket, Enem, Enem.*"

"Which basically means," continued Foggle for my benefit, "you've been weighed in the balance and found wanting." Everyone was in full delighted agreement.

Wise spoke up, bringing our small group back to the task in hand. "If Oggle, Foggle, and Boggle go with Zebaj, he will explain what he is setting out to achieve. Brave and Pockets can work on their side of the things and don't forget his cave must be destroyed as well. I will set a little surprise for Wizard Wonky in the centre of this slab of rock."

Our group broke up and set off to deal with our different tasks. Zebaj showed his three friends the path to the cave. "The challenge we have is blocking off each entrance to the paths we don't need, while making a new path, which needs to be the obvious one for him to flee down. We should start the path from the end point and work towards his cave; if Oggle and Boggle could do that, then me and Foggle will block off every other path."

In their pairs, the friends set about the task.

Chapter 12
Final Preparations

Meanwhile, Brave and I made our way to the covered roof of Wonky's cave. Lying down flat next to the small chimney stack, we listened carefully; Wizard Wonky was humming a little tune. "He seems to sound happy in an odd kind of way," whispered Brave.

Wizard Wonky started singing in a haunting kind of voice which was mingled with an evil chuckle. "I've got lies for Wise, I've got slavery for Bravery. And for Oggle, Foggle, and Boggle, I've got snod grass, navel rash and oodles and oodles of nits, gnats, and nasties." Brave was so angry, he was about to let out a huge roar when I dived on him, pinning him to the ground with my hand clamped over his mouth. After several minutes, Brave calmed down and we crept away.

"Thank you," whispered Brave. "I almost ruined everything."

"At least we know what he is up too," I replied with grim determination. Finding a secluded spot, Brave made a long, slim, torpedo shaped object.

"This is my smoke bomb but to finish it, I must soak it in the juice of a huge Nolemretaw, then when we want to light the smoke bomb, I will click my nails for a spark, which is all it will need and it will instantly give out huge clouds of smoke, filling his cave with eye-watering, throat-burning, nose-clogging smoke, which will last a long, long time. He will be forced to flee his cave or he will either suffocate or choke himself to death. I know where the Nolemretaw Tree is as well, we'll pick a suitable fruit on the way back to base," and with that we set off to collect the final piece of our preparations.

While we were busy, Wise had been very active. He had built what looked like an ancient hexagonal altar, standing three metres high with seven stone steps for Wizard Wonky to ascend. The altar was made out of logs and thick sticks created when they made their grand entry into Prickly Wood on their flying disc. On the top of this, he placed in a raised fashion what looked like two rare old books; the first one was called 'The Secrets of Eternal Magic' and the second was 'The Secret of Eternal Youth'. Both these books actually exist but no one knows where the real books are hidden. Wise was pleased with his handiwork.

A little while later, we all met up and shared what we had achieved. In short, all the preparations were ready. "All we need to do now is time everything to perfection," said Wise.

Brave being the action guy was keen to get started when Foggle spoke up. "If we wait a bit, the sun will be lower in the sky and he will be running into it, which means he will have the sun in his eyes as he is running away from his cave."

"That will create an element of surprise because he will be almost here before he realises what's happened to his cave and seeing the ancient altar will compel him to keep going and climb the steps."

"And that is when he will become very angry, because everything will collapse as he touches it," added Wise.

"Right then," he added, "I suggest that Brave and Pockets take up their position and the rest of us move off the rock and sit over there where we can watch without being seen," concluded Wise.

"What have you got there, Brave?" asked Boggle looking at the long, strange, dark green object he was picking up.

"This is our smoke bomb. It has to be this shape to slide easily down the chimney, and I've soaked it in Nolemretaw juice and wrapped it in a leaf from the Nugumba Tree so it stays damp."

"Are you ready, Pockets, let's get going."

"At your service," I smiled, "let the party begin." Brave and I decided to take a long circular route, so we could come to the cave without being seen. We got to our destination without any hassle. Lying on the ground near the chimney, we slowly made the hole slightly bigger. Wizard Wonky was still engrossed practising his new spell. He was dressed in his full wizard's outfit, the tall pointy hat, his long, flowing cloak, his grand, long, turned up, pointy shoes. All matching, sky blue with bright yellow stars all over it. The only addition was the shape of a new moon in the front of his tall hat and his tall magician's staff nearby.

"Some lies against Wise,
I'll make Brave my slave,
Cross eyes for Boggle,
Confusion for Foggle,
Oggle, Oggle won't be able to goggle,
And who says Zebaj has changed his ways,

I will add a little pinch of this,
And little pinch of that,
And hot it up and stir it up into a gooey mess,
And I will spray it all over The Land of Pleasant,
And it doesn't matter if it goes wrong
Because they will become a group of pheasants."

And with a loud cackling laugh filled with evil intent, Wizard Wonky continued mixing his destructive potion.

"Wizard Wonky, you need to listen carefully," I shouted down the chimney in a deep commanding voice. Before he had time to recover or time to answer, I shouted again, "*Nisrap, Leket, Enem, Enem.*" While I was engaged in my task, Brave unwrapped the smoke bomb, clicked his paw nails together, produced a spark and had the bomb smoking, silently he dropped it into the chimney while I was shouting. The chimney was longer than we had imagined, and it seemed to take an age before we heard the full effect. *SPLASH!!! BOOM!!!* The smoking bomb landed right in the cauldron, which increased the effect. Smoke billowed upwards and outwards, instantly filling the cave. Wizard Wonky started running around the cave in blind panic like a demented spinning top, his long cloak was flapping like a demented bat. The wizard was screeching and shouting, squawking, and crashing into anything and everything in his cave, creating total chaos; his throat was throbbing as if it were on fire. His nose felt as if it was swollen, it was that blocked. His eyes were burning so badly that he could barely see what he was doing. The smoke kept billowing out through the cave entrance. Brave and I crept around to the side of the cave to get a glimpse of what was going on, the noise was unbelievable, as Wizard Wonky was still crashing blindly into everything he had knocked over. Suddenly and very dramatically, he burst out of the cave into the fresh air, his famous cloak was in shreds, his tall hat was twisted, dented and stained, his long white hair was knotted and mated, and his long white beard was blowing in his face, inflaming his eyes, and impairing his vision even more.

"Run for your life," shouted Brave. As we did, there was an almighty explosion, the roof of the cave was sent sky high, followed by a huge crashing sound as the walls completely caved in with tremendous force. Long seconds later, there was another high crashing sound as the roof landed back on top of the rubble that was once the cave.

Wizard Wonky was racing down the path still in blind panic. Brave and I had very quickly retraced our steps in record time. As we re-joined the group on the far side of the rock, Wizard Wonky was stumbling his way into view. His throat was still throbbing, his nose was still clogged and his eyes were still streaming but not stinging as much. Through his blurred vision he caught sight of the big ancient altar. Seeing it made him stop and rub his eyes. Blinking back the tears, he looked again. Realising what this was, he rushed forward again. Our small group sat watching with bated breath. Closer and closer stumbled the wizard. We held our breath. "Is this what I think it is," muttered the dishevelled Wonky, "can this be the Ancient Altar?" Closer and closer he came. The silence among the small group of my friends was intense. The wizard's pace was getting quicker. His blind panic had turned into an excited hope.

He paused again to rub his eyes, "No, I'm not dreaming. I've never seen this before, it must have descended from the sky." Once again, he staggered forward as he stepped onto the rock, he realised how dazed and confused and exhausted he was. *Never mind all that*, he thought, *I must ascend the steps of the altar*. Very carefully, he approached it, feeling that he had been chosen. Believing his life must have accomplished something of value to be granted this great honour. As he placed his foot on the first stone step, he puffed his chest out in pride. We watched and waited. Wizard Wonky climbed the seven stone steps. We watched in absolute silence, not daring to breathe. Wonky had two more steps to the top. He paused, his eyes were still blurry and stinging, making them water. He wiped his tattered sleeve across his face. Then with renewed energy and pride, he climbed the last two steps and held his magician's staff high above his head. He let out an enormous "Wow", followed by "I do not believe it". He stared at the two ancient looking books; then he looked up into sky. Then he stared once again at the ancient books. As he placed his hand on what he thought was the ancient cover of 'The Secrets of Eternal Magic', he heard the booming voice again, "*Nisrap, Leket, Enem, Enem.*" I had cupped my hands around my mouth and shouted. Wizard Wonky was about to open the cover but it was too late. The makeshift book collapsed into a small pile of twigs. In desperation, he reached for the other book but the effect was the same, a pile of twigs.

"*Nisrap, Leket, Enem, Enem,*" I boomed again. Realising he had been tricked but he didn't know how the wizard became violently angry.

"No, no, no," he cried out, "not like this," and in his anger his temper boiled over and he threw himself at the altar which also disintegrated into a big pile of logs and sticks. Pulling himself up to his full height and spinning around slowly as if he were looking for someone, he bellowed out in violent temper. "I will have my revenge." *SLAM!!!* Instantly, the sides of the rock rose up and slammed shut like a great big cocoon of rock. Next, it started spinning clockwise at an incredible speed; this lasted a long time. Faster and faster it spun until it was just a blur. Instantly and without slowing down, it stopped spinning and opened in a violent manner. *SLAM!* It hit the ground in its original shape but with such force that it sunk into the ground so that it was impossible to distinguish it. The wizard, however, was still frantically spinning. We watched in silence not wanting to spoil the moment. After several minutes, Wonky came to a standstill but was so dizzy that he fell flat on his face. We stared at him wondering what would happen next. Finally, he slowly raised his head, "I'm still alive," he muttered. "How did I manage that?" Little by little he started to stand up. First of all, on all fours, gripping the ground with as much strength as he could muster. He slowly raised his head and looked around. Not far away driven into the ground was his wizard's staff; slowly he crawled towards it. Wizard Wonky did not feel well. This was definitely a bad hair-do day for him. We still watched in silence, wondering what would happen next. The wizard continued crawling on all fours. The closer he got to his staff the further away it seemed to be; finally, it was in reach, grasping hold of it Wonky breathed a sigh of relief. At that moment in time, he realised he had an audience. He was still on his knees hanging on to his staff and staring at our small group. We suddenly realised there was no longer an invisible barrier but still we sat in silence. Finally, the wizard spoke in a very angry voice, "I have survived. I have been chosen by the Grand Masters to be the master wizard in The Land of Pleasant. At last, I shall rule and bring about the changes, which shall destroy this land forever." Without warning, his wizard's staff was grabbed as if by an invisible hand. It suddenly had a life of its own as it started rotating in the air, then as quick as a flash it started beating the wizard around the head, digging him in the ribs, whacking him on the knees. We all rolled about on the grass laughing until our sides ached. The wizard couldn't get away or defend himself from his demented staff. *Thwack! Crack! Jab, Jab! Dig! Thwack! Crack! Jab, Jab! Dig!* Time and time again, it hit him until he was black and blue. Finally, the wizard's staff stopped beating him and it hovered vertically in the air. Wizard Wonky was completely dazed. He didn't know where he was or what was happening to him. It felt like a living nightmare. One minute he was working on a new spell. The next minute he was caveless, homeless, wandless, and powerless, and sitting opposite him was a small group; one was his prisoner, five were his archenemies, whom he was trying to destroy, and then there was a stranger, me, who he didn't recognise at all. His magician's staff was still hovering in the air just in front him. Wizard Wonky dived for it, but all he grabbed was fresh air. My small group of friends were finding his antics really amusing and laughed uncontrollably at him. Every time he dived or grabbed at the staff, he not only missed, he also fell over, flat on his face every time. After many failed attempts, getting angrier and looking extremely foolish, Wizard Wonky drew himself up to his full height, waved his left arm frantically at us and exploded in a fit of uncontrollable rage. "I, the Great Wizard Wonky, will make you all pay for this, especially you," he screamed at me. But he was too late!

Without any warning, Wizard Wonky seemed to dissolve from the feet up as a deep, dark, grey mist slowly swirled upwards from the ground. Around and around it swirled, gradually covering his feet. The cold, dark mist became denser as it swirled around his ankles. Around and around it swirled. It was like an increasing length of wide black ribbon. Finally, Wonky was totally enveloped in the cold dark mist. The mist continued swirling around him and climbed upwards until it was a huge column ascending into the sky. The wizard was caught inside the column, unable to escape. The screams of terror he was letting out made it sound as if he was a tormented prisoner. Suddenly, without warning, the huge column of mist collapsed and spread over the ground, hovering just above the heads of our small group, as we watched spellbound. Then, very slowly, the dark grey, damp mist started swirling around Wizard Wonky again, and as it began swirling around and rising up, he just evaporated in the dark grey cloud of mist. Slowly from his feet up, without collapsing and always screaming in terror, he slowly dissolved until there was nothing left, not even the point of his hat or the tip of his staff. The mist was very cold, like damp grey November fog.

"What's going on?" I cried.

"Going on where?" came a reply. I spun around, standing behind me in the fog was a tall man with a tall black hat and a toothless grin.

"Another successful adventure, thank you. Once again, the Land of Pleasant has been restored. Not perfect, but pleasant."

"Wait a minute, you're Misty, right?"

"Right, and you're Pockets, right? And you've just had a successful time in the Land of Pleasant and I have been sent by…" and pulling himself up to his full height, he continued, "…by The See Thru Man to say once again, thank you," and with that he disappeared. The cold, damp fog I was in swirled upwards in a clockwise motion like someone rolling up an old blanket; as it disappeared, I discovered that I was at the top of my street and the time was 16:36. It didn't take too long to walk home today after all, I smiled to myself. *I wonder when the next adventure will be.*

"Sooner than you think," said a voice from somewhere behind me.

Volume 6
The Ogre's Wife

A Brief Introduction

It has often been said that The Land of Pleasant isn't perfect, but it is pleasant. It has some main characters called Stabmows, a King, a Queen, another group of citizens called Stesomrams, and a variety of outsiders who must be dealt with so that the land remains pleasant. In the very first adventure, my reader encountered the Ogre of Gulberia. In this adventure, you meet his ugly, lumpy, bumpy, wart, and weeping, sore covered wife.

As with all the other adventures, occasionally you will have to translate messages and phrases from Rorrim, which is the national language of the Land of Pleasant into English.

I dedicate this story once again to my four grandchildren, whose imagination has helped me enormously.

Chapter 1
The Sliding Wall

The windowless room was stuffy and oppressive. The room consisted of a threadbare grey and pink carpet, a large scruffy square table with ten odd chairs around it, six were occupied. The four walls were almost identical; the same sad, dull, pale, lifeless grey colour dominated each one. There wasn't a single picture anywhere, the only wall that was different was the one with the windowless door in it and that too was the same sad, dull, pale, lifeless grey colour. Diagonally opposite the door was a tea trolley with four wonky wheels supporting it and on it were 12 chipped and badly stained mugs, six dirty glasses, some cheap tea bags, milk, cheap instant coffee, tarnished spoons, sugar, and a thermos flask of hot water, and a jug of water. Around the table sat senior social worker Ms Shirty Brainstorm—her father misspelt her name on her birth certificate at the time because he was drunk, but the name really suited her. She had a mop of unkempt, unruly, lifeless grey hair, and small horn rimmed glasses, which were too small for her large spotty face; Assistant Head Teacher, Mr M. T. Potts; the Minute Taker, Mr Ian N. K. Wells; a member of the local care team, Miss Shepherd; PC Drinkwater from the local drug squad, me and from the Safeguarding Children's Association, Dr P.R.E. Gular, originally from Newport, Gwent.

Ms Brainstorm spoke in a crisp rasping voice, smiling as she spoke, "Do you like our brightly painted office."

"I've used brighter undercoat," replied Mr Wells the Minute Taker.

"I'll have you know," she snapped back, "this is our best top coat."

"Top coat," interrupted a surprised Dr Gular, "I wear a better top coat when I'm gardening in winter."

PC Drinkwater joined in the conversation, "Did you hear about the young lad who was asked by his teacher to write a sentence with the word 'fascinate' in it, he wrote, I have a top coat with nine buttons, one is missing so I can only fasten eight."

Mr Potts joined in laughing, "In my first teaching post, we had a student with a big mouth. His PE teacher decided to use him as the school coach, so they took all his teeth out and replaced them with bus seats." By now everyone was smiling or laughing, everyone that is except for Ms Brainstorm. She was as humourless as her newly painted meeting room!!!

I wondered when they would get to the main part of the meeting, namely the wellbeing and the future of the young person we were discussing. Walking around the table to the hostess trolley, I asked in my strong Welsh accent, "Would anyone else like a glass of water?"

No one replied. Ms Brainstorm had called the meeting to order and was on a roll, her rasping voice rang out.

"I don't know what will become of our client, no matter what strategies I put in place, nothing seems to work—"

Dr Gular interrupted, his voice was icy cold as he asked, "Have you ever asked the young person what strategies he would like in place instead of assuming you know what is best. If you have the client as a person as your primary focus and their needs as an important secondary focus then you might be more successful."

You could cut the atmosphere with a knife. I was about to ask again if anyone wanted a drink, when, without warning, the wall behind the trolley slid noiselessly open revealing a long unlit passageway; I was so startled that I almost dropped the large jug of water I was holding. I blinked a few times thinking I was hallucinating. Staring further into the blackness, I could just make out a familiar figure; the tall black hat, the long black frock coat, the black trousers and the worn but highly polished black boots and that non-ghostly smile. The See Thru Man was beckoning me with a long, thin bony see thru finger. I opened my mouth to exclaim 'what are you doing here?' when I remembered no one else could see what was going on. Again, The See Thru Man beckoned me with his bony, see thru finger. Still holding the jug of water, I stepped towards The See Thru Man. Instantly, six bright spotlights came on in the initial part of the passage, transforming it into a grand ornate hallway as the wall silently closed behind me. The floor and walls were made of a blood red marble with silver streaks randomly running through them creating a psychedelic pattern. Every so often, fastened to the wall were huge silver candlestick holders, each one holding a very big burning cream candlestick, giving off a very faint glow. "What is this place?" I exclaimed.

"Not many people know this place exists," replied The See Thru Man with his non-ghostly see thru grin, "hang on tight, we need to move quickly." Without any warning, we were flying as if we had been jet propelled along the corridor. Every so often, a set of spotlights came on, lighting another long section of the corridor, while the hallway behind us was plunged into almost total darkness, except for a faint flicker of light given off by the candles, which cast their shadows in an eerie moving scene on the walls. On and on we flew. I suddenly became aware that I had flames coming out of my heels, which gave me the feeling of being thrust forward by a jet engine. After sometime of hurtling forwards in a dead straight line, I realised two more things; firstly, we were going steadily downwards, and secondly, I was still carrying the jug of water. The See Thru Man glanced at me as we continued flying through the tunnel and grinningly said, "You will need that where you are going."

Before I could answer, he accelerated ahead. "How did you do that?" I shouted.

"It's instinct that does it," came the reply. It took a few seconds before I realised what I had to do. Eventually, we stopped at a huge set of arch shaped, heavy oak wooden double doors. Each door was hung with six massive steel hinges and had a series of large black steel studs in both of them, giving the doors an imposing look.

"Now, listen carefully, this doorway is just inside the boundary of Gulberia. When you step through them, take in your surroundings because this is your escape route. The jug you are carrying will now be invisible to you. You will have freedom of movement with your right arm and hand but when you need it, it will be there for you. Your mission is to dissolve Noddaba, get rid of the Ogre's Wife and set Sir Woggle free; he is her greatest trophy. The Ogress is called Lebezej."

"Great," I replied dubiously, "but who and what is Noddaba and how do I dissolve it?"

"Outside these doors, you will see in the distance the back of the old castle in Gulberia. Your immediate surroundings will look familiar to you because they look like an ancient disused dilapidated cemetery. The sun never shines here so it is always dark, gloomy, cold, lifeless grey, and foreboding, and the howling icy cold wind never lets up. A secret entrance to the prison where Woggle is trapped is guarded by Noddaba. The problem you face is simple, the creature you want, often but not always, lies incredibly still and looks like any one of the gargoyles on display. You need the contents of the jug, but don't drink from it because it's no longer cold water. The only indicator you will have for knowing when to use it is this; steam will slowly rise from it. When that happens, you must throw the contents of the jug over Noddaba. If you are successful, he will dissolve and you will then be able to deal with Lebezej. Brave knows how to deal with her."

"Brave, how does he know and where is he now?" I spluttered as I digested the details from The See Thru Man.

"He's already outside these doors."

"Is there anything else I need to know?" I asked.

"Like what?" replied The See Thru Man.

"This Noddaba, what does it look like?"

"Think ugly dragon, then think huge, ugly dragon, then think massive, ugly dragon," replied The See Thru Man.

"Right," I said with some apprehension.

"Now, give it six huge legs and paws with massive claws. Four at the front and two at the back, with a long ferocious whip-like tail, a massive grotesque head with evil amber-coloured eyes, a black matted threadbare mane and a huge, ugly mouth, a double row of razor sharp teeth, a long, dark red, forked tongue. And one last thing, when it's aroused, it can be like a chameleon. I will leave you soon. Brave will be pleased to see you and remember this, don't use the jug until Brave has disappeared." And with that last comment, The See Thru Man vanished.

Chapter 2
Through the Doors

I stood and stared at the massive doors and wondered how to get through them. Grabbing the door handle and twisting produced nothing, pulling and pushing had a negative effect as well. Inspiration took hold and I calmly and confidently walked at the doors, remembering how this approach had worked in the past. *Wallop!* I hit the doors full on and bounced backwards landing on the floor. "This is proving to be more challenging than I anticipated," I muttered to myself. Picking myself off the floor, I decided a more careful examination was required. *Maybe it's one of the black studs,* I thought, *perhaps I need to gently push, twist, or press one, let's give it a go.* As I reached out and gently touched the right-hand door, they both completely dissolved, and I found myself outside. Instantly, I spun around looking for the doors I was behind a moment ago; behind me was an ancient, dead-looking tree, totally bare, dark dismal grey and seemingly lifeless; angry, grey, obscure clouds darted across the sky casting grotesque shadows all around me. The landscape consisted of bare cliffs, jagged mountains, small hills, and thousands of grotesque looking statues. There were no bushes, no shrubs, and no birds, and as far as I could tell, there was no life anywhere.

This place is a living nightmare, I thought to myself as I made a careful note of my surroundings. I shuddered. It was a desolate, lifeless wilderness. Everywhere I looked, I saw hundreds of grotesque statues of unrecognisable creatures, like a defeated army from a war long forgotten. Some of the statues were grey stone-like while others were a dull black marble, all massive and ugly but none that resembled Noddaba. Looking into the distance, I could see on the horizon the back of Narcaervon Castle towering upwards. Remaining still, I wondered where Brave was. Behind me and some distance away, one of the black marble like creatures stirred slightly, its eyes glowing amber, full of evil intent. Out of the corner of my eye, I was distracted, looking sharply to my left, I stared. All I could see was dark grey gargoyles and the barren, lifeless, grey wasteland of the wilderness, while the howling icy wind cut into me. Slowly turning my head in the direction of the distraction, I got a better look. Some of these statues were like prehistoric creatures, others were just massive skeletons and others like ancient mythical gargoyles from a distant era. Most of them were incomplete; wings were missing from some, and limbs and heads missing from others. In this lifeless, desolate place, these seemed more grotesque and horrifically ugly. Finally, I muttered beneath my breath. "This is a godforsaken place."

"No, it's not," replied a familiar voice in a whisper behind me. "But don't turn around just yet. Just stay calm and listen carefully." The familiar voice continued, "You are not a pretty sight at the moment."

"Am I pleased to hear you," I replied whispering with relief, "but what do you mean by your first comment?"

"Well, if it was godforsaken, you wouldn't be here," answered Brave. "But right now, we have work to do."

Behind us, the black marble monster stirred slowly, its amber-coloured eyes gleaming and its long dark-red forked tongue flicked quickly out and in again as it returned to its motionless state. Keeping his voice in a whisper, Brave continued explaining certain things about our mission. "Firstly, The Old Tree behind us is very important. Secondly, you will eventually be chased by the Ogre's Wife. She is ugly and covered in warts, scabs, and weeping sores; she's not a pretty sight. Thirdly, when that happens, you must head back to the tree. Fourthly, throw yourself upon it. Don't hesitate. Don't stop and think about it and don't hold back. Throw yourself on it. The tree is your protection and escape, it will save you, but for Lebezej it will be her destruction," and with a chuckle, Brave continued, "and fifthly, don't look in a mirror because you won't like what you see."

"What's that supposed to mean?" I asked in bewilderment.

"Right now and for our protection, we look like one of them," replied Brave. I slowly glanced over my shoulder expecting to see my friend Brave, instead I had the shock of my life. Instead of seeing Brave, I saw a dark grey stone-like gargoyle; I almost jumped of my skin.

Suddenly, I felt a tap on my shoulder and a voice saying, "That's not me, this is me," turning around the other way, I almost jumped out of my skin again.

The gargoyle I was looking at, spoke to me in a familiar voice. "You must stop doing that," it whispered, "you won't look very pleasant if you leave your skin behind."

"Brave, do I look like you?" I stammered, as I stared at my friend.

"Of course, you don't," replied Brave, "you are not that good looking, but never mind. We must use our disguise to our advantage. What we mustn't do is rush around, that will give the game away."

Chapter 3
First Encounter

"What is this place? And what is the meaning of all these grotesque looking statues?" I asked.

"This is the Wilderness of Niz," replied Brave. "Many, many years ago, there was a fierce war between the Land of Pleasant and a prehistoric race, back then these gargoyles were real monsters. They hated everything good and pleasant and came to destroy us. Their plan was to capture Gulberia first then launch an attack on the Land of Pleasant, but they had underestimated our King and Woggle the Wanderer. It was only the courage and quick wit of Woggle, who had heard of what was happening, so he organised the citizens of our land, which eventually saved the day. We were still taken by surprise and the battle was very fierce, raging for several days with losses on both sides; there was blood and severed limbs everywhere, which led to this place looking like this. The last great battle happened here, Woggle, Wise, the King of Gulberia, and myself trapped the Ogre and imprisoned him in the deepest dungeon in the castle and you were involved in defeating him forever. The moment he was captured in battle, all the remaining forces were robbed of their power and were frozen in time, which secured victory for us. Everything here became like stone, with their broken severed limbs lying all around, and this place became a howling desolate wasteland known as the Wilderness of Niz.

"The Stabmows were the heroes and were celebrated throughout the Land of Pleasant. Only Wise knew that it wouldn't last. He knew the Ogre's Wife wasn't involved in the battle and would someday come seeking vengeance and retribution, and she almost succeeded by imprisoning Woggle and guarding the tunnel, which leads to the inner cell in the dungeon with Noddaba. What makes it more challenging is the Ogre's Wife is in the same cell; how she is torturing him is anybody's guess. Destroying Noddaba will bring her out of the cell enraged and in full flight along the underground passageway, which Noddaba is guarding. Hopefully, in her panic-stricken rage, she will flee from the cell, forgetting Woggle and giving him the chance to escape. I will give you more details later. For the moment, it's back to the task in hand."

I was miles away, lost in thought as I digested Brave's story and trying to work out how we would succeed when Brave whispered again, "We might look like these ugly statues for the moment, but it will change later, which is useful."

"That's all very well, but how are we going to search this place and find Noddaba?" I asked. While we were busy talking it through, the ferocious wind, which was howling like a baying banshee, ripped some rocks off the top of a nearby cliff face, starting an avalanche that was heading in our direction.

"When I shout run, run for your life over there," yelled Brave, shouting above the noise of the wind and the rockslide. "Not yet, wait, but be ready. Hold on just a few seconds longer." Cold sweat was running down my face and back as Brave restrained me, my heart was pounding in my chest and the pulse in my temples was thumping as I watched the avalanche hurtling closer. The seconds passed slowly, the roar of the rockslide was deafening. Smaller pieces of stone were bouncing around us like shrapnel.

Finally, Brave yelled, "NOW." We raced as fast as possible out of the path of the oncoming avalanche, finally diving for cover behind a huge ugly statue.

"That was close," I panted, gasping for breath, "but why did you leave it to the last minute?"

"To give us cover as we changed our position. Noddaba was behind us," replied Brave. The howling icy wind was as relentless as ever; the noise from the rockslide was slowly subsiding. High on the cliff behind us, Noddaba was scanning the landscape, looking for the two unwelcomed guests.

One he knew, the other was unknown. "Whatever it is that they are after, whatever it is that they want, they must get past me first," snarled the ugly creature, its evil forked tongue flicking out and in menacingly.

After a long silence, Brave spoke, "From the cover of the cliff face we should be able to slowly work our way around a large area of this place and that way, find out where this creature is lurking. It will have a lair or a den, and it will have the entrance to guard, which will be concealed and that's what we must find for a successful mission."

Time dragged by. The wind was relentless. The desolate wilderness was incredibly depressing; the dark grey, angry clouds continued scurrying across the sky casting weird and obscure shadows over the ground, which made the search even harder as their very presence seemed to eat into our souls.

After a long and fruitless search with the icy ferocious winds biting into us, I whispered, "Do you know what we're looking for?"

"I do," replied Brave, "but I've been more concerned about the smell."

"What smell?" replied Pockets.

"Exactly. Remember, we are after the Ogre's Wife, so we can free Woggle. What I'm concerned about is the lack of smell. The creature guarding the entrance gives off an awful smell."

"Hmmm" was all I could say as I was lost deep in thought. Finally, I said, "What if the creature is always downwind from us. In other words—"

"Of course, how foolish of me," interrupted Brave. "I will never get the better of him. We'd better change tactics."

Together we started moving slowly in a different direction; the wind's icy fingers digging deeply into our faces. From one gargoyle to another, we kept moving as we continued our search, doing our best to keep covered. As I rested against one stone creature for cover, it crumbled to dust exposing my hiding place. Instantly, I froze, looking like one of the grotesque statues nearby. Suddenly, the air was filled with a defining roar.

"That's Noddaba," whispered Brave, "he's not as close as you think; quickly, follow me." The pair of us dashed off, darting from one stone statue to another. The howling icy wind continued cutting into our faces with intense ferocity.

Chapter 4
Chased

As we rested for a moment, Brave began whispering to me, his companion, "You have to dissolve Noddaba, right, and to do that you must throw the contents of the jug over him, but not until you see the steam rising from it, and that won't happen until I've disappeared, right, and the only way I can do that is to stand close enough to his ugly face so that when he opens his great, ugly mouth to roar, to terrify us, I must leap inside him and disappear, at that precise moment steam will rise from your jug and you must throw it over him. He will dissolve and I will be standing there in front of you."

I listened intently to everything Brave said, after a long pause I finally spoke. "Why do you have to leap inside him, that seems an odd thing to do?"

"It's simple; sometimes we get an ultimate victory from within. All you must do is be ready."

"Look out," I shouted as I rugby tackled Brave, diving him out of the path of a huge boulder, which had been hurled at us with the intention of crushing us both.

After many minutes of laying in the dust, we slowly stood to our feet and as we dusted ourselves down, Brave spoke first, "You just saved my life, thank you."

"You would have done the same for me, Brave, and it proves we can't afford to relax," I replied.

"Because Noddaba is watching us," concluded Brave.

We made our way through the formidable graveyard; the howling icy wind was relentless as it stung our faces and ripped into our skin, tearing into our protective clothing. Finding a group of grotesque statues, which gave the impression that we were in a rugby scrum, the two of us rested awhile, then speaking in hushed tones and pointing, I said, "That's where we were just now when the boulder was hurled at us, which means Noddaba must have been up there, and if he was up there, then the entrance he is guarding must be in that direction too."

Brave thought long and hard before answering and when he finally spoke he didn't give the answer I was expecting.

"We need to go the long way around for the following reasons: That cliff face is too shear to climb quickly, it offers no cover or protection; the direction of the wind is wrong and will blow our cover and the way the cliff face is bulging right there, it looks as if it will burst at any moment." As Brave finished speaking, there was a deafening explosion as the cliff face erupted and a huge torrent of icy cold water burst out like a huge waterfall. "Run for it," shouted Brave urgently. Forgetting about cover and protection, the two of us went dashing through the desolate wilderness, Brave taking the lead with me close on his heels. On and on we ran, dodging around different groups of statues as the icy cold water raced after us. Brave shouted over his shoulder, "That path up there, we need to go there, come on." All thoughts of concealment were abandoned as we raced towards a mountain path. Swerving past some statues, leaping over severed limbs, which were strewn across their path, we raced on as the floodwaters thundered after us getting dangerously close by the second. As we jumped over a mangled pile of ancient limbs and wings, I caught my foot, stumbled, and fell headlong amongst them all. The icy cold water thundered over me, Brave watched in horror, too far ahead to save me.

Chapter 5
With the Ogre's Wife

Meanwhile, in the deepest, darkest dungeon in the Castle of Gulberia, the Ogre's Wife, Lebezej, had thrown her trophy, which lay curled up like a big ball into the far corner of the cell. Now Lebezej was not very intelligent and what she lacked in brainpower she made for in brute force. Hence the phrase, all brawn and no brain. And because her brainpower was pea-sized, she had chosen the most secure dungeon in the castle but not the biggest one. In fact, it wasn't big enough for her to stand up straight in. In fact, it wasn't big enough to swing a cat in, and unknown to her, Sir Woggle the Wanderer wasn't unconscious, he wasn't even asleep, but he was acting dead extremely well.

Having flung Woggle into the cell, Lebezej made several unsuccessful attempts to follow after him but the cell she had chosen had a small doorway, small that is for an Ogre's Wife. Each attempt to enter was completely unsuccessful because she didn't bend her broad knobbly back or duck her huge wart covered head. Instead, she crashed into the ancient heavy stonework and heavy wooden doors. Each time she grew angrier and angrier. The angrier she got, the louder she shouted her threats at Woggle, who remained stone dead in the corner. Exhaustion started to take its toll and eventually she sagged to the floor like a wet sack of coal. Her big, ugly face was dripping with sweat.

Great drops of the stuff fell off her huge lumpy, bumpy nose. She sweat so much, it made a greasy, slimy, stinking stream, which unknowing to her, ran down the tunnel. While she was sagging and gasping for breath on the floor, she thought she saw her opportunity to grab Woggle who was still curled up like a ball. With a deafening roar she lunged forward, her big knobbly arm with its huge hand with its twisted ugly fingers and black ragged nails stretching out to grab or stab Woggle, but the doorway was too narrow for her bulky, knobbly body. Stretch as she might, Woggle remained just out of harm's way. Her stinking, greasy sweat continued dripping frantically from every pore, turning the stream of sweat into a small river; on and on it flowed, slipping and slopping, slushing and gurgling down the long tunnel. The Ogre's Wife was getting more frantic by the second. The more frantic she became, the more she sweat, and the more she sweat, the deeper the sticky, greasy, stinking sweaty river became. Suddenly, Woggle stood upright, turned to face the cell entrance and pressed himself into the cell wall. Lebezej tried forcing her head in through the cell door but with her arm and shoulder almost filling the entrance, there wasn't room. She was so desperate to get at her trophy that whatever common sense she should have, deserted her in her frantic state. Sir Woggle now began enjoying the moment. First, he jeered at her, then he insulted her, next he called her names; each time he succeeded in making her more angry and more frantic, and she sweat a lot more sweat, and the river of slimy, stinking sweat was up to her knees, and she was struggling to keep her grip and balance on the old stone floor. Woggle continued tormenting Lebezej.

'There once was an Ogre's Wife,
The ugliest thing, I've seen in my life.
She was covered in warts and weeping sores,
And she cannot fit through my cell door.
Tra la. Tra la la la la.'

This little ditty made Lebezej madder than ever. Finally, she lost her balance and hit the floor flat on her back, with her wart-covered legs thrown in the air. Crash. *Ooomph*! All the wind was knocked out of her and she began sliding down the very long tunnel in the greasy smelly river of her own sweat.

Chapter 6
Not Like This!

Back in the howling wilderness, Brave watched in horror as he yelled out, "No, no, no, not like this." Brave sat in silence, staring at the spot where he'd last seen me, memories flashed before him, flooding his mind of different adventures we had shared together; finally with a grief-filled heart and fresh grim determination, he made his resolve as he muttered to himself, "Somehow and I don't know how yet but for the sake of my friend, I will succeed in our mission, just for him," and with that thought filling his mind, Brave turned around and began climbing to higher ground. His eyes were burning, he had a lump in his throat, his heart was heavy, his legs felt like lead, and his feet like lumps of stone. It was as if he was enveloped in a cloak of sadness. The ridge he was aiming for suddenly seemed a long way off. The so-called path was littered with stones and boulders and shattered remains of fallen monsters, making the up-hill climb more dangerous. After what seemed like an eternity, Brave sat down on the grey stone ledge and looked all around him, from this vantage point he could see a huge area of this wilderness and it looked more terrifying than he had anticipated. The lump in his throat was worse, feeling bigger than ever and the burning in his eyes was unbearable. He tried holding back the tears but it was no use, suddenly it was as if the floodgates opened and Brave began sobbing, quietly at first, then as he gave into his emotions his sobbing grew louder as he gave expression to his pain and loss. As the tears finally subsided, Brave looked up and through his tear-stained face, he looked around him; there was an eerie silence on this sheltered ledge. It was while Brave was here, he remembered again how we first met and how the man from the other side became firm friends with him and his friends, and now he would be the bearer of sad tidings. Brave sat staring into the middle distance, reaffirming his commitment to the job at hand; he was suddenly aware he was being watched. Instantly, he was ready for action, every sinew, and every sense was on red alert. Slowly, looking up, he saw a gargoyle hovering in front of him about 50 metres away. It was motionless as it hung in the icy cold air. For a few moments, Brave studied this phenomenon he was aware of, something familiar about it. The hovering gargoyle slowly smiled; the non-ghostly see thru smile he was famous for, then he spoke, just one phrase, "You're looking in the wrong place for your friend," and then he vanished, which is another thing he is famous for. Brave sat motionless but now he had a fresh surge of hope flowing through him. Without wasting another second, Brave carefully and secretively made his way back down the path until he reached the place where he had last seen me. By now, the floodwaters had stopped and the ground around him was soggy. Standing still as stone, he slowly and deliberately began an intense eye search, scanning the immediate area, nothing. Again he looked, this time widening his search. Slowly and deliberately, again there was nothing. Six times he intensely scanned the area and each time was fruitless. He remembered the phrase, "You're looking in the wrong place for your friend." The ground beneath his feet began to move slowly from side to side and up and down as if a huge earthworm was wriggling just beneath the surface. Moving slowly to one side, Brave watched as the ground continued to heave and twist in a series of weird contortions.

"It's like something long imprisoned is waking from the dead and is desperately trying to escape," murmured Brave quietly as he watched in silence. As it started, so it stopped; the ground gave a final heave and a twist as it settled down. Brave scratched his head in bewilderment as he continued staring at the ground. Once again, a flood of grief swept over him and his eyes started burning, and the lump in his throat returned as he remembered the sudden loss of me and how helpless he felt because he was unable to rescue me; this was quickly followed by the surge of hope as he remembered the recent statement, "You're looking in the wrong place for your friend." *If that's the case and it must be, then surely*... a loud and deafening roar filled the air, shattering Brave's thoughts. Instantly, he froze, blending in with his surroundings. Slowly and cautiously, Brave scanned the desolate wilderness, nothing moved. The only sound was the howling icy wind, which was relentless. High above the stone ledge at the top of the cliff, Noddaba lay scanning the wilderness, wondering where the second intruder was. Behind Brave, the ground slowly heaved, twisted, and writhed again. As Brave turned to watch it, another movement caught his eye, quickly looking to his left, he found himself staring at a group of grey marble like monsters that were intertwined and horrific. The ground behind him slowly cracked open and a huge slug-like creature slithered closer to Brave, its ugly mouth with huge fangs yawning open ready to swallow him. Closer and closer it slithered almost silently to him. The sucking noise its huge body made as it slithered closer was drowned out by the howling wind. "Behind you," Brave heard the shout, side stepped and *thwack*, he struck the creature with his right arm just behind its head. Instantly, it shrivelled and died making a dreadful hissing noise as it did. Brave watched it disappear, remembering the voice which called him and turning he saw the scrum like group of gargoyles.

As he studied them, one spoke in a whisper, "I'm in here." Brave's heart was racing, his head was spinning as elation drove out the final remains of despair and his excited relief gave wings to his grief as it took flight and fled from him. Brave forgot about discretion and the need for the cover. He flew across the ground and did a flying drop kick near the top of the mangled mess of interlocking statues. As his feet struck the structure, it crumbled, collapsing and turning to dust. Brave stood to his feet and turning around he discovered one statue was still complete, he watched as it slowly stretched out and untangled itself, then it slowly stood up, still dazed and looked around. Finally, it spoke; the voice was haggard and confused. "Where am I?" Brave was ecstatic and again he felt the lump in his throat and the burning in his eyes only this time it was relief he felt not grief. Putting his arm around my shoulder, he made me slowly sit down. The howling icy wind soon revived my memory of where I was and the mission we were on. The two of us spoke at the same time.

"I am sorry I was too far away to…"

"I'm sorry for…"

There was no need for any apology, we were safe and reunited and that was all that mattered.

After a long silence, I spoke, "Noddaba is up there. It's his evil amber eyes which give him away."

Chapter 7
Face to Face

"What's that awful smell?" I concluded.

"I don't know, it's not Noddaba," replied Brave. High up on the cliff Noddaba was surveying the desolate wilderness when suddenly the stinking, slimy, greasy, sweaty river washed around him taking him completely by surprise and catching him off guard. Leaping into the air, he let out a huge angry roar. As he landed heavily, the ground beneath him gave way, causing him to slide down the cliff face.

"Get ready," shouted Brave above the noise of the relentlessly icy cold wind, "we've got company." We watched as Noddaba failed to stop his chaotic slide; every attempt he made to slow down failed.

"Come on," yelled Brave, "this is our moment." Once again, caution was thrown to the wind, which was still relentless, icy cold and howling with a wolf's head. Rolling and tumbling, Noddaba came hurtling down the mountainside. With about 350 metres to go, the creature succeeded in righting himself but while he was up the right way, he still couldn't slow down.

"This way," shouted Brave as he suddenly changed direction and raced in front of the oncoming Noddaba. "Now we wait and stay ready, he'll soon be close enough." The seconds ticked slowly by. The howling wind never let up, howling with an intensity which was unnatural, its long, icy cold fingers digging deep into our faces as we watched and waited as Noddaba got ever closer.

Brave glanced at me, as I subconsciously held my right hand as if I was holding something. "Are you ready?" asked Brave. "You look as if you've got everything you need."

It was only then I realised that I was holding the invisible jug. "I guess I am," I replied with grim determination, not taking my eyes off Noddaba as I spoke. Closer and closer the ugly monster came. Soon it would be at the base of the cliff. As I continued taking it all in, I realised how ugly this beast was. There was nothing about it you could admire, he was ugliness personified. Seeing an extremely large rock jutting up from the ground, Brave made his way to it with me following close on his heels. "Perfect," he whispered to himself. Suddenly, the two of us shivered, as the icy wind continued to cut into us with its long cold fingers. Looking at one another, we realised that we were back to our true selves, no protection, no looking like and blending in with our surroundings. This was it. The sickly, stinking smell was getting stronger and stronger.

"That's not Noddaba," shouted Brave above the wind.

"Up there," I yelled. Looking up to where Noddaba had been, we saw what looked like a dirty yellow ribbon unfurling from the side of the mountain.

As Noddaba continued sliding down the mountainside, his four front legs became trapped in a horizontal crevice, he was sliding too fast to do anything, and with his front legs trapped, his momentum flung him into a painful somersault. Suddenly, there was a terrible cracking, snapping, tearing sound. The two of us watched spellbound, as if it was in slow motion. The beast looked much bigger as it was tumbling through the air. Each of its four legs broke at the same time. Noddaba hit the ground on his back. His front legs were freed but not before each one was wrenched out of its sockets, dislocating them. The pain was unbearable and the beast let out an agonising roar. "Quick, on to the rock," shouted Brave, as he scrambled up it.

As we stood up right on top of it, Brave said, "We have a phrase in the Land of Pleasant which in Rorrim is: '*Em rof tfelc sega fo kcor*'. It simply means the safest place anywhere is on the rock."

Brave and I stood rooted to the spot as Noddaba finally came to halt about 50 metres from the bottom of the cliff. He was completely dazed, in agony, and a lot bigger close up. The two of us stood side by side motionless. We watched and waited.

This creature is absolutely grotesque, I hope we are successful, I thought.

Brave nudged me and whispered, "Get ready, Noddaba's playing crafty." As we watched Noddaba, we could see the muscles in his massive body rippling like the waves on the ocean.

Chapter 8
Support (Back-Up)

Hours earlier, the citizens of Gulberia had been disturbed by the commotions generated by Lebezej deep in the underground cell. Curiosity had over-taken their fear of the Ogre's Wife and most of them were mingling in the castle courtyard or the market square, which was just outside its main gates. There were all sorts of speculation and rumours flying about. Some said, "She must be murdering him." Others said, "She'll be torturing him and inflicting intense pain on him." Those who were more positive had a very different approach. "This is Sir Woggle the Wanderer we are talking about, he will outsmart her, remember she's all brawn and no brain." While the comments were flying around, a small group had climbed onto the castle wall, which overlooked the Wilderness of Niz; they were carefully scanning the horizon. While all this commotion and activity was going on, a small group of visitors arrived at the main castle gates. Zebaj the Stesomram had been off on one of his explorations when he was confronted by a familiar figure in a tall black hat, long black frock coat, very shiny but worn black boots. His friendly, non-ghostly, see thru smile was the same as ever. "Where are you going, my fine friend?" he said to Zebaj, which totally surprised him because he was at that precise moment in time examining a very deep hole that was in front him.

Looking up, Zebaj was totally surprised to see The See Thru Man standing just a few metres off the ground. "I wouldn't go down there if I were you, but if you're up to it, I have a very important mission for you."

"I'm more than willing," replied Zebaj. Without hesitation, The See Thru Man gave Zebaj all the information, then sent him to the Stabmows with the following instructions:

"They must all go to Gulberia. Mobilise the citizens to head out into the Wilderness of Niz. Form five groups at strategic points, which will become obvious and at the right moment raise a big shout of constant encouragement."

"That's it?" replied Zebaj.

"Yes," was the reply and with that last word, he vanished.

Zebaj was true to his word and hurried off to find Oggle, Foggle, Boggle, and Wise. They were outside their tree trunk home discussing their future and the whereabouts of Brave and Woggle when he raced up. "Here's a friend on a mission," said Oggle, who saw Zebaj first.

"You look as if you've run along way," added Wise. Zebaj gave them the news and passed on all the instructions from The See Thru Man. Finally, he came up for air. The four friends took in the information.

After a few seconds, Foggle and Boggle spoke at the same time. "What are we waiting for? Come on, it's time for action."

The journey to Gulberia was uneventful and soon they were at the castle gates. As the locals realised who had arrived, a huge cheer went up followed by a constant buzz of excitement. Wise brought order and asked Zebaj to introduce himself and to pass on the message he was given. As Zebaj was bringing his instructions to a close, a huge cheer of support and agreement went up from the crowd. "And if there are any citizens absent, will you go quickly and bring them here, we need as many of you as possible." A few Gulberians disappeared and within a few minutes returned with 250 more Gulberians. Wise organised the full thing, dividing the crowd into five groups, next the group leaders were taken up onto the parapet at the rear of the castle. This enabled them to look out over the Wilderness of Niz.

"What a dreadfully forsaken and barren place this is," murmured Zebaj to Oggle. Now, Stabmows have extraordinary eyesight when they focus on things in the distance and it wasn't long before Boggle spotted Brave and me as we were dashing for the rock. Then Wise spotted Noddaba hurtling uncontrollably down the mountainside. Quickly speaking to his four friends, Wise instructed them to take their groups to strategic places in the wilderness and to wait for his command. No questions were asked as they set off to their individual stations, close enough for a good view but far enough away to stay safe. Each group crouched in silence, watching and waiting.

Chapter 9
On the Rock

Back on the rock, Brave and I remained motionless as we stood staring at Noddaba. Is whispered, "I feel incredibly vulnerable and amazingly secure all at the same time, while standing on the rock." Brave nodded in agreement.

Noddaba's long, dark, red-forked tongue flicked slowly out and in. His evil amber eyes were half-open. We remained motionless, prepared to play the waiting game. Once again, the long, dark, red-forked tongue flicked slowly out and back in again. The seconds ticked slowly by.

The groups in the distance waited patiently.

Lebezej continued frantically sliding down the tunnel in the river of her own dirty, smelly sweat, unable to stop.

Crack! The whip-like tail of Noddaba snaked through the air. Because of the pain he was in, his aim and speed was off. *Crack, Crack, Crack*, three times in quick succession his tail whistled through the air. The groups watched and waited.

The Ogre's Wife continued on her frantic journey.

Brave and I remained immovable. *Crack, crack,* again his tail whistled through the air. This time it caught Brave on his back and me on my left shoulder; we were both bleeding. Time and time again, Noddaba flicked his tail whistling through the air, cracking like a gun shot and ripping into our skin causing the blood to flow freely. A murmured conversation of concern was gaining momentum as it spread through the distant groups like an invisible spider's web. "Why are they just standing there? Why don't they do something? They can't take much more of this."

"*Ssshhhh.* Be patient," replied Wise. "Brave knows what he is doing."

Meanwhile in the tunnel, Lebezej had been flung upside down and spun around 180 degrees and was now travelling head first on her back, through the slimy river of her own sweat.

Crack, crack, Noddaba's tail streaked through icy cold air again cracking in front of me, then in front of Brave. It was his big mistake. As quick as lightening, Brave caught the tail and dug his claws in deeply and in one swift movement had bitten off a length of Noddaba's tail. Thick reddish, black blood gushed out as Noddaba's tail swung dementedly in the air. "Are you ready?" shouted Brave.

"Ready" was my reply. Noddaba was almost defenceless, his four shoulders were dislocated, his front legs broken and now his whip tail useless. In sheer desperation, he rose up on his hind legs letting out an angry and terrifying roar. His breath was like a stinking, stormy wind but the moment his huge ugly mouth and cavernous throat were open to their widest, Brave sprang forward flying through the air and disappearing into the abyss of the beast; as he was in mid-flight, steam started rising from the jug just in front of my right hand. Noddaba snapped his jaws tight; I flung the contents of the invisible jug at Noddaba's face. Instantly, a lifeless grey liquid spread out in the air, the full force of it hit the ugly beast fully in the face and continued enveloping him completely in it. Noddaba roared again and again in total agony, but it was no use, he was totally trapped, the grey liquid did its job. The grey substance slowly contracted, crushing Noddaba, squeezing the life out of him while dissolving him at the same time. The crunching, squeezing, squelching, sizzling sound continued until all that remained on the lifeless grey floor of the desolate wilderness, surrounded by the shrieking howling wind, which was as icy cold as ever, was Brave and he was triumphant. The five groups were about to cheer when Wise signalled for them to remain silent. "Not yet. Hold on until the time is right." The groups became composed and silence settled on them once more.

Meanwhile in the tunnel, Lebezej was still slipping and sliding head first in a frantic fashion. She had managed to roll over onto her front but was still travelling headfirst and gaining speed with no way of slowing down. Unknown to her, Sir Woggle, who is a talented Stabmow and able like all Stabmows to climb up almost anything, cling to most things, leap over most obstacles and run upside down on any surface including tunnels like this one, which is what he was doing right now, running upside down along the roof of the tunnel, a few metres behind the Ogre's Wife. Closer and closer they got to the entrance of the tunnel. Lebezej became suddenly aware that Noddaba was not at his post. She couldn't stop sweating, and she couldn't stop slipping and sliding and hurtling headlong in the stinking, slimy river of her sweat. The river of sweat was forced in front of her like a bow wave of a ship, forcing the stinking river out of the tunnel and down the mountainside. With less than ten metres to go, Woggle gave an increase of speed, somersaulted through the air and landed in the centre of the ugly Ogre's lumpy, bumpy back. Digging his claws deeply into her sweating flesh, Lebezej let out a blood-curdling roar as Woggle inflicted more pain. Suddenly, an icy blast of cold air rushed into the tunnel and Woggle knew the entrance was getting closer, as they flew around the final bend, still slipping and sliding and hurtling at a frantic rate, the entrance came into view, Woggle braced himself. The Ogre's Wife burst out of the tunnel roaring more loudly as Woggle continued digging his claws in her sweaty, knobbly, lumpy back.

Chapter 10
The Ogre's Wife

On the rock, Brave and I were celebrating our first major victory when suddenly, "Up there," shouted Brave, pointing up the cliff face which Noddaba had recently come down. They watched in amazement with their eyes and mouths wide open as the huge ugly body of Lebezej burst out of the unguarded tunnel, forcing the river of ugly, slimy sweat over the edge of mountainside like an ugly tidal wave. To our amazement, we watched as Sir Woggle the Wanderer stood erect on the Ogre's broad back, as is if he was riding a surfboard and with a triumphant shout leapt off her back to safety. The Ogre's Wife was rolling and spinning, tumbling, and bouncing frantically down the mountainside. Woggle came leaping down the cliff face by a slightly different route. I was about to leave the rock and race across to meet Woggle when Brave restrained me. "You're safer on the rock, trust me, Woggle won't be long." Brave was right, in a few moments, we were joined by our friend and as we watched the Ogre's Wife continuing on her bumpy journey, he told us everything that had happened in the cell.

Then placing his big paw on my right shoulder, he said encouragingly, "I hope you're ready for the race of your life; The Old Tree is about six miles that way. You must run in a straight line, don't dodge anything, don't leap over anything and above all don't hold back. Everything will crumble before you as you run at it. And more than anything else, when you get to The Old Tree, you must not hesitate, throw yourself at it. The tree is your only way of escape." I simply nodded in agreement. Then turning around, I looked where Woggle was pointing; all I could see was the desolate wilderness, the howling wasteland of Niz, complete with its ugly statues and grotesque monsters from a defeated army of long ago. The howling, icy wind suddenly felt colder and fiercer than ever and as I looked around myself again, despair and hopelessness engulfed me like a heavy black cloak. "Don't look at your surroundings, fix your eyes on the tree. Focus not on what you can see but on what you can't see at the moment."

"Right," I replied.

A crashing, rumbling sound was heard behind us. Spinning around, we watched as the ugly Ogre's Wife came crashing down the last few hundred metres of the mountainside with the stinky, dirty, river of her own sweat, swirling around her like a deepening whirlpool as she finally stopped at the base of the cliff. The three of us watched and waited. Slowly, like someone drunk, she staggered to her feet, desperately trying to focus her dull brain on all that had happened; eventually, she made it. Standing almost upright she didn't make a pretty sight. Her long, dirty, lifeless grey hair was more matted than usual, with her sickly sweat running out of it and down her lumpy, bumpy, wart covered face, which was bright red with anger and exhaustion. Her rough, ragged clothing was in shreds, but as she straightened herself up to her full height, she slowly realised how she had been tricked and with a bellowing roar called out, "NODDABA," but Noddaba didn't answer. Slowly, Lebezej raised her ugly face and slowly and deliberately looked around her. She looked up the cliff face she had recently tumbled down but there was no Noddaba. Next, she looked into the distance of the bleak barren wasteland; again, there was nothing. Her huge frame started shaking with rage. Once again, she bellowed, "NODDABA," again there was only the almost desolate silence of the lifeless wilderness. The howling icy wind was no respecter of persons, it cut deeply into her ugly skin making the sores in her skin weep. Finally, her gaze was focused on her immediate surroundings; as her gaze came into focus, she found herself staring at three full of life figures. Sir Woggle she recognised instantly, he was her trophy. Staring at him in disbelief seemed to make the wounds in her back, which he had inflicted, burn and sting even more. Shaking her huge, ugly, fat wart covered fists at him, she bellowed again, "NODDABA," but Noddaba didn't respond to her cry. Firmly planted on the rock, the three of us stood motionless and secure. As Lebezej continued staring at us slowly and painfully, she worked out that the other Stabmow must be Brave. Who else could it be? But who was the third character?

Woggle half-turned his head to me and whispered, "Get ready to run."

The stinking river of her sweat was slipping down the mountainside and swirling waist deep like a dirty pond around her. While it did, the Ogre's Wife continued staring at Brave when the penny dropped. It was him who enticed her husband to his death. Rage began welling up inside her. Her anger reached boiling point once more as her greasy, smelly sweat started streaming from her pores. I whispered to my friends, "She is an ugly creature."

"Believe me, she's much worse close up," replied Woggle with a grin.

Lebezej bellowed again, "NODDABA," but the creature didn't come to her command. "NODDABA," she bellowed again. The only reply was the howling, icy wind wailing like a tormented banshee. For a brief moment, the wind ceased and the eerie silence was broken as Brave spoke a short, icy cold sentence.

"Noddaba has been dissolved." The eerie silence returned as Lebezej allowed the impact of the short statement sink slowly into her brain. 'Dissolved'. Once again, the penny dropped and glaring at Brave for the second time, she opened her mouth to bellow in anger but no sound was heard, as she was about to shout out, she realised what he meant by 'dissolved'. It finally made sense and finding her voice, the ugly giant of a woman raised a huge ugly lumpy, wart covered arm and pointing her huge, fat, knobbly finger with its dirty broken finger nail at my face, she bellowed, "You, wait till I get my hands on you." Simultaneously, Woggle and Brave put a restraining paw on me.

"Not yet," they whispered. "To run now will give the impression you are running scared and that won't help you. Be patient and play the waiting game."

The Ogre's Wife continued in her raging angry outburst, with her dirty, greasy sweat pouring from her, making the dirty pond bigger and deeper. The stench was unbelievable. Continuing to point and wave her horrible, scraggy finger, Lebezej continued to bellow, "You. You…" words failed her. A few moments later, she bellowed again, "Wait 'til I get my hands on you, I'm going to tear you limb from limb," with that last rant she took her first huge step forward.

"Not yet," said Brave as he kept a restraining paw on me.

Chapter 11
The Race

The slimy sticky mess moved with Lebezej as she took another step towards the three of us. Closer and closer she slowly came. The huge sticky pond was starting to stretch out behind her as if it was a large piece of dirty elastic. Brave whispered to his friend, "How are you feeling about the next part of this adventure?"

"If I'm honest with you, right now I'm feeling good because I know there's a victory to be won for everyone else, which means this race is not about me, but it is about the bigger picture."

Lebezej took a few more strides and bellowed again, "I'm gonna break every bone in your scrawny body as soon as I get my hands on you." Again, I was restrained. The stinking, sweaty mess continued slowly stretching out behind her as she made a few more strides towards us and bellowed again, desperately trying to intimidate them, "I'm gonna crush the three of you in one go when I get my hands on you. You will regret the day you were born. I'm going to turn your bodies into pulp and then make you into Ogre stew."

In the distance, the five groups watched and waited. They could hear the bellowing voice of Lebezej as it was carried to them on the wind's icy wings. A murmuring spread amongst their ranks. "What are they waiting for? Why doesn't Pockets make a run for it?" And so the murmuring went on.

Having slowly calmed their groups down, each leader explained, "Timing is everything, to run too soon will demonstrate fear and to run too late will be disastrous for us all."

Back on the rock, the three of us comrades waited. The howling, swirling, icy wind continued in its relentless, restless manner. Woggle slowly leaned slightly closer to me and whispered in Rorrim: "*Lruh lla ruoy fles otno eht eert esuaceb eh serac rof ouy.*"

Brave nodded and murmured. "Memorise it."

The Ogre's Wife was 20 metres away. Everything about her was a hundred times uglier. Her breath was ugly. Her mouth was ugly.

Her whole body was ugly. Even her warts, sores, lumps, and bumps were uglier. There was nothing about her that was 'pleasant'. Everything was absolute ugliness. *Like Noddaba, she is ugliness personified,* I thought to myself. Turning to Woggle, I whispered, "You are right about her ugliness." At that precise moment, the howling, icy wind changed direction in Lebezej's favour, carrying my voice and comment to her huge, ugly, cauliflower, wart covered ears.

"I heard that," she bellowed. Her breath was a vile mixture of rotten eggs, gone-off cabbage and stale fish that was as old as her. She lurched forward, her huge, ugly, lumpy, bumpy arms out stretched, with her big, fat, knobbly fingers reaching for me.

At the last minute, Brave shouted, "RUN." Instantly, Brave and Woggle dived left and right, and I took off in a dead straight line on the six-mile race of my life. Ignoring Sir Woggle and Brave, Lebezej was after a new prize and this time she wouldn't fail. With her huge, fat, ugly hands and arms outstretched clawing the air between her and me, she started her chase.

The first obstacle in my path was a huddled group of grotesque gargoyles. "It's now or never," I muttered and just as I raced at them, they disintegrated turning to dust.

"Wow," was all I could say as the lifeless, grey dust was picked up by the wind and carried spiralling into the grey sky above. The Ogre's Wife continuing in hot pursuit was having some bother of her own. She was still sweating and the dirty, sticky, smelling sweat pond she had created at the bottom of the cliff was clinging to her and stretching out behind her like dirty, grey, yellow, ragged ribbon on a desolate landscape. *Crash*, another group of gargoyles turned to dust as I kept on with my straight-line race.

Back on the rock, Brave and Woggle watched in hopeful admiration. "He will succeed," observed Brave. Woggle nodded in agreement.

On and on I ran, running a true course, leaving behind me a trail of dirty, dry grey clouds of dust, which spiralled into the dirty grey sky. Lebezej was plodding on behind me, taking huge steps and getting closer and closer with each stride. The stinking, sweaty stream continued trailing out behind her like a long, dirty grey yellow ribbon across the barren wasteland. The straight line I was running included going up and down a number of hills and cliffs but it excluded going to the left or the right. Every so often, I would quote the memorised phrase '*Lruh lla ruoy fles otno eht eert esuaceb eh serac rof ouy*'. I had been running for about an hour, the going was difficult through the desolate wilderness, the ferocious icy wind making it harder to run a true course than I had imagined. Up and down mountainsides, some more challenging than others and as far as I could tell, I was still running in a straight line. As I reached a high ledge on a hillside, my legs gave way causing me to stumble. Lebezej saw her chance; as she was reaching the ledge and stretching out her long, fat, ugly arms and long, knobbly fingers, she made a grab at my legs.

On the rock, Woggle and Brave were watching. Further away five groups watched with bated breath, some gasping and crying out, "No, not like this." Suddenly, they heard Woggle and Brave cheering and shouting encouragement. The five groups joined in. I heard their encouraging shout as the Ogress was trying to grasp my legs, she heard the shouts as well. I felt as if I was enveloped in their encouragement. I felt I was surrounded by a great crowd of witnesses all urging me on, which gave me a fresh burst of energy and strength. Regaining my balance, I raced on. In her anger and frustration, Lebezej turned and faced the distant crowds and shook her massive arms and fists at them. Turning her back on them, she started racing after me, bellowing and shouting threats after me. "When I get my hands on you—" the rest of the threat was drowned out by the citizens of Gulberia and the Stabmows as they shouted encouragement again to me.

Chapter 12
The Tree

Woggle and Brave signalled to the five groups to change their positions and leading the way, they set off through the desolate wasteland so they could keep the race and chase in their focus. Their continued shouts of encouragement reached me and became like fireballs of energy within me as I raced down the other side of another mountain. On the descent, I remembered a piece of advice a schoolteacher had given me years earlier, "When running, always save some energy for the home straight." *I must remember that and use it to my advantage.* Again, I heard her bellowing insults at me and this time I felt the ground vibrating beneath me as she came charging down the mountain like an enraged bull. Her vile hot breath was getting closer. As I reached the base of the mountain, I looked up and ahead of me, away in the distance, I saw for the second time The Old Tree. Woggle's advice was ringing in my ears. Brave's instructions were surging through my veins. Unknown to Lebezej and I, the cheering crowd kept on changing position to keep the chase in focus and again they roared their encouragement, which reached me, carried on the icy wind like it was echoing down the corridors of time. Their shouts seemed to engulf me. Another group of grotesque gargoyles turned to dust as I raced at them.

The Old Tree was very slowly getting closer. Lebezej was closing in on her prey. *Crash!* Another ugly creature turned to dust and another column of grey dust spiralled into the bleak sky. Lebezej bellowed again hurling more insults and accusations at me. Again, the roar of the crowd urged me on as they continued following at a safe distance, their messages of encouragement faithfully carried to me by the icy fingers of the wind and my legs found fresh strength. Behind me, I could feel the hot, vile breath of Lebezej on my neck and back. Again, I remembered the advice from my junior schoolteacher, "Don't look over your shoulder to see where the opposition is. Many a race is lost this way." Lebezej hadn't spotted the tree yet, she was so focused on her prey and was getting closer with every stride of her fat, ugly, bulky, wart-covered, sore infested legs. Her huge, fat feet with their six toes and claw-like nails, constantly made the ground tremble with every stride she took. The wind was as relentless as ever. A few more gargoyles turned to dust. Once again, I looked up; the tree was about a mile and a half away. Again, I remembered advice given by Mr Dobbs, his junior schoolteacher, "Don't slow down until you've crossed the finishing line." Without any warning, I suddenly felt the dirty, scraggy fingernails of Lebezej scratching my back, the pain was sharp and fierce like a hot knife. I lifted my head as the pain went deep into my flesh and seeing The Old Tree getting closer spurred me on. The Ogre's Wife looked in the same direction and for the first time she saw The Old Tree and bellowed as if in agony, "No, not the tree." But it was no use, driven by anger and hatred, she was compelled to pursue her prey. She was furious and to catch me, who had dissolved Noddaba, was her only aim. Again, she stretched out her long, fat, ugly arms, and again she managed only to scratch the surface of my skin. Blood was flowing freely from the open wounds in my back. The wind's long, icy fingers seemed to cut deep into the wounds causing them to sting. The dirty ribbon of sweat continued streaming out behind her over the desolate wilderness, she continued in her chase, she was close but not close enough, yet.

Once again, Woggle and Brave led the groups to a new location in the wilderness. The five groups had now gathered as one with Sir Woggle and Brave on the top of a rugged hill. From this new elevated position, the large crowd could regularly see clouds of dust spiralling upwards as one gargoyle after another crumbled to dust. Then they watched as Lebezej made a grab for me and just missed. Wise spoke up, "Understand this, my friends, he's not running from her, he is fleeing to the tree." They watched again as she scrapped and scratched my back. They watched, and they shouted their encouragement to me as I kept running just out of harm's way.

I looked up again as yet another group of ugly stone creatures turned to dust and again the roar of the pursuing crowd urged me on. I had never felt so isolatedly un-alone. It was a strange feeling out running Lebezej while surrounded by a cheering crowd whose peace depended on my success. Looking up once more, I realised The Old Tree was about three quarters of a mile away, it suddenly felt as if it were in touching distance. Again, Lebezej bellowed out in defiance, "Not The Old Tree," but her anger drove her on after me and this time she would succeed. She, Lebezej the Terrible, would catch her prey and crush me slowly. She would show no mercy. Another group of prehistoric looking monsters crumbled to dust and another cloud of dust rose into the air. The circling, icy wind caught up the dust and threw it fully into her ugly face, blinding her and causing her to choke. Frantically rubbing her eyes while coughing and spluttering and losing ground, she continued chasing me. The crowd cheered and roared again. The Old Tree was less than 350 metres away, I held back on my pace. Lebezej bellowed again and continued pounding after me. Her long strides covered a lot of ground. "I'm going to crush you. When I get my hands on you—" *Crash!* Another group of gargoyles crumbled to dust. I recited the phrase again as I raced on towards my goal. '*Lruh lla ruoy fles otno eht eert esuaceb eh serac rof ouy*'. Lebezej was gaining ground behind me, I could feel her vile, hot breath. The long, stinking ribbon of sweat stretched out behind her, the icy wind spreading the stench across the desolate wilderness covering it as if it were in a rotten blanket. Over another hill and down the other side, columns of dust spiralled into the angry clouds above, onto more level ground I looked ahead, again The Old Tree was looming larger and larger. It looked as dead and as lifeless as ever. Crash, more dust as another gargoyle crumbled. Just over 200 metres to go.

The Ogre's Wife bellowed again and made another grab at her prey, again her scraggy nails gouged my flesh and again more blood flowed. "About 180 metres, I'm getting closer. Come on legs don't give up now," I muttered to myself. Lebezej started gaining on him. The icy wind was as ferocious as ever. The crowd continued shouting. Lebezej continued sweating. The dirty ribbon of sweat continued snaking out behind her. I kept on running; 160 metres to go. The Old Tree was looming closer.

The Ogre's Wife bellowed again, "Anything but the tree," but it was no use. Driven by enraged anger, she kept chasing her prey. One hundred fifty-five metres to go; once again I heard another encouraging roar from the crowd, another crashing of gargoyles and another cloud of dust, again Lebezej lashed out and again my back bled. Once again, the encouraging crowd cheered and changed position; this time she saw them, and slowly realising they were following her and her prey, she stopped for a second and shook her huge, ugly fists at them before continuing after her prey. I kept on running, The Old Tree was about 115 metres away. I raced on. Lebezej kept plodding after me. Her huge strides making up the lost ground. Seventy-five metres to go; I started sprinting, punching as it were the ground with my feet, something I learned long ago. The Old Tree was getting closer with each stride. The Ogre's Wife chased after me; her stinking stream of sweat snaking out behind her as she dragged it across the wasteland. The crowd continued cheering. Crash and crumble, another column of dust spiralled into the sky. The icy wind was howling with a wolf's head as it continued screaming. Sixty-two metres to go. I raced at an ugly group of huddled gargoyles, once again they crumbled to dust. Lebezej grabbed at me again; her knobbly fingers reaching for my shoulders but all she succeeded in doing was scratching my skin with her broken black nails. Fifty metres, the crowd let out a deafening cheer. I raced on. Lebezej raced after me, grabbing again at my shoulders but all she got was a fist full of air. *Crash!* Another group of stone creatures crumbled to dust, again Lebezej grabbed at her prey, again the crowd cheered as they raced closer. *Crash!* More grey dust spiralled into the grey sky, spinning upwards in the ferocious wind. The Old Tree was 33 metres away. The crowd was much closer now than they had ever been and their shouts were deafeningly encouraging. *Crash*, crumble, more dust, 27 metres to go. I raced on taking short sharp fast steps as I continued sprinting to my destination. On and on, towards my ultimate prize. Again, the ugly Ogress lunged at me, the huge fingers on her right hand grabbing my shoulder. The on-looking crowd gasped as some shouted, "No, no, it can't end like this."

All the Stabmows and Zebaj cried out in one voice, "Keep your eyes on The Tree." I was wriggling as I was running. Unfortunately for Lebezej, her lumpy, bumpy, knobbly hands were too slippery with her sweat to secure a good grip and I escaped, but the pain in my shoulder was severe. The Old Tree was just 15 metres away; suddenly, to me, this dead, lifeless looking tree appeared beautiful. Nothing had changed about it, it just looked beautiful. Eleven metres to go, these last few metres seemed the longest part of the race. A deathly hush like a well-fitting coat, settled over the anticipated crowd as they watched the last gargoyle in my path crumble and the dust spiral upwards like a huge, grey, disfigured column, 8 metres to go. "Timing is everything," I muttered. In stony silence, the crowd watched with growing anticipation. With her huge, ugly arms swinging like a demented windmill, Lebezej made several unsuccessful attempts to grab her prey. Five metres, 4, 3, 2, with just over a metre to go, Lebezej made a last attempt but it was no use, in a flying bear hug with my arms outstretched, I hit the massive trunk of The Old Tree and instantly disappeared. Hard on my heels and with no way of stopping, Lebezej hit the ancient tree with full force. The Old Tree remained rock solid, immovable, and impenetrable.

As Lebezej crumbled at the foot of The Old Tree, her dirty, stinking ribbon like river of sweat completely engulfed her. The dust in it made her choke while the river of her smelly sweat suffocated her causing her to drown in her own liquid stench, until all that was left was a mangled disfigured lifeless mound. The crowd burst into rapturous applause. Forgetting the cold icy wind, they started dancing and partying as they made their way back to their castle. As they did, the icy wind subsided, the angry clouds slowly parted and the sun started shining through.

"It will always be a wilderness," said Wise.

"But no longer will it be a desolate wasteland with a howling, icy wind," added Sir Woggle.

Meanwhile, I gave a slight cough, shivered, and blinked several times and interrupted the meeting as I asked in my strong Welsh accent, "Why has this jug of water got steam coming off it?" Nobody replied but Ms Brainstorm continued looking very embarrassed. And as I stared at the lifeless grey wall behind the hostess trolley, I caught the glimpse of a non-ghostly, see thru smile grinning at me, then it vanished.

Some readers may wonder and ask 'What's it really like in 'The Land of Pleasant' or you might ask are there any stories about a typical day in the Land of Pleasant. Or you might wonder 'What do Oggle, Foggle, Boggle, and Wise get up to when there are no dangers to be averted, or adventures to go on, no enemies threatening their safety and what about Brave and Sir Woggle the Wanderer, not to mention the visitor from the other side?'

Well, all those questions will be answered for you in another short story, which is called 'The Dundalion'.